Amy's Diary

charmz™

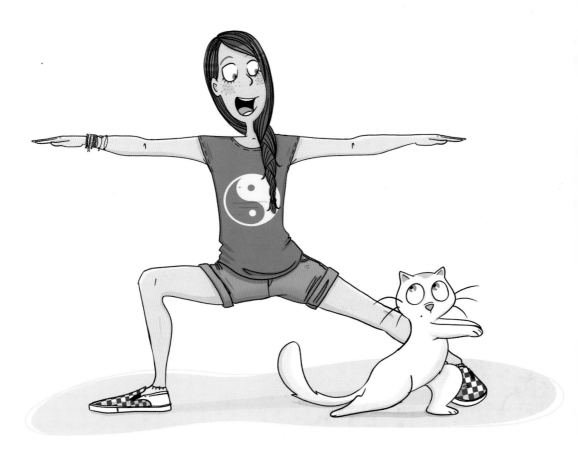

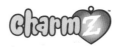

MORE GRAPHIC NOVELS AVAILABLE FROM charmz™

Amy's Diary
Space Alien... Almost?
India Desjardins

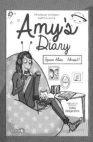

AMY'S DIARY #1 "SPACE ALIEN... ALMOST?"

Amy's Diary
The World's Upside Down
India Desjardins

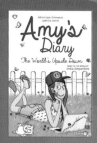

AMY'S DIARY #2 "THE WORLD'S UPSIDE DOWN"

Amy's Diary
Moving On

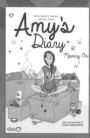

AMY'S DIARY #3 "MOVING ON"

STITCHED
The First Day of the Rest of her Life

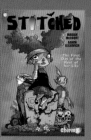

STITCHED #1 "THE FIRST DAY OF THE REST OF HER LIFE"

STITCHED
Love in the Time of Assumption

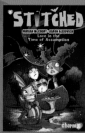

STITCHED #2 "LOVE IN THE TIME OF ASSUMPTION"

Chloe
The New Girl

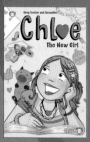

CHLOE #1 "THE NEW GIRL"

Chloe
The Queen of High School

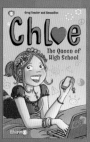

CHLOE #2 "THE QUEEN OF HIGH SCHOOL"

Chloe
Frenemies

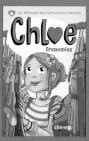

CHLOE #3 "FRENEMIES"

Chloe
Rainy Day

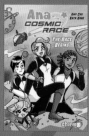

CHLOE #4 "RAINY DAY"

Ana and the Cosmic Race
The Race Begins

ANA AND THE COSMIC RACE #1 "THE RACE BEGINS"

PATRICIA LYFOUNG
The Scarlet Rose

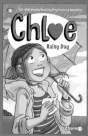

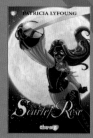

SCARLET ROSE #1 "I KNEW I'D MEET YOU"

PATRICIA LYFOUNG
The Scarlet Rose
I'll Go Where You Go

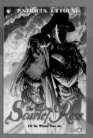

SCARLET ROSE #2 "I'LL GO WHERE YOU GO"

PATRICIA LYFOUNG
The Scarlet Rose
I Think I Love You

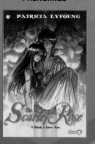

SCARLET ROSE #3 "I THINK I LOVE YOU"

PATRICIA LYFOUNG
The Scarlet Rose

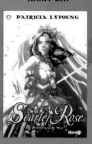

SCARLET ROSE #4 "YOU WILL ALWAYS BE MINE"

GFFs
Ghost Friends Forever

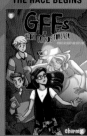

G.F.F.s #1 "MY HEART LIES IN THE 90s"

GFFs
Ghost Friends Forever
Witches Get Things Done

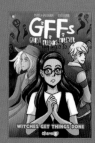

G.F.F.s #2 "WITCHES GET THINGS DONE"

Monica
Who Can Afford the Price of Friendship Today?!

MONICA ADVENTURES #1

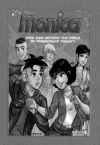

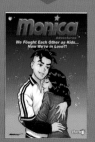

Monica
We Fought Each Other as Kids... Now We're in Love?!

MONICA ADVENTURES #2

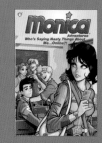

Monica
Who's Saying Nasty Things About Me...Online?!

MONICA ADVENTURES #3

Sweeties
Cherry Skye

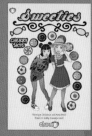

SWEETIES #1 "CHERRY SKYE"

SEE MORE AT PAPERCUTZ.COM

Amy's Diary

Diary

Moving On

Based on the novels by INDIA DESJARDINS

Adaptation — VÉRONIQUE GRISSEAUX

Illustration — LAËTITIA AYNIÉ

charmz

NEW YORK

Véronique and Laëtitia, a team on fire that's really captured Amy's world. Elsa Lafon, my accomplice overseas. Annabelle, Laetitia Lehmann, Mélanie Rouzière, Corinne De Vailly, and the whole Michel Lafon and Jungle teams.
—*India*

Thanks to Amy for making me live such a long, beautiful adventure with two talented authors and two awesome editors!
—*Laëtitia*

What a pleasure to have worked with you, Laëtitia!
Thanks to the awesome Jungle and Lafon team.
And especially a huuuuge thanks to India!
I love this Amy Von Brandt, I love her!
—*Véronique*

Amy's Diary

#3 "Moving On"

Le journal d'Aurélie Laflamme [AMY'S DIARY] volume 3 *"Ça Déménage"* © 2016 Jungle/Michel Lafon. All Rights Reserved. www.editions-jungle.com. Used under license.

Based on the novels by INDIA DESJARDINS
VÉRONIQUE GRISSEAUX—Comics Adaptation
LAËTITIA AYNIÉ—Art, Color, Design
JOE JOHNSON—Translation
BRYAN SENKA—Lettering
LÉA ZIMMERMAN—Production
IZZY BOYCE-BLANCHARD—Editorial Intern
JEFF WHITMAN—Managing Editor
JIM SALICRUP
Editor-in-Chief

Thanks to Véronique and Laetritia,
a team on fire that's really captured Amy's world.

Special thanks to FLORA BOFFY

Charmz is an imprint of Papercutz.
Papercutz.com

Hardcover ISBN: 978-1-5458-0344-8
Paperback ISBN: 978-1-5458-0345-5

Printed in China
November 2019

Charmz books may be purchased for business or promotional use. For information on bulk purchases please contact Macmillan Corporate and Premium Sales Department at:
(800) 221-795-7945 x5442.

Distributed by Macmillan
First Charmz printing

On Cloud Nine

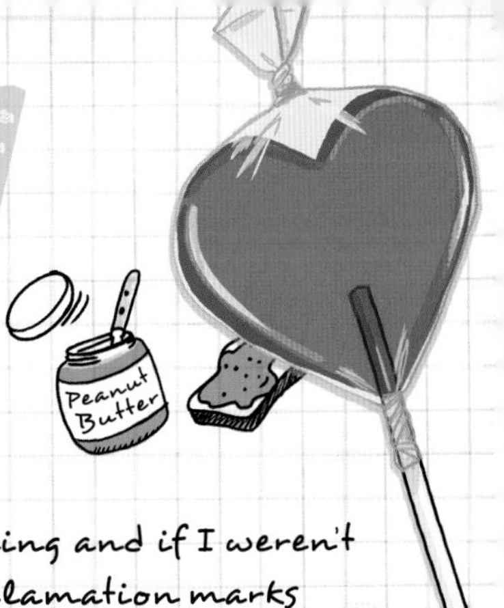
Peanut Butter

- Friday, January 5th:

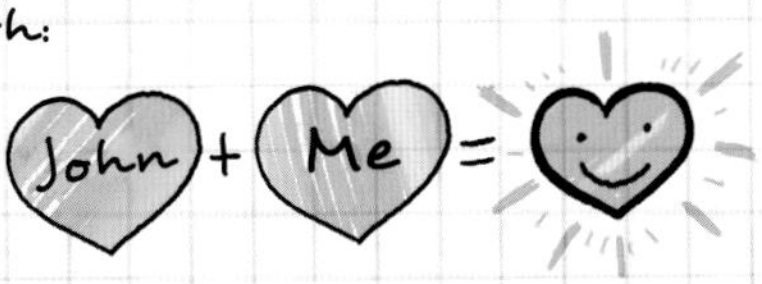
John
+
Me
=

9:52am:

Everything's great!
(If I hadn't become hyper-aware about global warming and if I weren't worried about saving trees, I'd fill this page with exclamation marks to illustrate the true intensity of my happiness.)

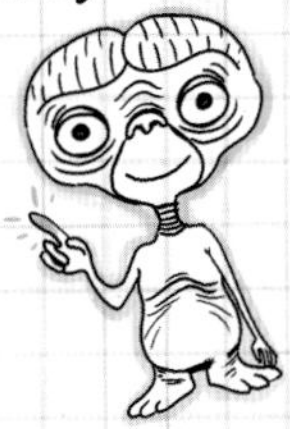

Everything's going so great, I wonder if it can be possible to be this happy? So much so, I have nothing to talk about.

NOTHING!

Now I'm part of that category of happy people with no problems. That's new for me. Me, who so often feels like aliens abandoned me on Earth after an intergalactic voyage (yes, yes, apart from the fact that ET is truly ugly, I've identified with that character for a long time).

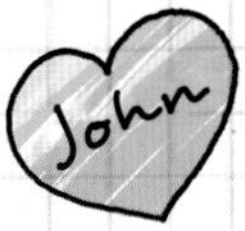
John

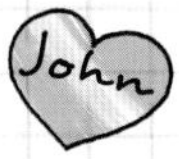
John

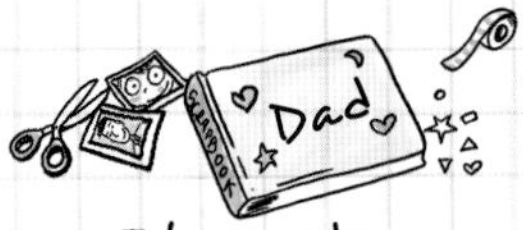
Dad

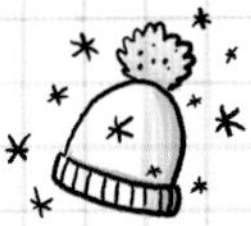

9:54am:

This morning, when I woke up, I turned on my new TV that I placed right in front of my bed. (The one I got for Christmas from my mom. I also got a super awesome present from my Granny Von Brandt: she gave me pictures of my dad to make a scrapbook of his life. That way he'll always be close to me!). So, back to TV... just in time for the music video I've been wanting to watch... Craaaazy!

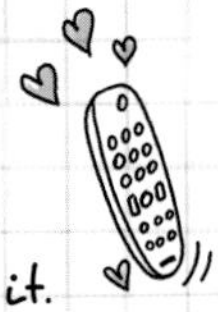

And when I hit the "on" button and the video I was wanting to see popped up on my screen, I just knew it was going be a great day. That life was giving me exactly what I wanted right when I wanted it.

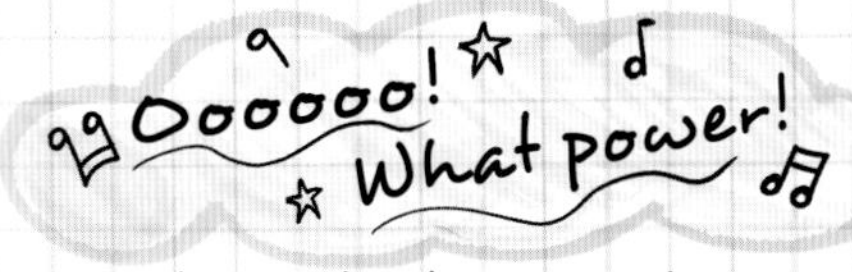
Oooooo!
What power!

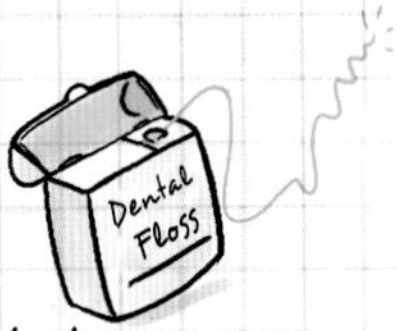
Dental Floss

9:56am:

What can I fantasize about, now that all my dreams have come true? I know what I could do. I could dream of not being in a dentist's chair, with a dental hygienist energetically scratching away at my teeth with a scaler while, in the neighboring room, an instrument's making the sound zweeeee, zweeeeee, which is splitting my eardrums.

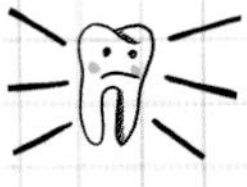

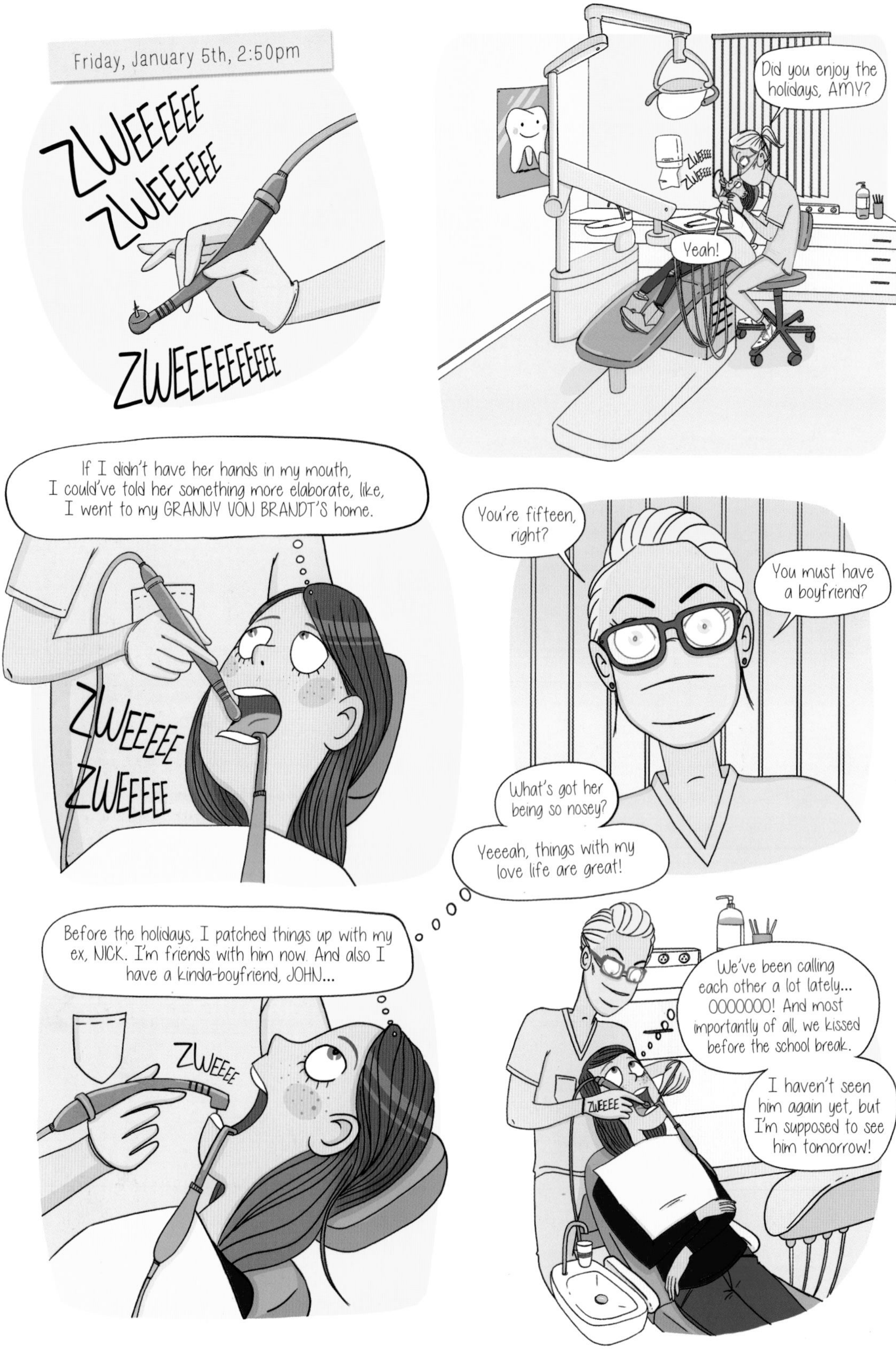
Friday, January 5th, 2:50pm
ZWEEEEEE
ZWEEEEEE
ZWEEEEEEEEEE
Did you enjoy the holidays, AMY?
Yeah!
If I didn't have her hands in my mouth, I could've told her something more elaborate, like, I went to my GRANNY VON BRANDT'S home.
ZWEEEEE
ZWEEEEE
You're fifteen, right?
You must have a boyfriend?
What's got her being so nosey?
Yeeeah, things with my love life are great!
Before the holidays, I patched things up with my ex, NICK. I'm friends with him now. And also I have a kinda-boyfriend, JOHN...
ZWEEEE
We've been calling each other a lot lately... OOOOOOO! And most importantly of all, we kissed before the school break.
I haven't seen him again yet, but I'm supposed to see him tomorrow!
ZWEEEE

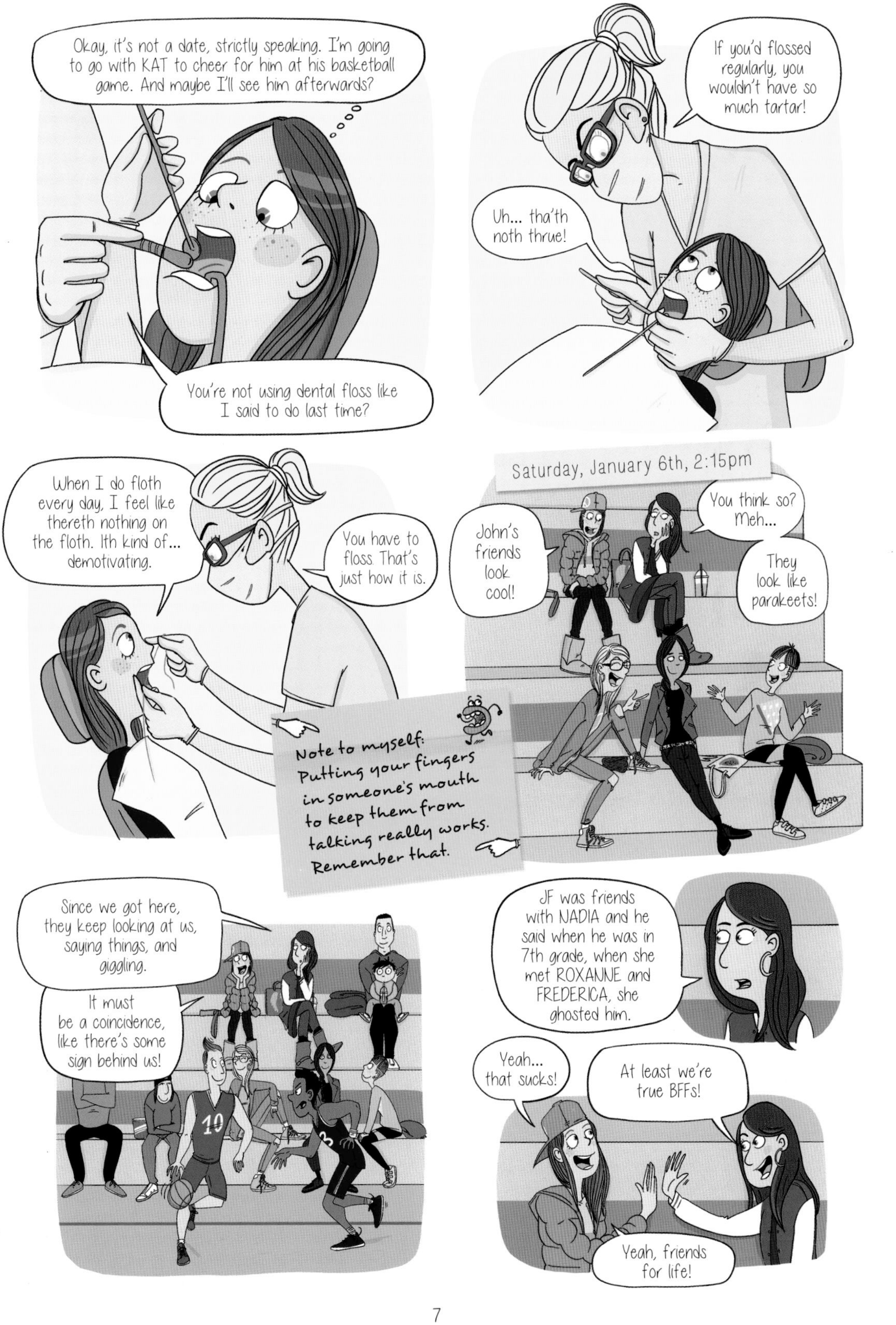
Okay, it's not a date, strictly speaking. I'm going to go with KAT to cheer for him at his basketball game. And maybe I'll see him afterwards?
You're not using dental floss like I said to do last time?
If you'd flossed regularly, you wouldn't have so much tartar!
Uh... tha'th noth thrue!
When I do floth every day, I feel like thereth nothing on the floth. Ith kind of... demotivating.
You have to floss. That's just how it is.
Note to myself: Putting your fingers in someone's mouth to keep them from talking really works. Remember that.
Saturday, January 6th, 2:15pm
John's friends look cool!
You think so? Meh...
They look like parakeets!
Since we got here, they keep looking at us, saying things, and giggling.
It must be a coincidence, like there's some sign behind us!
JF was friends with NADIA and he said when he was in 7th grade, when she met ROXANNE and FREDERICA, she ghosted him.
Yeah... that sucks!
At least we're true BFFs!
Yeah, friends for life!

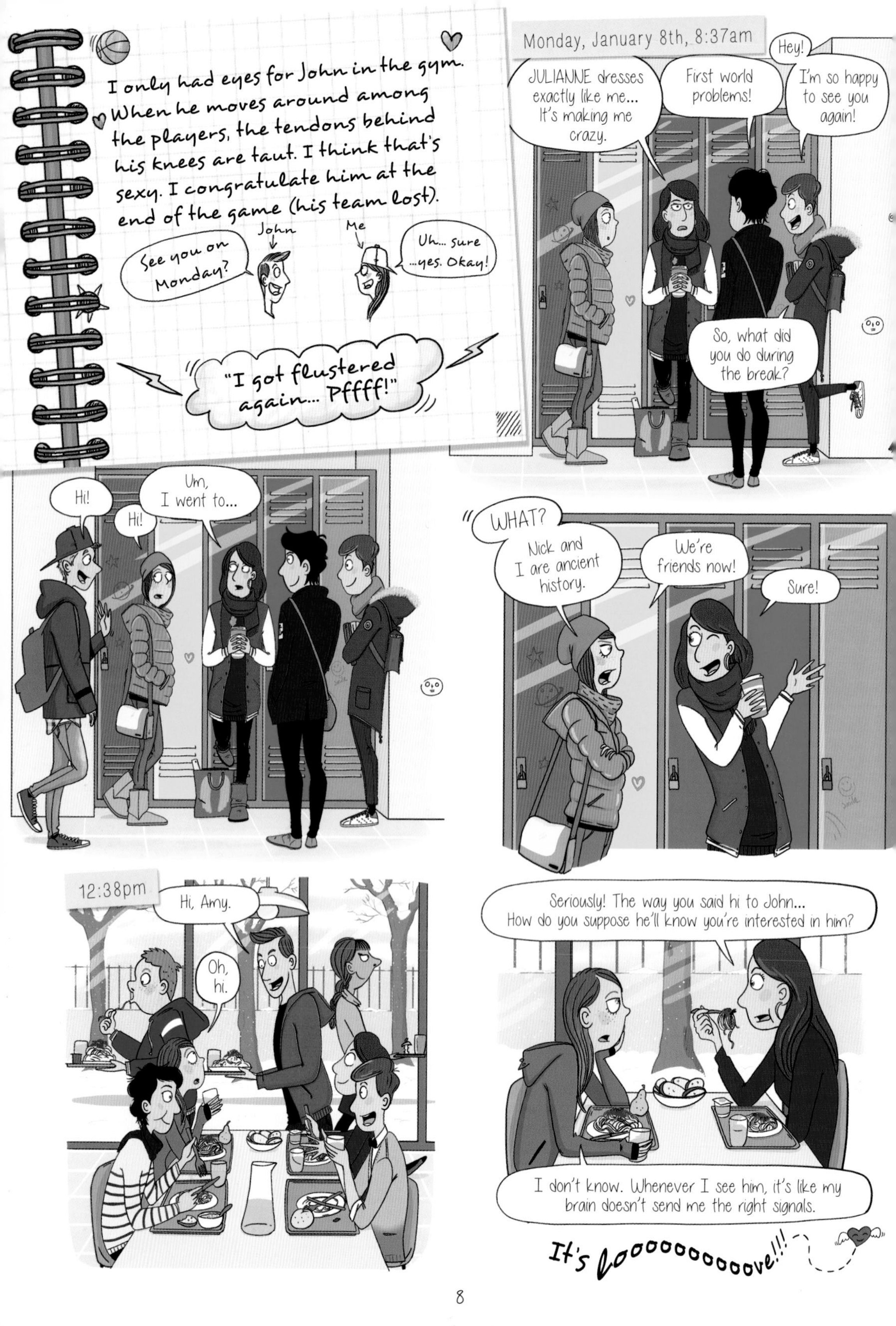
I only had eyes for John in the gym. When he moves around among the players, the tendons behind his knees are taut. I think that's sexy. I congratulate him at the end of the game (his team lost).
John
Me
See you on Monday?
Uh... sure ...yes. Okay!
"I got flustered again... Pffff!"
Monday, January 8th, 8:37am
JULIANNE dresses exactly like me... It's making me crazy.
First world problems!
Hey!
I'm so happy to see you again!
So, what did you do during the break?
Hi!
Hi!
Um, I went to...
WHAT?
Nick and I are ancient history.
We're friends now!
Sure!
12:38pm
Hi, Amy.
Oh, hi.
Seriously! The way you said hi to John... How do you suppose he'll know you're interested in him?
I don't know. Whenever I see him, it's like my brain doesn't send me the right signals.
It's loooooooooove!!!

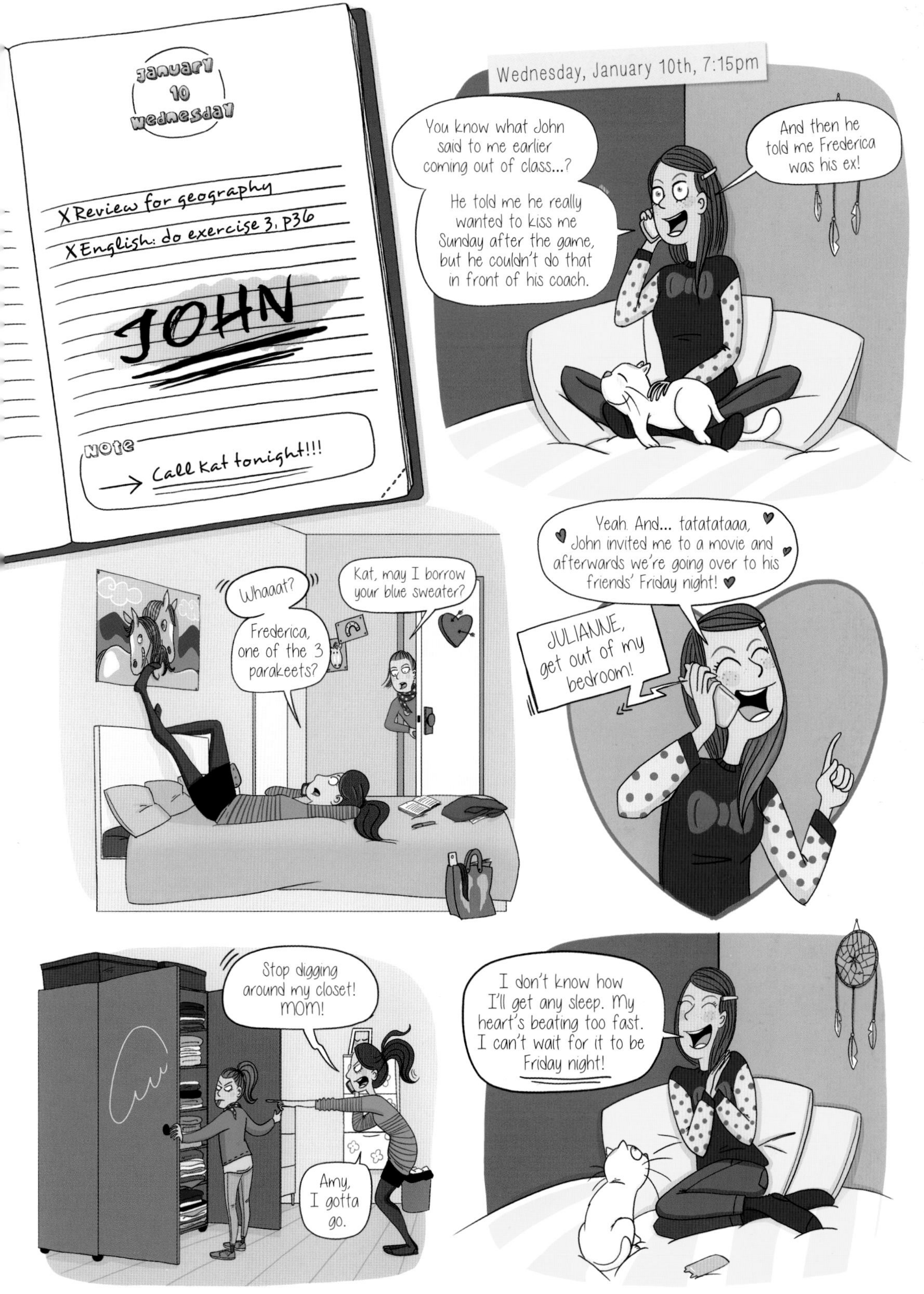
January 10 Wednesday
X Review for geography
X English: do exercise 3, p36
JOHN
Note
→ Call Kat tonight!!!
Wednesday, January 10th, 7:15pm
You know what John said to me earlier coming out of class...?
He told me he really wanted to kiss me Sunday after the game, but he couldn't do that in front of his coach.
And then he told me Frederica was his ex!
Whaaat?
Frederica, one of the 3 parakeets?
Kat, may I borrow your blue sweater?
Yeah. And... tatatataaa, John invited me to a movie and afterwards we're going over to his friends' Friday night!
JULIANNE, get out of my bedroom!
Stop digging around my closet! MOM!
Amy, I gotta go.
I don't know how I'll get any sleep. My heart's beating too fast. I can't wait for it to be Friday night!

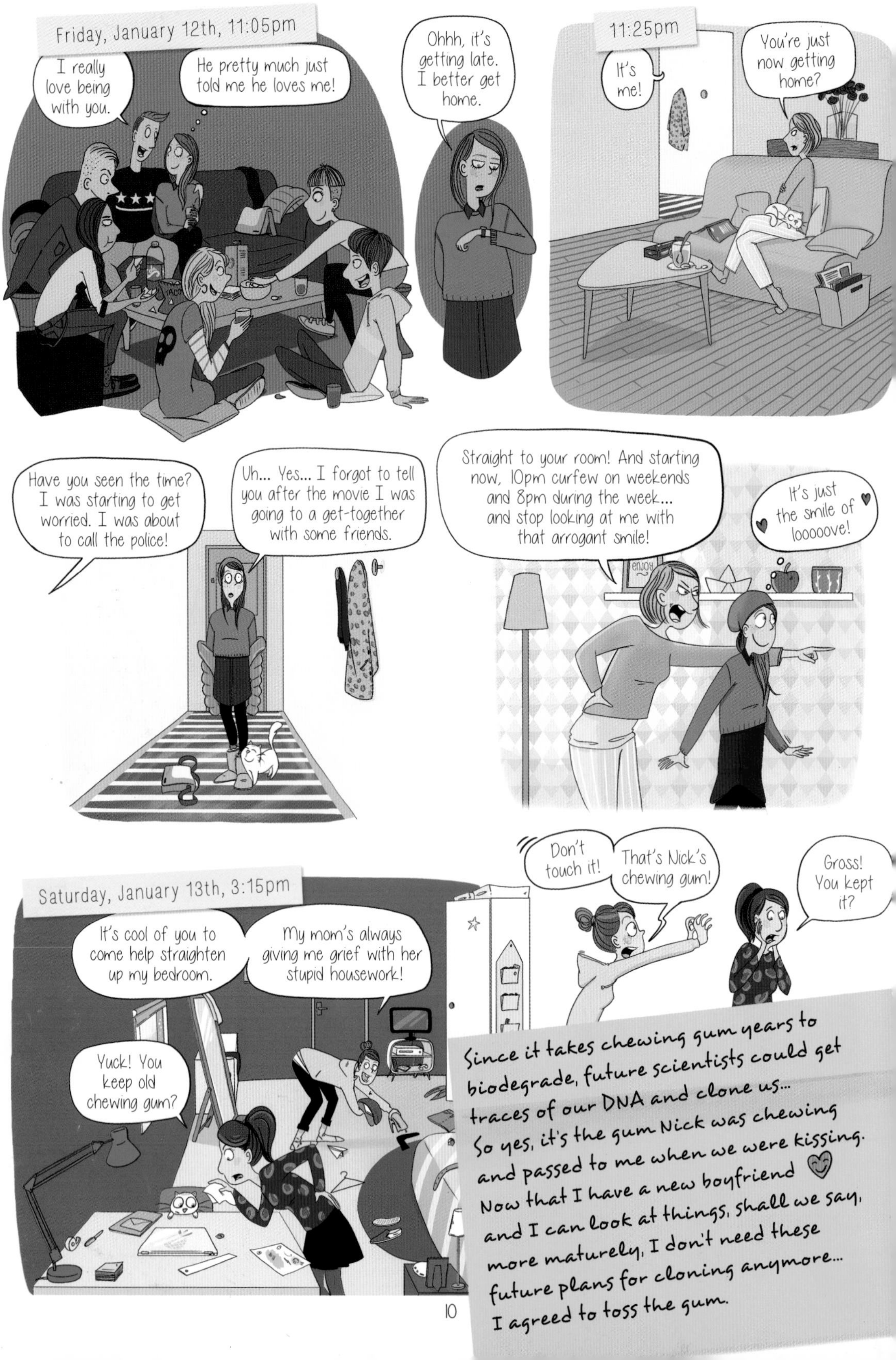

Friday, January 12th, 11:05pm
I really love being with you.
He pretty much just told me he loves me!
Ohhh, it's getting late. I better get home.
11:25pm
It's me!
You're just now getting home?
Have you seen the time? I was starting to get worried. I was about to call the police!
Uh... Yes... I forgot to tell you after the movie I was going to a get-together with some friends.
Straight to your room! And starting now, 10pm curfew on weekends and 8pm during the week... and stop looking at me with that arrogant smile!
It's just the smile of looooove!
Saturday, January 13th, 3:15pm
It's cool of you to come help straighten up my bedroom.
My mom's always giving me grief with her stupid housework!
Yuck! You keep old chewing gum?
Don't touch it!
That's Nick's chewing gum!
Gross! You kept it?
Since it takes chewing gum years to biodegrade, future scientists could get traces of our DNA and clone us...
So yes, it's the gum Nick was chewing and passed to me when we were kissing.
Now that I have a new boyfriend and I can look at things, shall we say, more maturely, I don't need these future plans for cloning anymore...
I agreed to toss the gum.

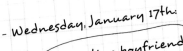

— Wednesday, January 17th:

Life with a boyfriend is totally <u>awesome</u>!

Everything seems lighter to me, different. Food is better. The floor doesn't look so hard. Jokes are funnier. The cold doesn't penetrate the pores of my skin...

(but using that argument with my mom as a reason for not wearing a hat is impossible).

Thursday, January 18th, 9:02am

Oh, my God! I'm an assassin!

I attempted unpremeditated murder!

But it's not your fault.

John is allergic to peanuts. You ate some peanut butter toast this morning, you kissed him on the lips, so here we are.

I don't dare think of what might have happened if I'd kissed him more, let's say... passionately!

Don't worry, I'm not mad at you I should've told you I was allergic.

I'm a horrible killer and I think John has Stockholm Syndrome.

Stockholm Syndrome:
Noun: Stockholm Syndrome is a complex psychological phenomenon (because it's paradoxical) of sympathy between the victim and his or her executioner.

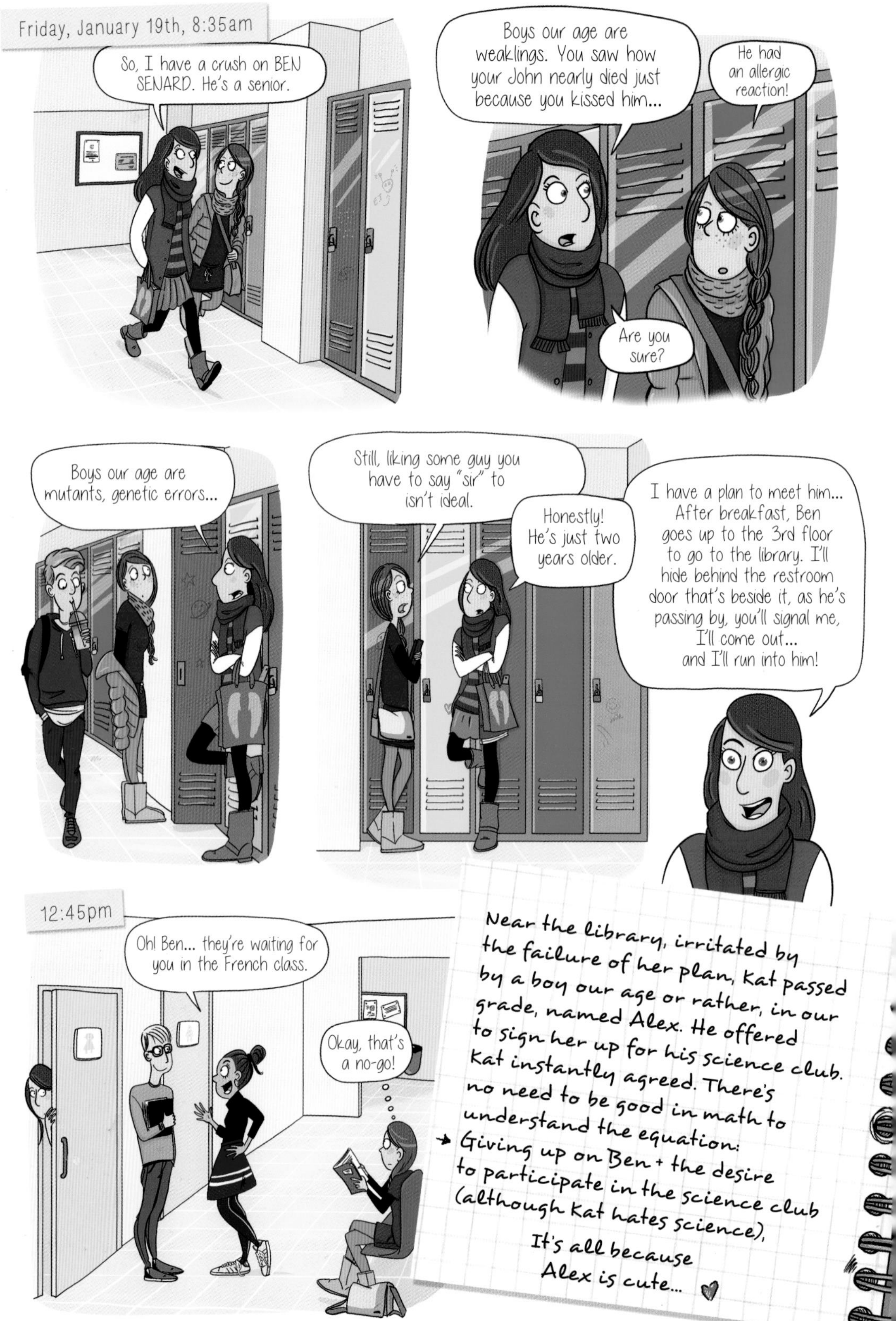
Friday, January 19th, 8:35am
So, I have a crush on BEN SENARD. He's a senior.
Boys our age are weaklings. You saw how your John nearly died just because you kissed him...
He had an allergic reaction!
Are you sure?
Boys our age are mutants, genetic errors...
Still, liking some guy you have to say "sir" to isn't ideal.
Honestly! He's just two years older.
I have a plan to meet him... After breakfast, Ben goes up to the 3rd floor to go to the library. I'll hide behind the restroom door that's beside it, as he's passing by, you'll signal me, I'll come out... and I'll run into him!
12:45pm
Oh! Ben... they're waiting for you in the French class.
Okay, that's a no-go!
Near the library, irritated by the failure of her plan, Kat passed by a boy our age or rather, in our grade, named Alex. He offered to sign her up for his science club. Kat instantly agreed. There's no need to be good in math to understand the equation:
→ Giving up on Ben + the desire to participate in the science club (although Kat hates science),
It's all because Alex is cute...

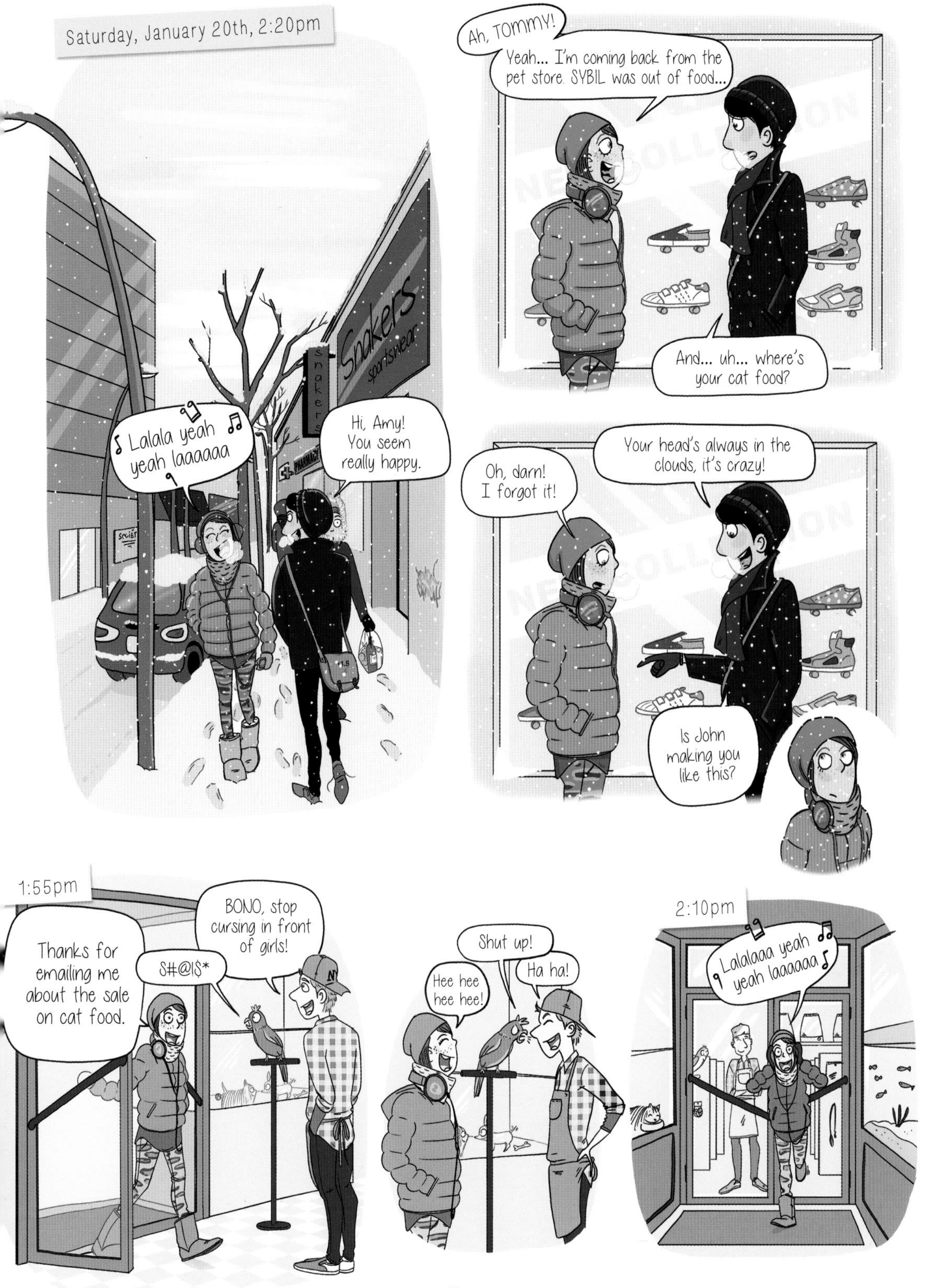
Saturday, January 20th, 2:20pm
Lalala yeah yeah laaaaaa
Hi, Amy! You seem really happy.
Snakers sportswear
snakers
PHARMACY
Ah, TOMMY!
Yeah... I'm coming back from the pet store. SYBIL was out of food...
And... uh... where's your cat food?
Oh, darn! I forgot it!
Your head's always in the clouds, it's crazy!
Is John making you like this?
1:55pm
Thanks for emailing me about the sale on cat food.
S#@!$*
BONO, stop cursing in front of girls!
Hee hee hee hee!
Shut up!
Ha ha!
2:10pm
Lalalaaa yeah yeah laaaaaa

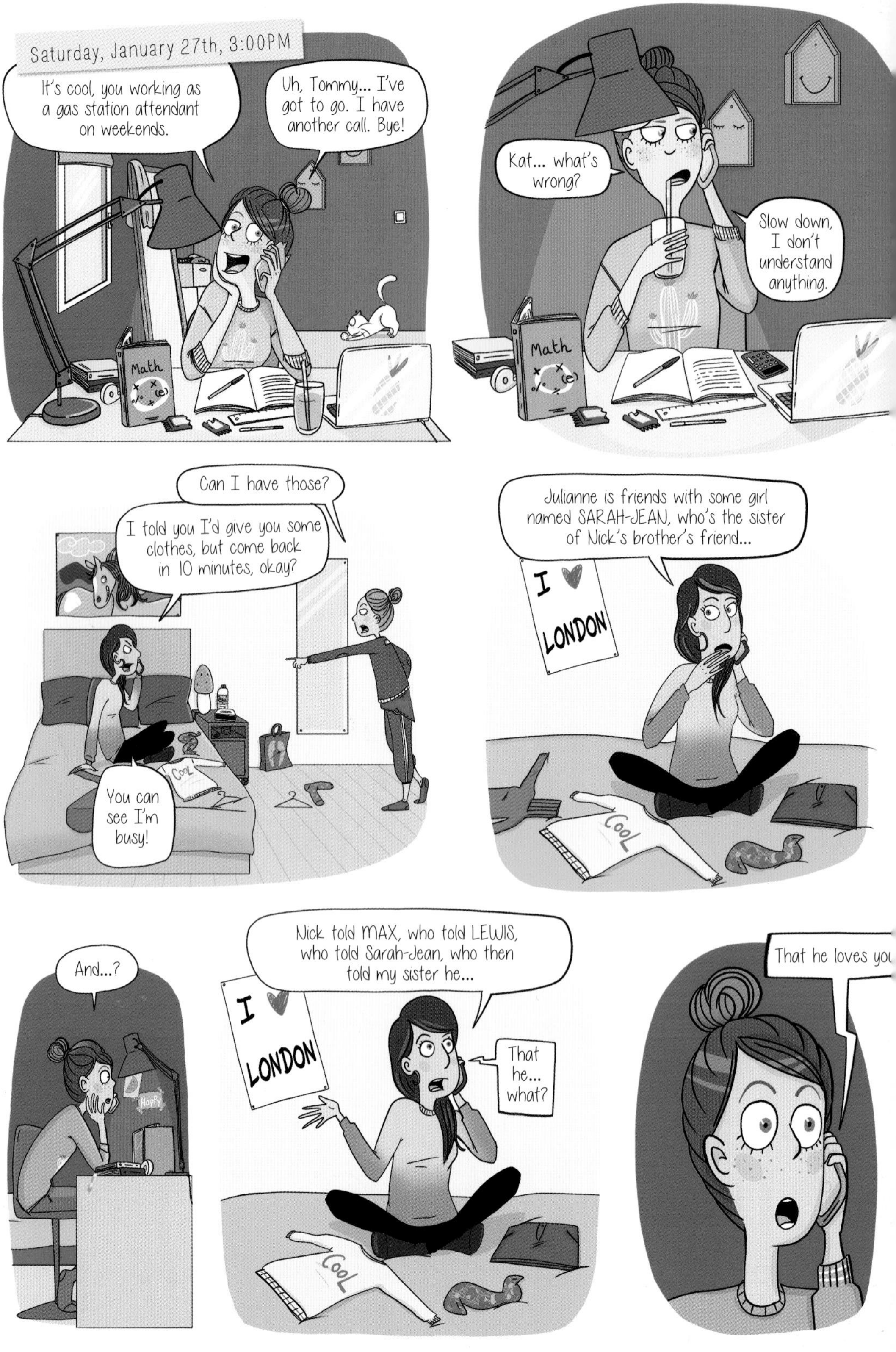
Saturday, January 27th, 3:00PM
It's cool, you working as a gas station attendant on weekends.
Uh, Tommy... I've got to go. I have another call. Bye!
Kat... what's wrong?
Slow down, I don't understand anything.
Can I have those?
I told you I'd give you some clothes, but come back in 10 minutes, okay?
You can see I'm busy!
Math
Cool
Julianne is friends with some girl named SARAH-JEAN, who's the sister of Nick's brother's friend...
I LONDON
And...?
Nick told MAX, who told LEWIS, who told Sarah-Jean, who then told my sister he...
That he... what?
That he loves you

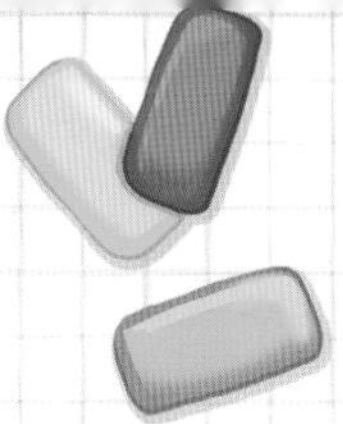

FEBRUARY
A Thousand Points of Light

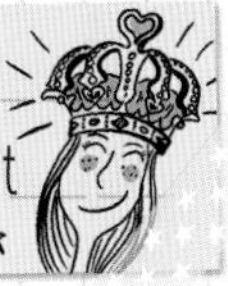

- Friday, February 2nd:

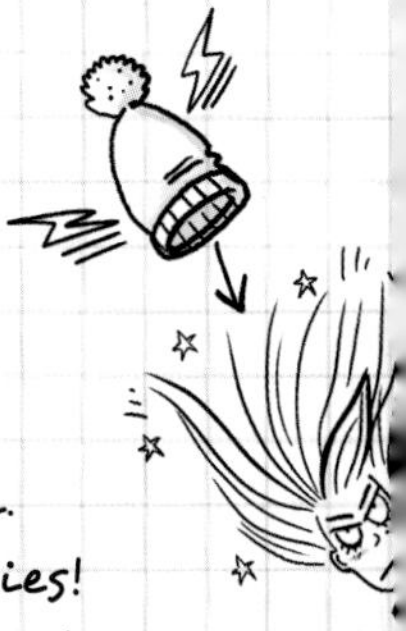

7:15pm:

I have a super busy schedule!
If cloning were more advanced, I'd totally go for that solution.
In short, I think it's almost exhausting having so many activities!
What's more, I'm meeting more and more people at school. Yesterday, Sophie-Anne Menard, a girl from my elementary school who didn't even like me, said hello to me!

Weirdly, the fact the Sophie-Anne would say hello to me (timidly, too) is almost like, shall we say, personal revenge.

I'm popular... I'm popular?
Me?!? Popular! **Woo-hoo!**

8:00pm:

Being really busy with my homework, John's basketball practice, my friends and my family, I haven't had much time to ponder this:
Nick still loves me!
In fact, I think I've been totally stunned the last few days by that news. I can't believe it... He still ♥ me?

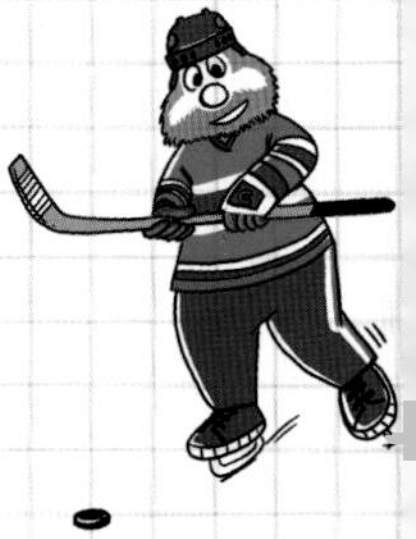

Okay, let's be clear (well, let it be clear to me), I love John.
He's so cool. He's handsome, kind, awesome, marvelous,
and he has magnificent tendons behind his knees.

8:08pm:

With John, it's not love like with Nick. I don't spend my time wanting to breathe in his scent or wanting to save his chewing gum.
And nothing's going "teeleeteelee" in my head.

With him, I sometimes can't control my brain anymore, but it's that way with all the boys I meet. The best thing with John is that he's helping me make new friends.
I like the girls Kat calls "parakeets."

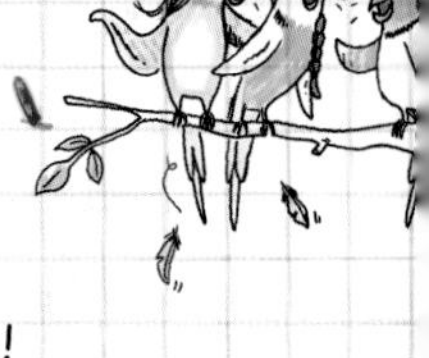

And the fact that Frederica (one of the parakeets) is John's ex doesn't bother me. They're friends. It's kind of like me and Nick!

Hurray for maturity!

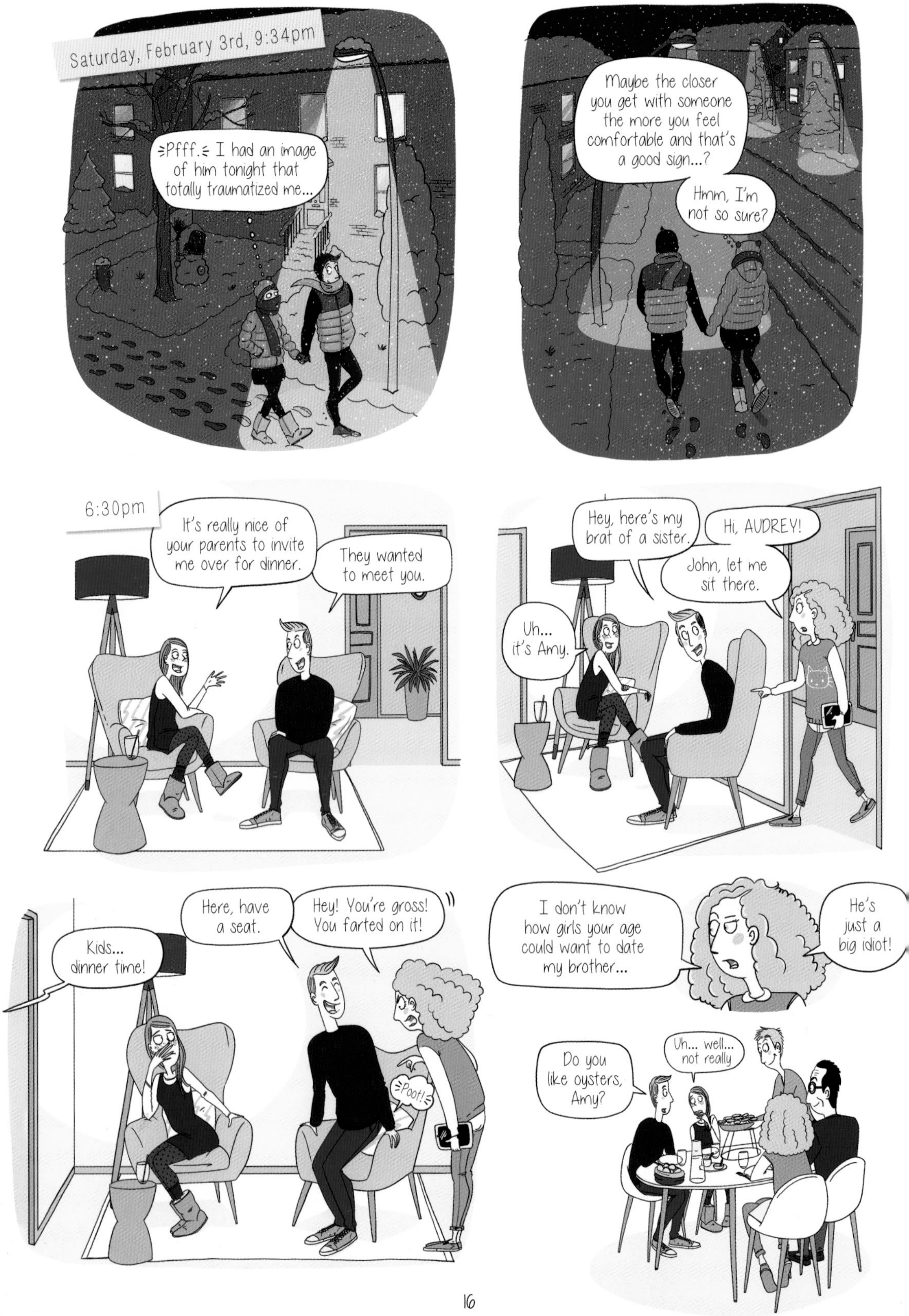
Saturday, February 3rd, 9:34pm
Pfff. I had an image of him tonight that totally traumatized me...
Maybe the closer you get with someone the more you feel comfortable and that's a good sign...?
Hmm, I'm not so sure?
6:30pm
It's really nice of your parents to invite me over for dinner.
They wanted to meet you.
Hey, here's my brat of a sister.
Hi, AUDREY!
John, let me sit there.
Uh... it's Amy.
Kids... dinner time!
Here, have a seat.
Hey! You're gross! You farted on it!
Poot!
I don't know how girls your age could want to date my brother...
He's just a big idiot!
Do you like oysters, Amy?
Uh... well... not really

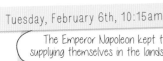
Tuesday, February 6th, 10:15am

The Emperor Napoleon kept the English from supplying themselves in the lands of the Baltic Sea...

What a dictator! He reminds me of my mom!

She refuses to let me get supplies in malls! I need new clothes to become more of a woman...

EMPEROR NAPOLEO

Hey... you got a thing for the boy in the science club...

Go on, fess up!

Why don't you ask John to have a party at his house on Friday... that way I could invite Alex!

A little quiet, please!

EMPEROR NAPOLEON

I'll talk to him after school.

Cool!

Thursday, February 8th, 12:30pm

I'll save seats in the cafeteria.

Okay, coming!

Hi!

Oh... hi!

Ever since Kat told me the "gossip," I really haven't tried to be in touch with Nick. It makes me uncomfortable knowing he's still _in love with me_...

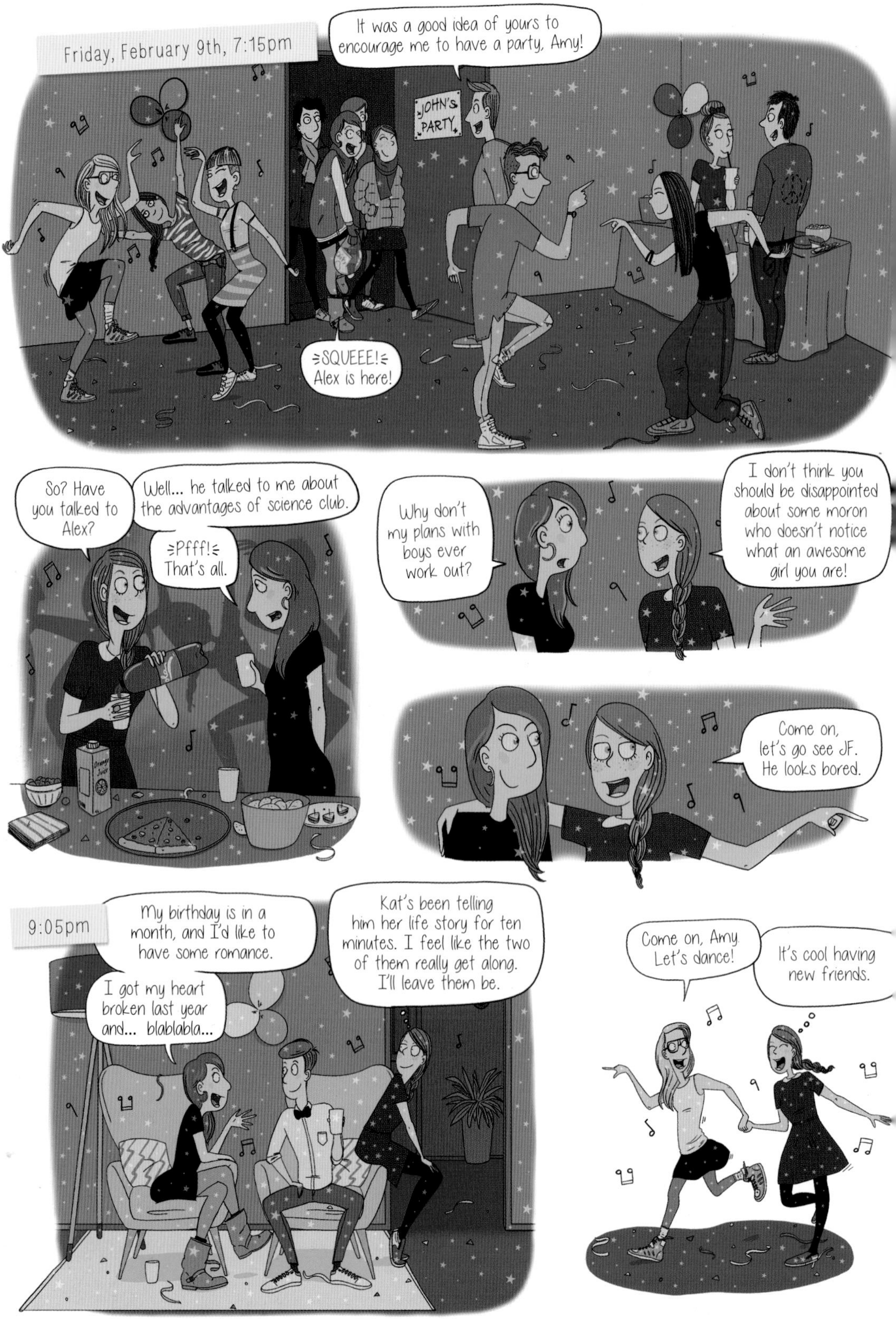
Friday, February 9th, 7:15pm
It was a good idea of yours to encourage me to have a party, Amy!
JOHN'S PARTY
SQUEEE! Alex is here!
So? Have you talked to Alex?
Well... he talked to me about the advantages of science club.
Pfff! That's all.
Why don't my plans with boys ever work out?
I don't think you should be disappointed about some moron who doesn't notice what an awesome girl you are!
Come on, let's go see JF. He looks bored.
9:05pm
My birthday is in a month, and I'd like to have some romance.
I got my heart broken last year and... blablabla...
Kat's been telling him her life story for ten minutes. I feel like the two of them really get along. I'll leave them be.
Come on, Amy. Let's dance!
It's cool having new friends.

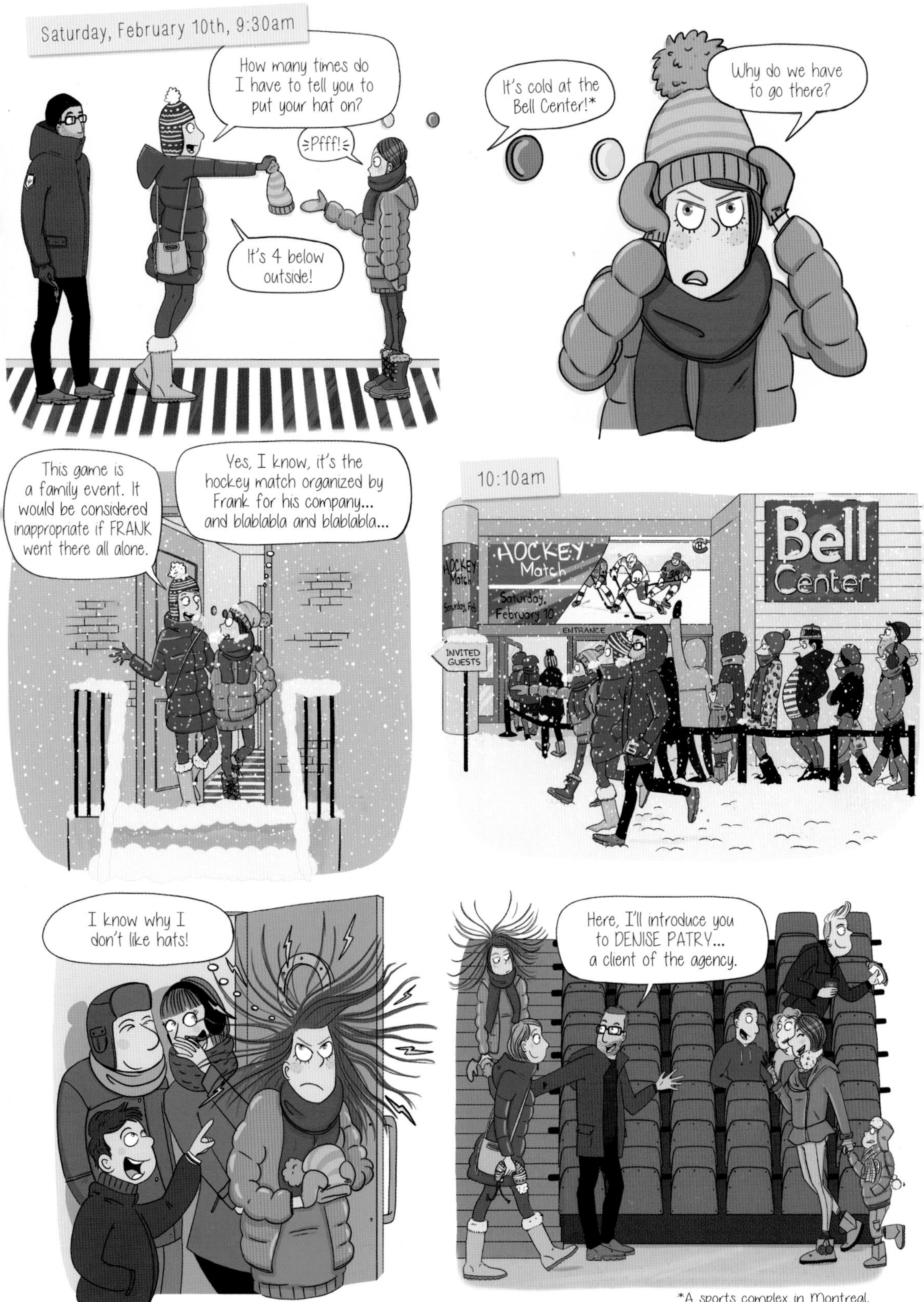

Saturday, February 10th, 9:30am
How many times do I have to tell you to put your hat on?
Pfff!
It's 4 below outside!
It's cold at the Bell Center!*
Why do we have to go there?
This game is a family event. It would be considered inappropriate if FRANK went there all alone.
Yes, I know, it's the hockey match organized by Frank for his company... and blablabla and blablabla...
10:10am
HOCKEY Match
Saturday, February 10
Bell Center
ENTRANCE
INVITED GUESTS
I know why I don't like hats!
Here, I'll introduce you to DENISE PATRY... a client of the agency.

*A sports complex in Montreal.

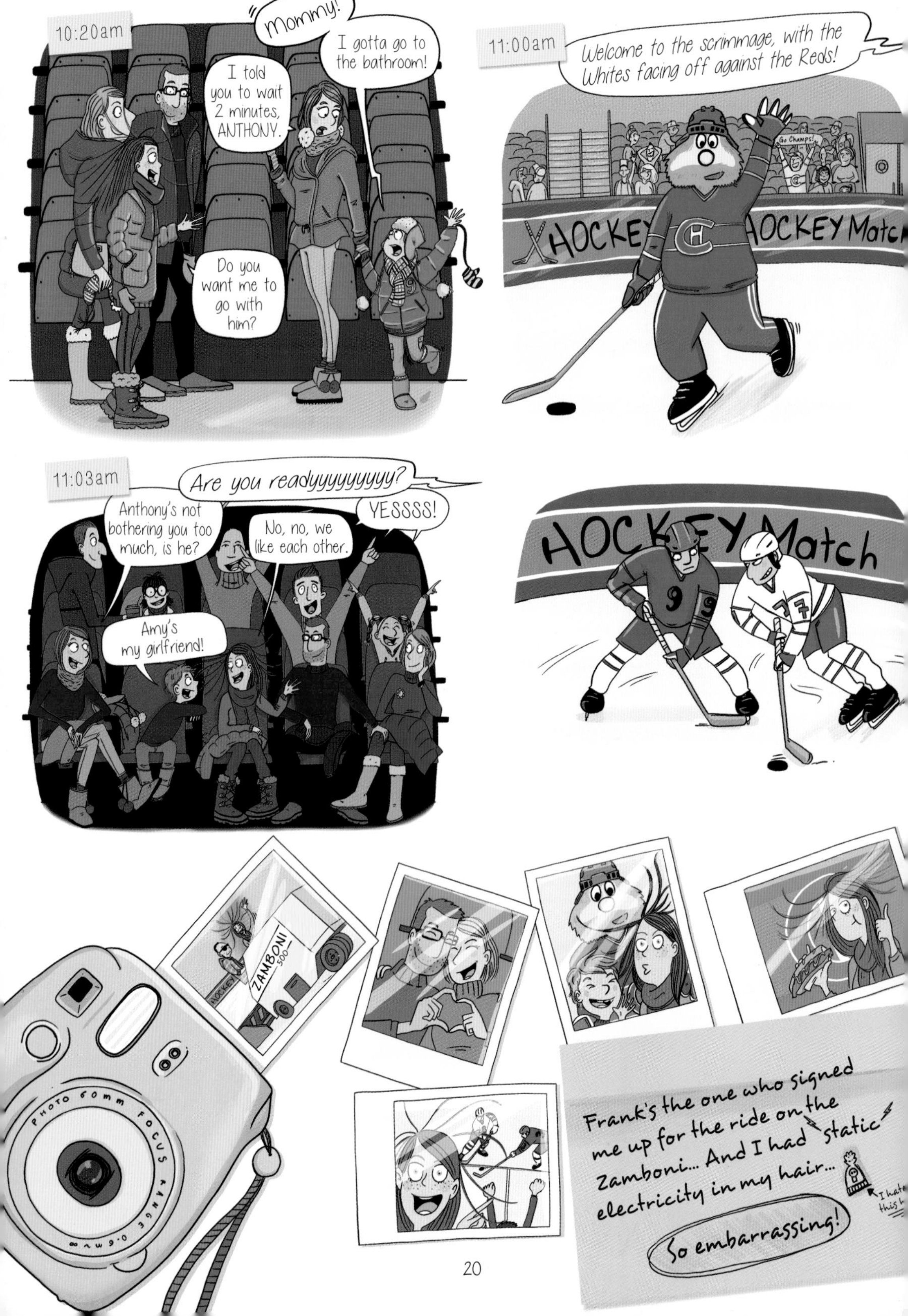
10:20am
Mommy!
I gotta go to the bathroom!
I told you to wait 2 minutes, ANTHONY.
Do you want me to go with him?
11:00am
Welcome to the scrimmage, with the Whites facing off against the Reds!
Go Champs!
HOCKEY
HOCKEY Match
11:03am
Are you readyyyyyyyy?
Anthony's not bothering you too much, is he?
No, no, we like each other.
YESSSS!
Amy's my girlfriend!
HOCKEY Match
ZAMBONI
HOCKEY
Frank's the one who signed me up for the ride on the Zamboni... And I had static electricity in my hair...
So embarrassing!

Monday, February 12th, 9:00am

You know Denise Patry, one of Frank's most important clients, loved you yesterday.

I'm really proud of you, hon.

Little Anthony is nice!

- Wednesday, February 14th:

Huge blizzard yesterday. School's closed. I spent my day sending email....

It's February 14th and It's ... tatatataaa Valentine's Day!

☑ Mail

To	John Martel
From	Amy Von Brandt
Subject	Happy Valentines!
Date	Wednesday, February 14, 10:22am

Hi!
I just wanted to wish you a Happy Blizzard!
No, just kidding! Happy Valentine's Day!
I love you.
Amy

☑ Mail

To	Amy Von Brandt
From	Nick Dubuc
Subject	Hockey
Date	Wednesday, February 14, 10:52am

Hello, Super girl!
How was your hockey match the other day?
Nick :) :)

☑ Mail

To	Nick Dubuc
From	Amy Von Brandt
Subject	RE: Hockey
Date	Wednesday, February 14, 10:54am

Hi!
It was cool! I've discovered an unsuspected passion for hockey! And I even took a ride around the rink on the Zamboni... Crazy!
Amy ;)

☑ Mail

To	Amy Von Brandt
From	John Martel
Subject	RE: Happy Valentine's Day
Date	Wednesday, February 15, 10:32am

Hi, beautiful!
I've been trying to make you a Valentine all morning long, but the power went out. I got so annoyed, I almost tossed my computer out the window. It's too bad, it was kinda funny, with funny snowmen... it's too long to explain.
All that to tell you, Well...
Happy Valentine's! I love you!
John
P.S. I'm coming by your place in an hour to give you a Valentine's kiss.

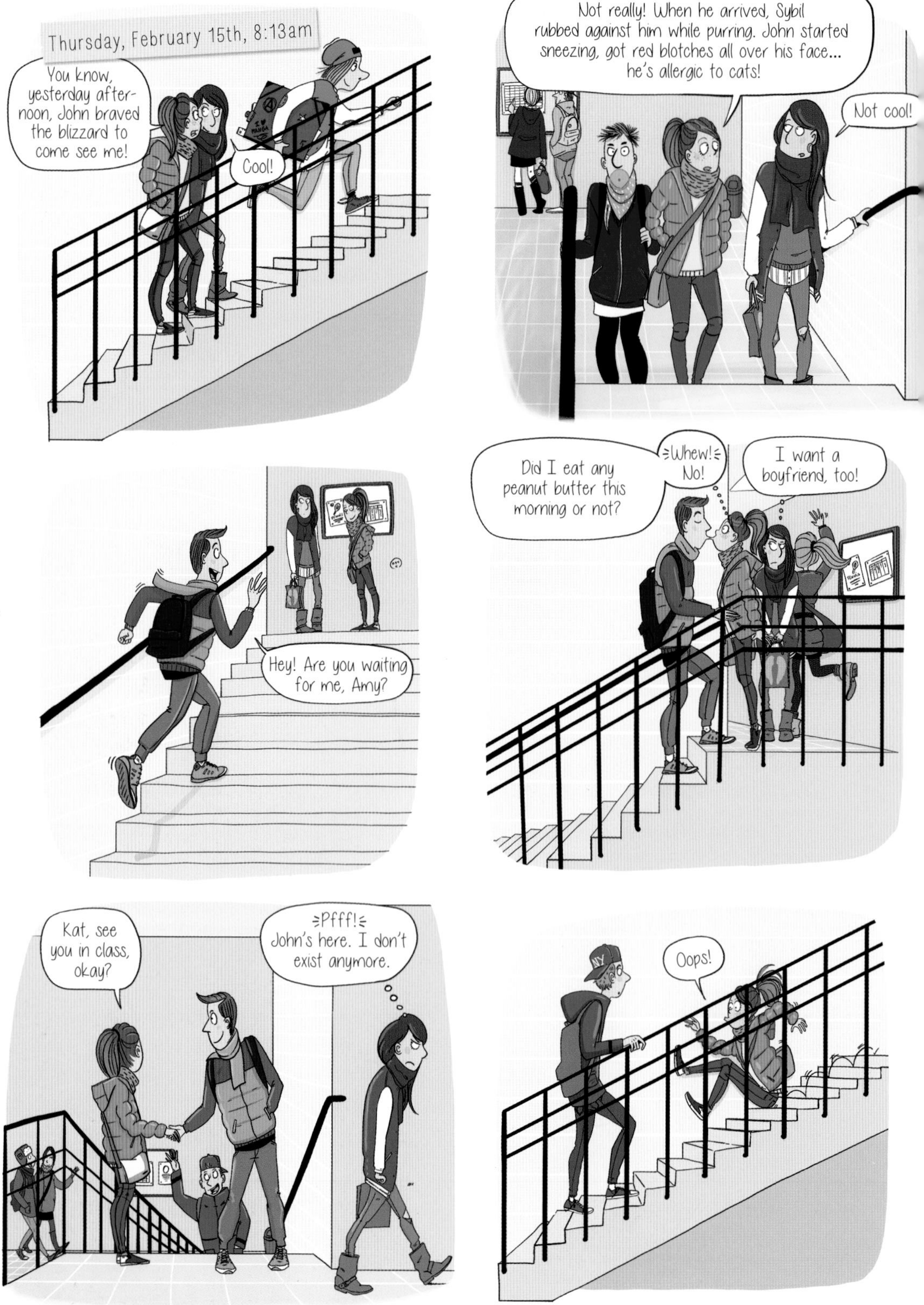
Thursday, February 15th, 8:13am
You know, yesterday after-noon, John braved the blizzard to come see me!
Cool!
Not really! When he arrived, Sybil rubbed against him while purring. John started sneezing, got red blotches all over his face... he's allergic to cats!
Not cool!
Hey! Are you waiting for me, Amy?
Did I eat any peanut butter this morning or not?
Whew! No!
I want a boyfriend, too!
Kat, see you in class, okay?
Pfff! John's here. I don't exist anymore.
Oops!

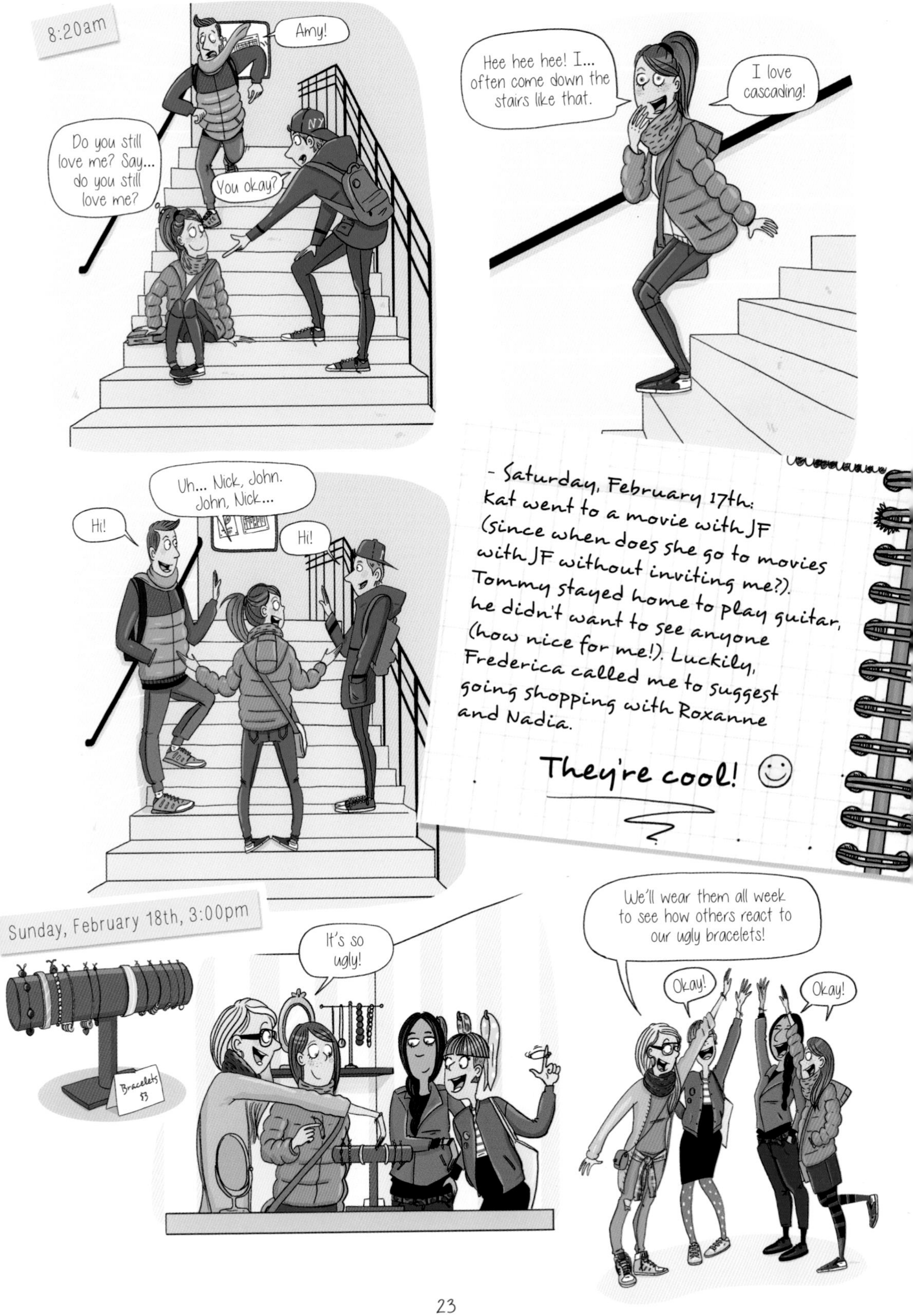
8:20am
Amy!
Do you still love me? Say... do you still love me?
You okay?
Hee hee hee! I... often come down the stairs like that.
I love cascading!
Uh... Nick, John. John, Nick...
Hi!
Hi!
- Saturday, February 17th:
Kat went to a movie with JF
(since when does she go to movies
with JF without inviting me?).
Tommy stayed home to play guitar,
he didn't want to see anyone
(how nice for me!). Luckily,
Frederica called me to suggest
going shopping with Roxanne
and Nadia.
They're cool!
Sunday, February 18th, 3:00pm
Bracelets $3
It's so ugly!
We'll wear them all week to see how others react to our ugly bracelets!
Okay!
Okay!

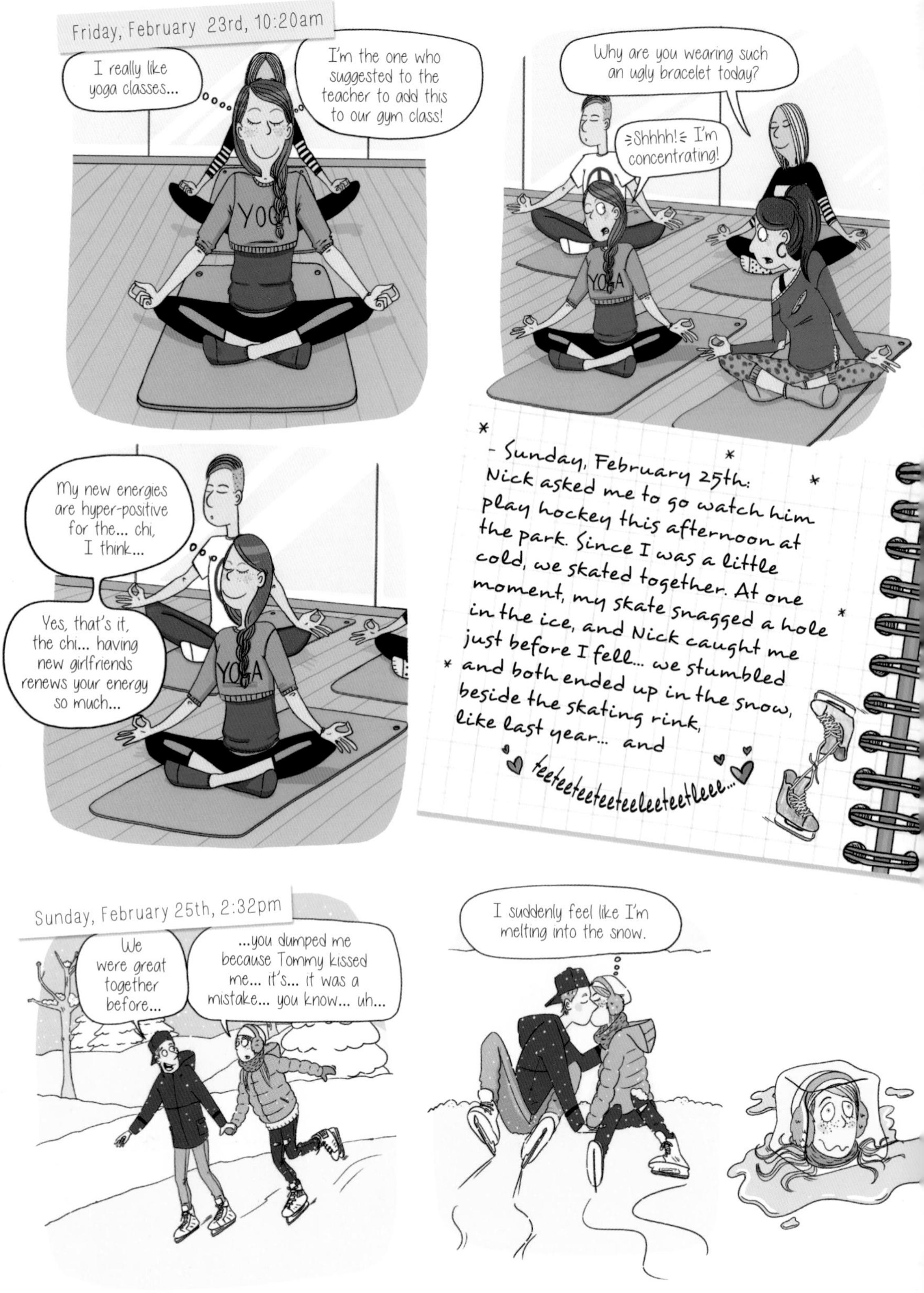
Friday, February 23rd, 10:20am
I really like yoga classes...
I'm the one who suggested to the teacher to add this to our gym class!
YOGA
Why are you wearing such an ugly bracelet today?
Shhhh! I'm concentrating!
My new energies are hyper-positive for the... chi, I think...
Yes, that's it, the chi... having new girlfriends renews your energy so much...
- Sunday, February 25th:
Nick asked me to go watch him play hockey this afternoon at the park. Since I was a little cold, we skated together. At one moment, my skate snagged a hole in the ice, and Nick caught me just before I fell... we stumbled and both ended up in the snow, beside the skating rink, like last year... and
teeteeteeteeteeleeteetleee...
Sunday, February 25th, 2:32pm
We were great together before...
...you dumped me because Tommy kissed me... it's... it was a mistake... you know... uh...
I suddenly feel like I'm melting into the snow.

MARCH

The Flip Side of the Coin

It moved all by itself!

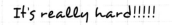

- Thursday, March 1st:

5:52pm:
I think choosing a deodorant is the most complicated thing in the universe! Am I more "wild berry"? "Funny melon"? "Gourmet strawberry"? Or "springtime breeze"? ..."Morning freshness," maybe?

It's really hard!!!!!

Deo

I'd love for my life to already be written down in a book (that wouldn't have been written by me) so I could consult it at times when I have choices to make. I'd just have to look twenty pages later. Or even at the end, that way, I'd know what to do as a career.

And I'd know what to do about my love-life!

ENAMEL

I wouldn't have to make any decisions, because everything would be decided in advance. I wouldn't be forced to invent the next part myself. Let's just say it would be relaxing!

That would also keep me from having surprises. For example, if I'd known my dad was going to die, I could've prepared myself for it. We could've spent his final moments together...

And if I'd known Tommy was going to kiss me in front of the windows of MusicPlus, last year, I wouldn't have gone there. Maybe I'd still be dating Nick now. But I wouldn't have my marvelous friend Tommy.

6:02pm:
Without any great conviction, I chose "wild berry." Simply because it's the deodorant stick I had in my hands when the cosmetics saleswoman suspiciously scowled at me, like: "You're a teenager, so you're probably going to steal something." Pffffffffffff!

Hair spider!

- Friday, March 2nd, 10:10am:
Awkward... Nick and I pretend not to see each other by the lockers...

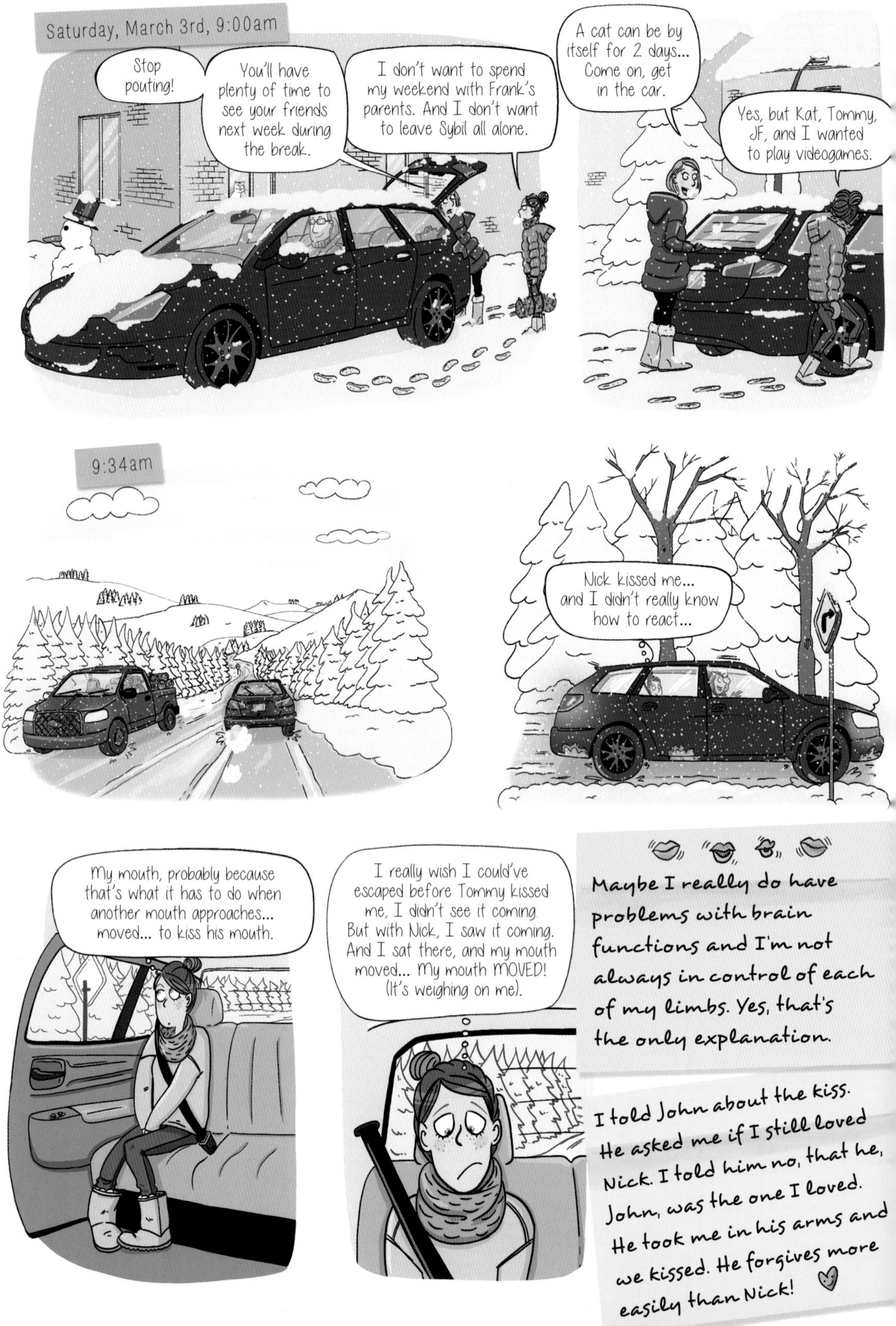
Saturday, March 3rd, 9:00am
Stop pouting!
You'll have plenty of time to see your friends next week during the break.
I don't want to spend my weekend with Frank's parents. And I don't want to leave Sybil all alone.
A cat can be by itself for 2 days... Come on, get in the car.
Yes, but Kat, Tommy, JF, and I wanted to play videogames.
9:34am
Nick kissed me... and I didn't really know how to react...
My mouth, probably because that's what it has to do when another mouth approaches... moved... to kiss his mouth.
I really wish I could've escaped before Tommy kissed me, I didn't see it coming. But with Nick, I saw it coming. And I sat there, and my mouth moved... My mouth MOVED! (It's weighing on me).
Maybe I really do have problems with brain functions and I'm not always in control of each of my limbs. Yes, that's the only explanation.
I told John about the kiss. He asked me if I still loved Nick. I told him no, that he, John, was the one I loved. He took me in his arms and we kissed. He forgives more easily than Nick!

Aaaargh!

- Sunday, March 4th, 9:00am:

While washing my hair this morning, I screamed, there was a huge spider in the bathtub... Frank's mom ran into the bathroom. And since there was no lock, she saw me completely naked!!!! Aaaargh! In fact, the spider was a ball of my hair. Real smart! And we almost couldn't escape this isolated chalet out in the country. There was a snowstorm, but fine, we got on the road to come home. And tomorrow is spring break! Yippee!

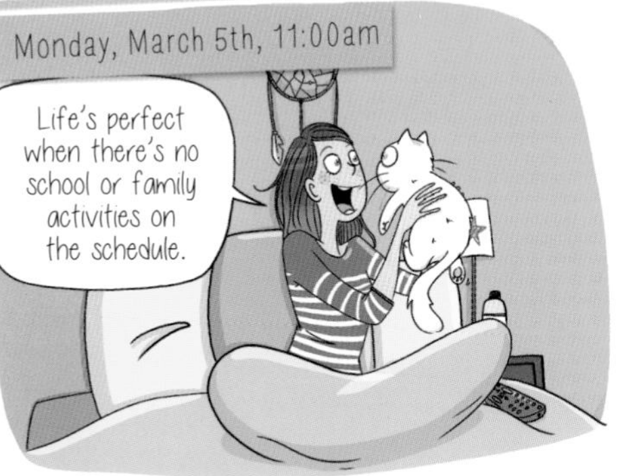

Monday, March 5th, 11:00am
Life's perfect when there's no school or family activities on the schedule.

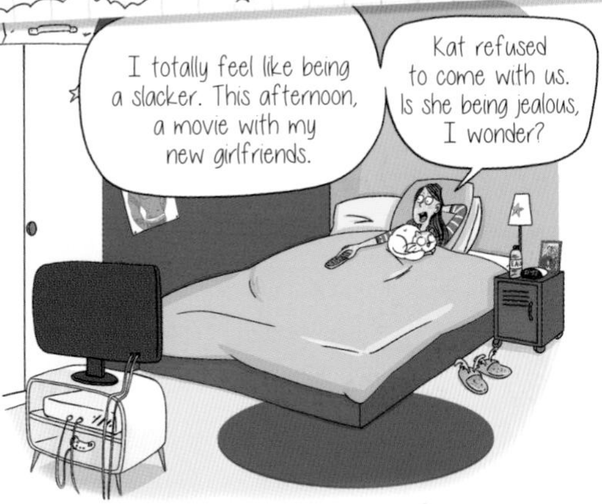

I totally feel like being a slacker. This afternoon, a movie with my new girlfriends.
Kat refused to come with us. Is she being jealous, I wonder?

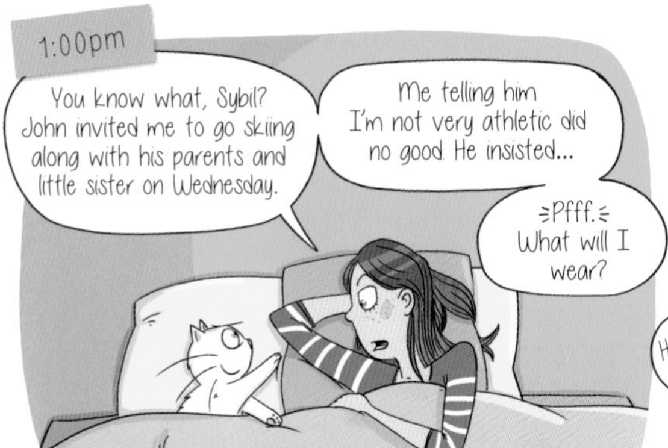

1:00pm
You know what, Sybil? John invited me to go skiing along with his parents and little sister on Wednesday.
Me telling him I'm not very athletic did no good. He insisted...
Pfff. What will I wear?

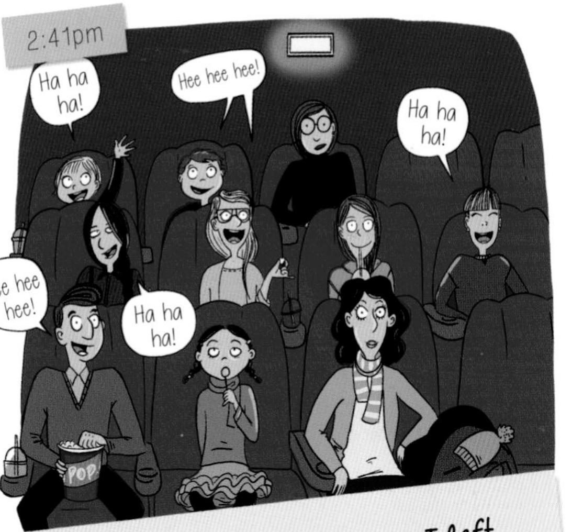

2:41pm
Ha ha ha!
Hee hee hee!
Ha ha ha!
Hee hee hee!
Ha ha ha!
POP

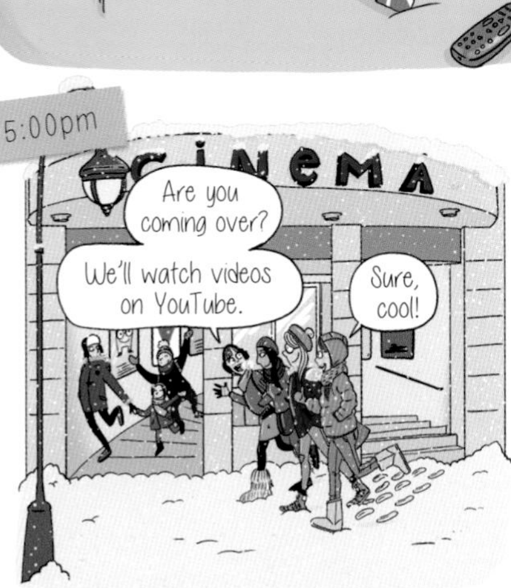

5:00pm
CINEMA
Are you coming over?
We'll watch videos on YouTube.
Sure, cool!

I didn't see the time when I left Roxanne's, but it was past 7pm. My mom was furious I got home so late without calling her. And like usual, she was worried. She said to me: "I bought you a cellphone, if it's always going to be out of power, what use is it?"

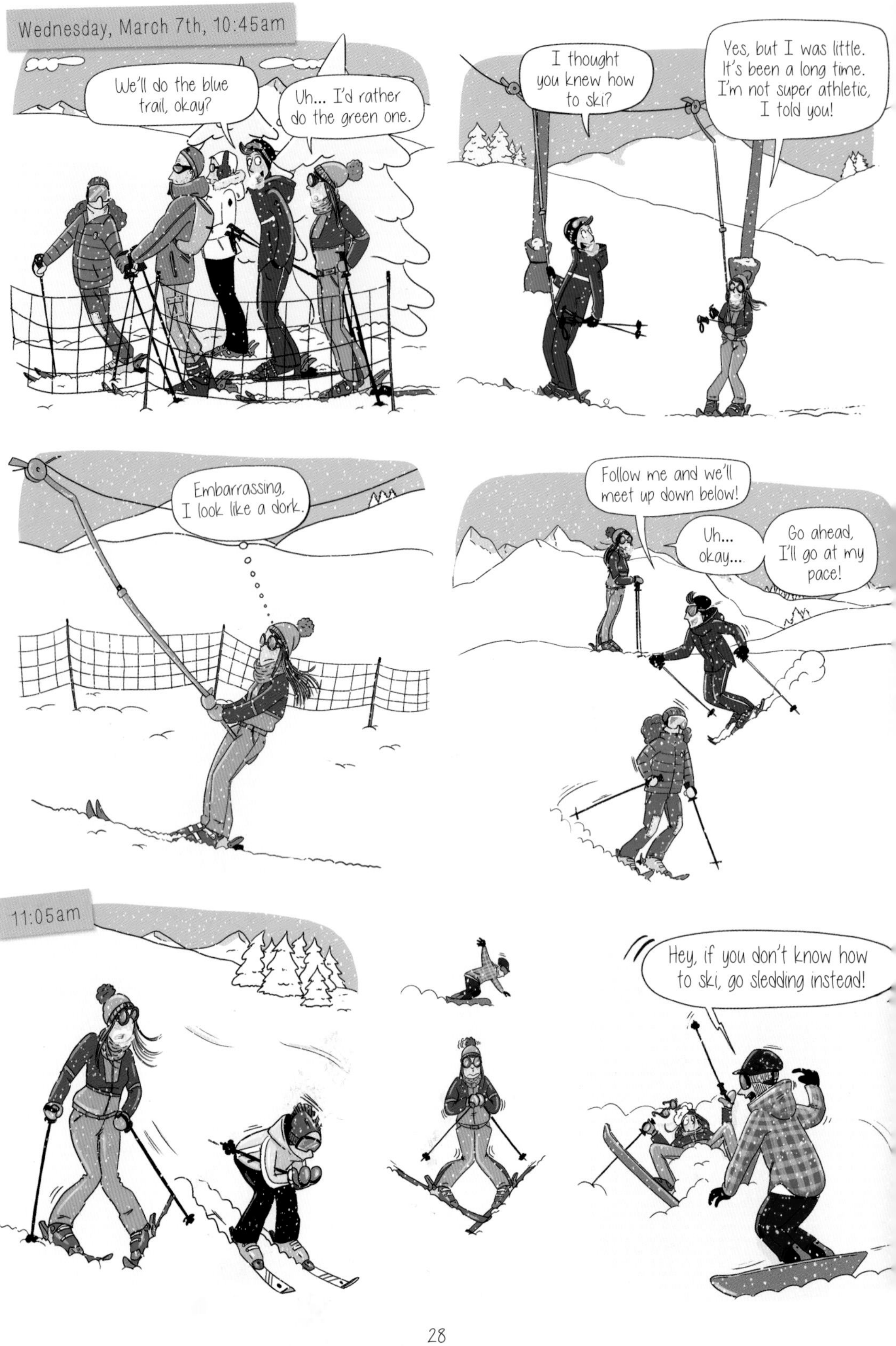
Wednesday, March 7th, 10:45am
We'll do the blue trail, okay?
Uh... I'd rather do the green one.
I thought you knew how to ski?
Yes, but I was little. It's been a long time. I'm not super athletic, I told you!
Embarrassing, I look like a dork.
Follow me and we'll meet up down below!
Uh... okay...
Go ahead, I'll go at my pace!
11:05am
Hey, if you don't know how to ski, go sledding instead!

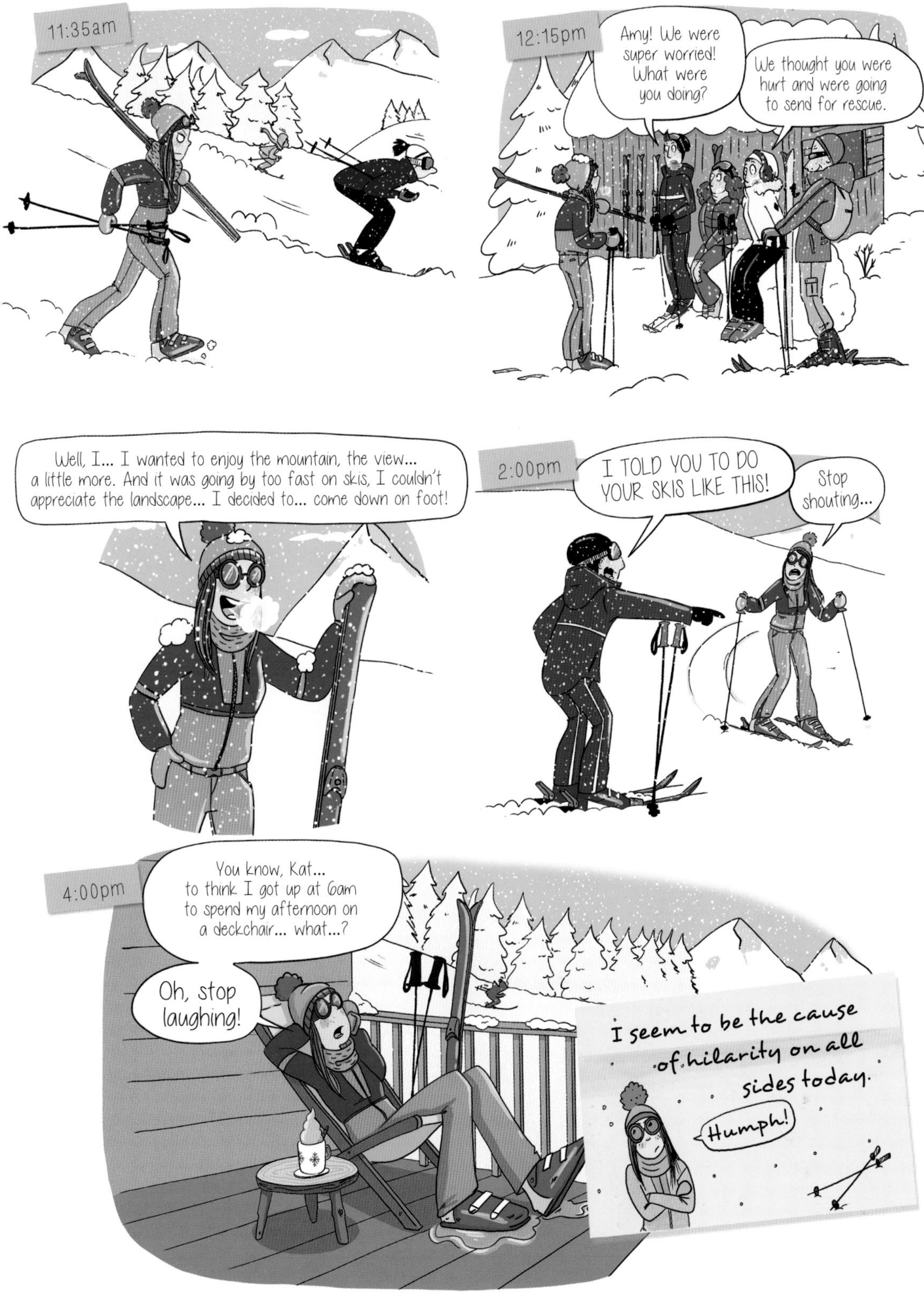
11:35am
12:15pm
Amy! We were super worried! What were you doing?
We thought you were hurt and were going to send for rescue.
Well, I... I wanted to enjoy the mountain, the view... a little more. And it was going by too fast on skis, I couldn't appreciate the landscape... I decided to... come down on foot!
2:00pm
I TOLD YOU TO DO YOUR SKIS LIKE THIS!
Stop shouting...
4:00pm
You know, Kat... to think I got up at 6am to spend my afternoon on a deckchair... what...?
Oh, stop laughing!
I seem to be the cause of hilarity on all sides today.
Humph!

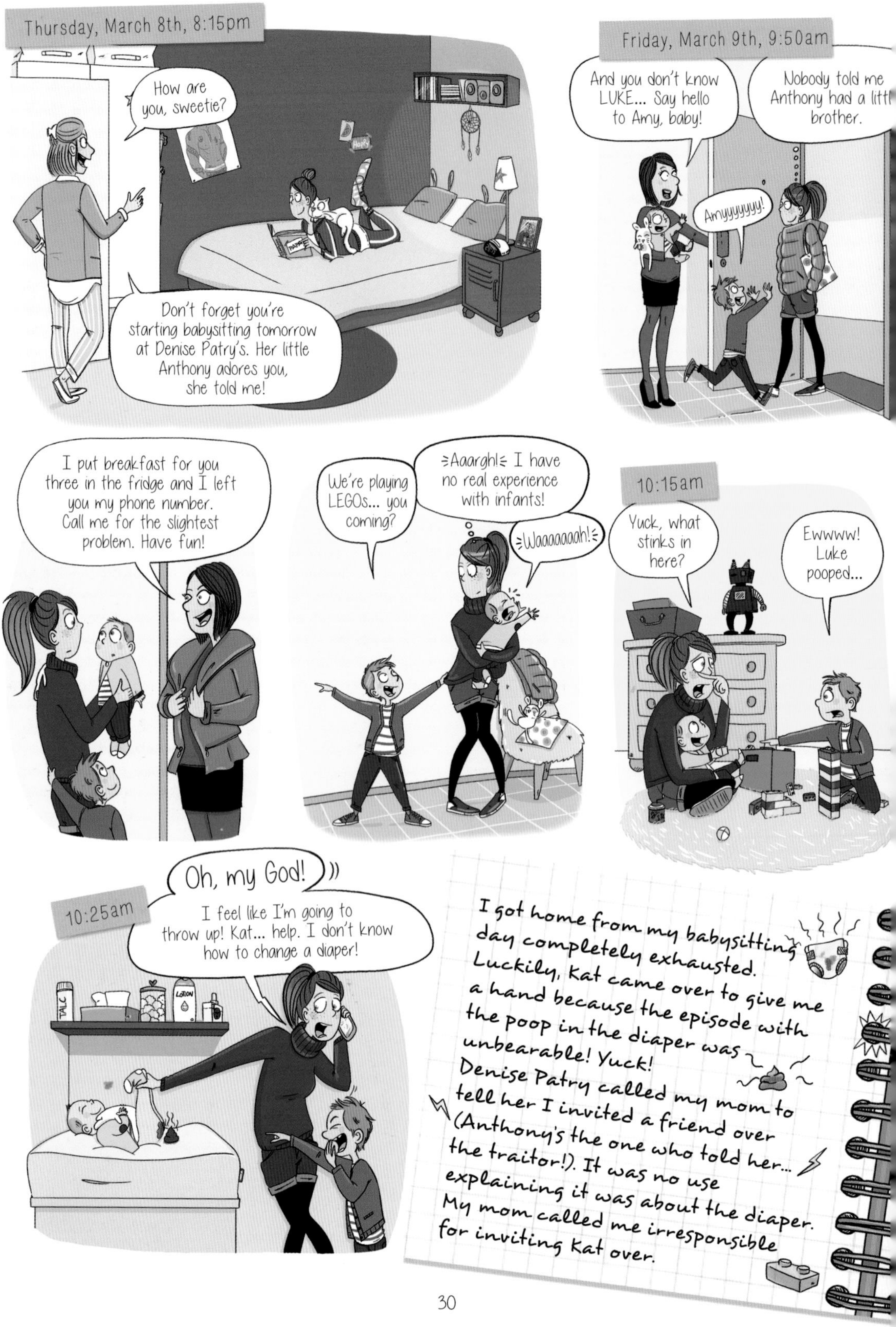
Thursday, March 8th, 8:15pm
How are you, sweetie?
Don't forget you're starting babysitting tomorrow at Denise Patry's. Her little Anthony adores you, she told me!
Friday, March 9th, 9:50am
And you don't know LUKE... Say hello to Amy, baby!
Nobody told me Anthony had a little brother.
Amyyyyyyy!
I put breakfast for you three in the fridge and I left you my phone number. Call me for the slightest problem. Have fun!
We're playing LEGOs... you coming?
Aaargh! I have no real experience with infants!
Waaaaaaah!
10:15am
Yuck, what stinks in here?
Ewwww! Luke pooped...
10:25am
Oh, my God!
I feel like I'm going to throw up! Kat... help. I don't know how to change a diaper!
TALC
LOTION
I got home from my babysitting day completely exhausted. Luckily, Kat came over to give me a hand because the episode with the poop in the diaper was unbearable! Yuck!
Denise Patry called my mom to tell her I invited a friend over (Anthony's the one who told her... the traitor!). It was no use explaining it was about the diaper. My mom called me irresponsible for inviting Kat over.

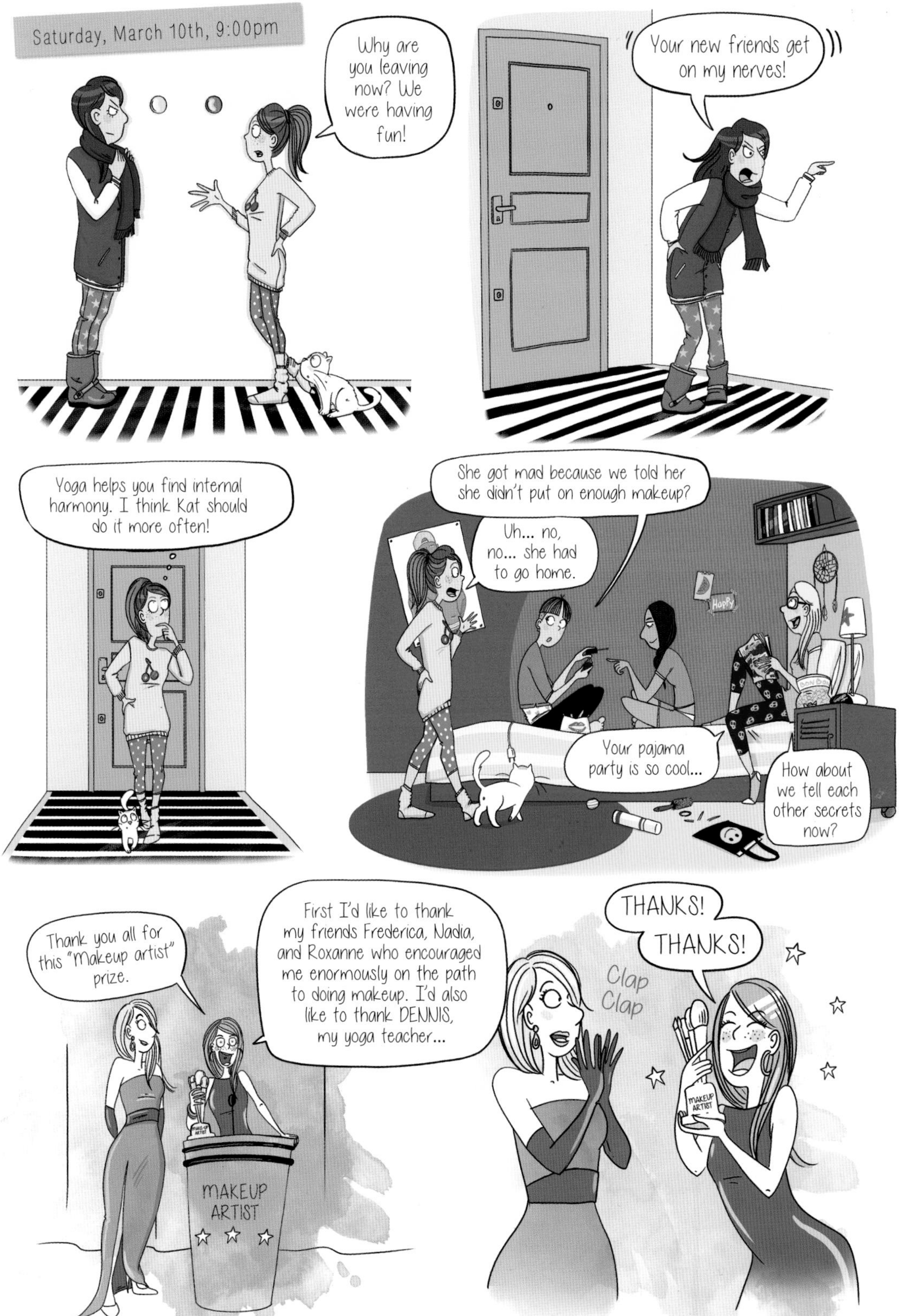

Saturday, March 10th, 9:00pm
Why are you leaving now? We were having fun!
Your new friends get on my nerves!
Yoga helps you find internal harmony. I think Kat should do it more often!
She got mad because we told her she didn't put on enough makeup?
Uh... no, no... she had to go home.
Happy
Your pajama party is so cool...
How about we tell each other secrets now?
Thank you all for this "Makeup artist" prize.
First I'd like to thank my friends Frederica, Nadia, and Roxanne who encouraged me enormously on the path to doing makeup. I'd also like to thank DENNIS, my yoga teacher...
MAKEUP ARTIST
THANKS!
THANKS!
Clap Clap
MAKEUP ARTIST

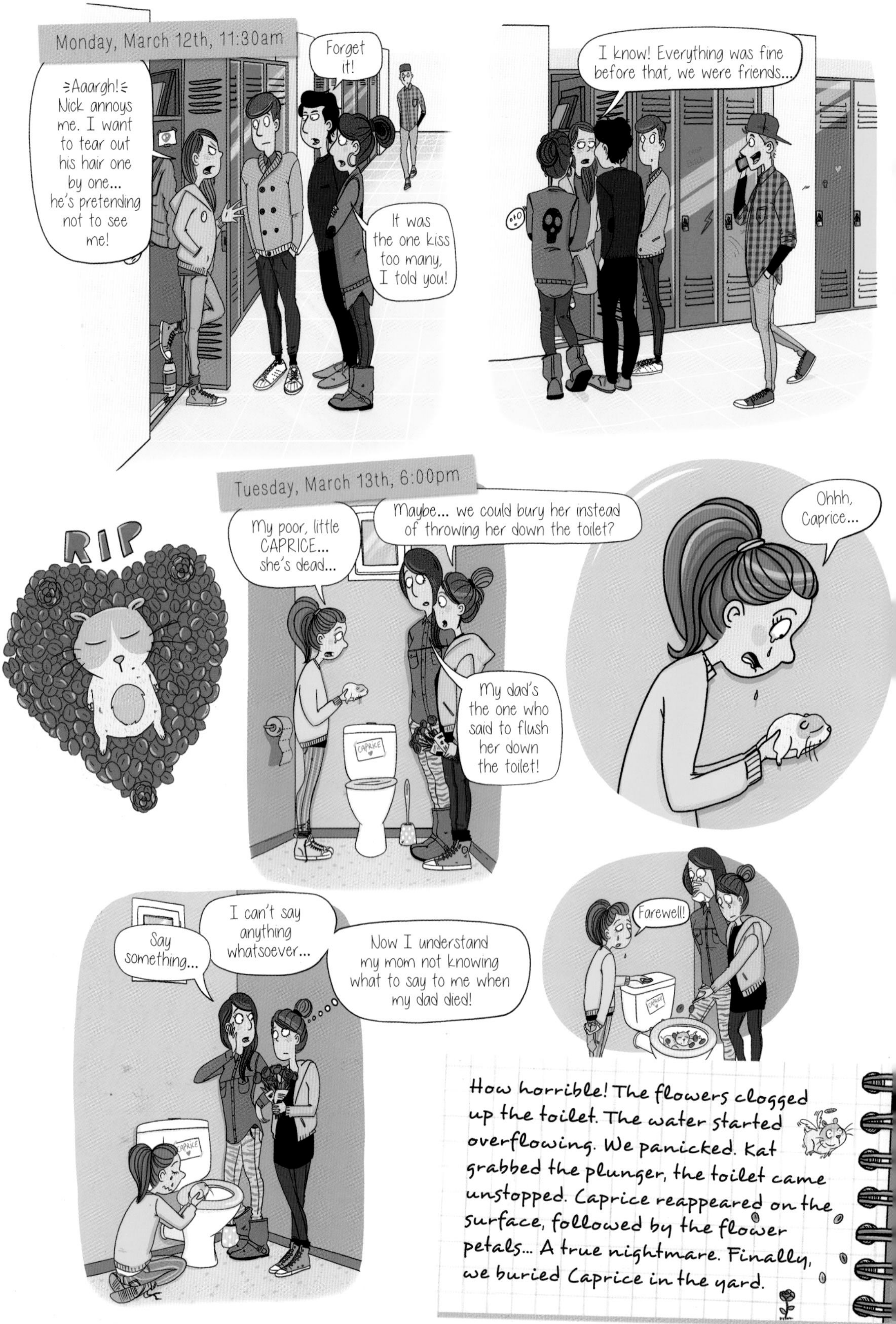

Monday, March 12th, 11:30am
Aaargh! Nick annoys me. I want to tear out his hair one by one... he's pretending not to see me!
Forget it!
It was the one kiss too many, I told you!
I know! Everything was fine before that, we were friends...
Tuesday, March 13th, 6:00pm
RIP
My poor, little CAPRICE... she's dead...
Maybe... we could bury her instead of throwing her down the toilet?
My dad's the one who said to flush her down the toilet!
Ohhh, Caprice...
CAPRICE
Say something...
I can't say anything whatsoever...
Now I understand my mom not knowing what to say to me when my dad died!
Farewell!
How horrible! The flowers clogged up the toilet. The water started overflowing. We panicked. Kat grabbed the plunger, the toilet came unstopped. Caprice reappeared on the surface, followed by the flower petals... A true nightmare. Finally, we buried Caprice in the yard.

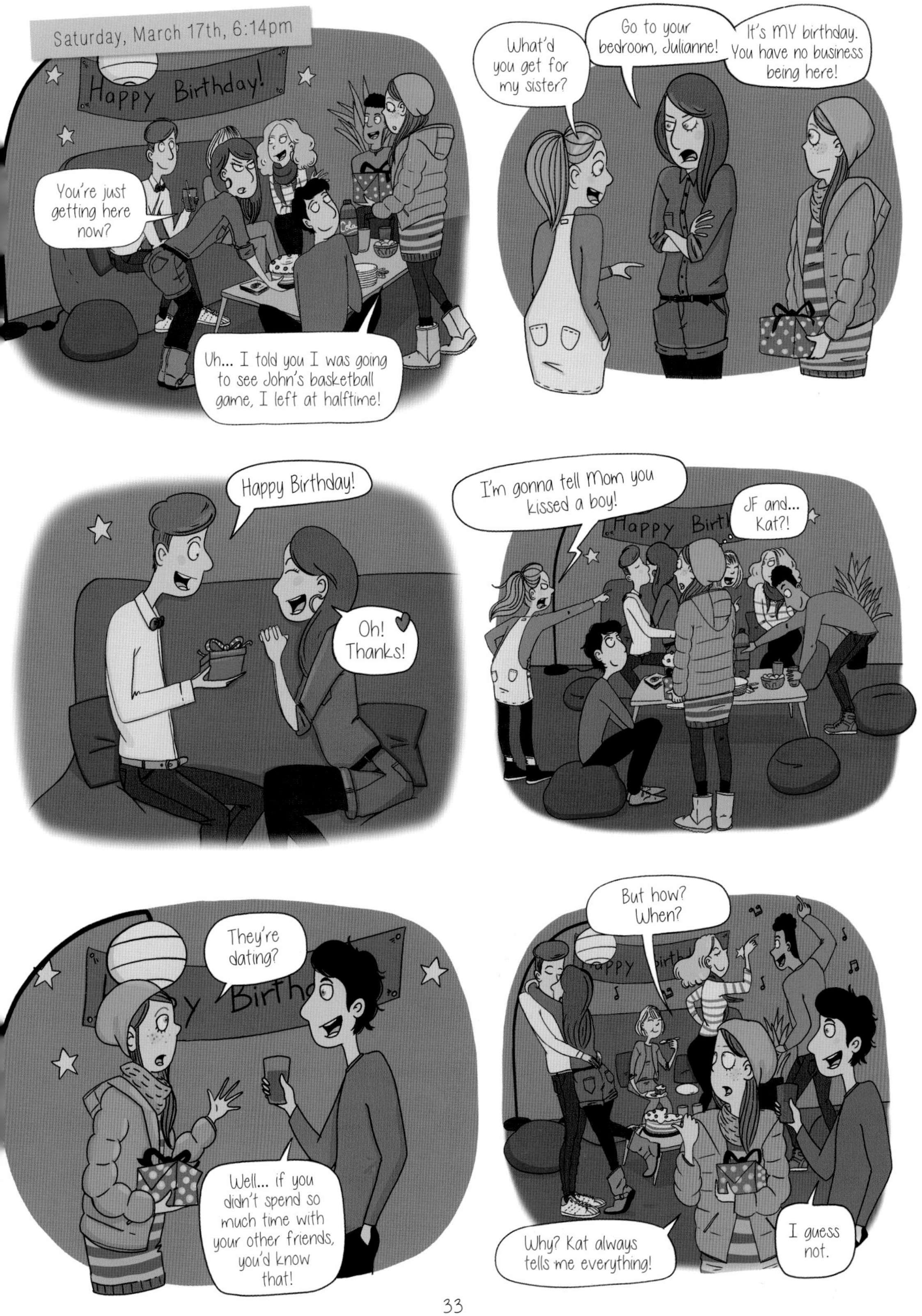
Saturday, March 17th, 6:14pm
Happy Birthday!
You're just getting here now?
Uh... I told you I was going to see John's basketball game, I left at halftime!
What'd you get for my sister?
Go to your bedroom, Julianne!
It's MY birthday. You have no business being here!
Happy Birthday!
Oh! Thanks!
I'm gonna tell Mom you kissed a boy!
JF and... Kat?!
They're dating?
Well... if you didn't spend so much time with your other friends, you'd know that!
But how? When?
Why? Kat always tells me everything!
I guess not.

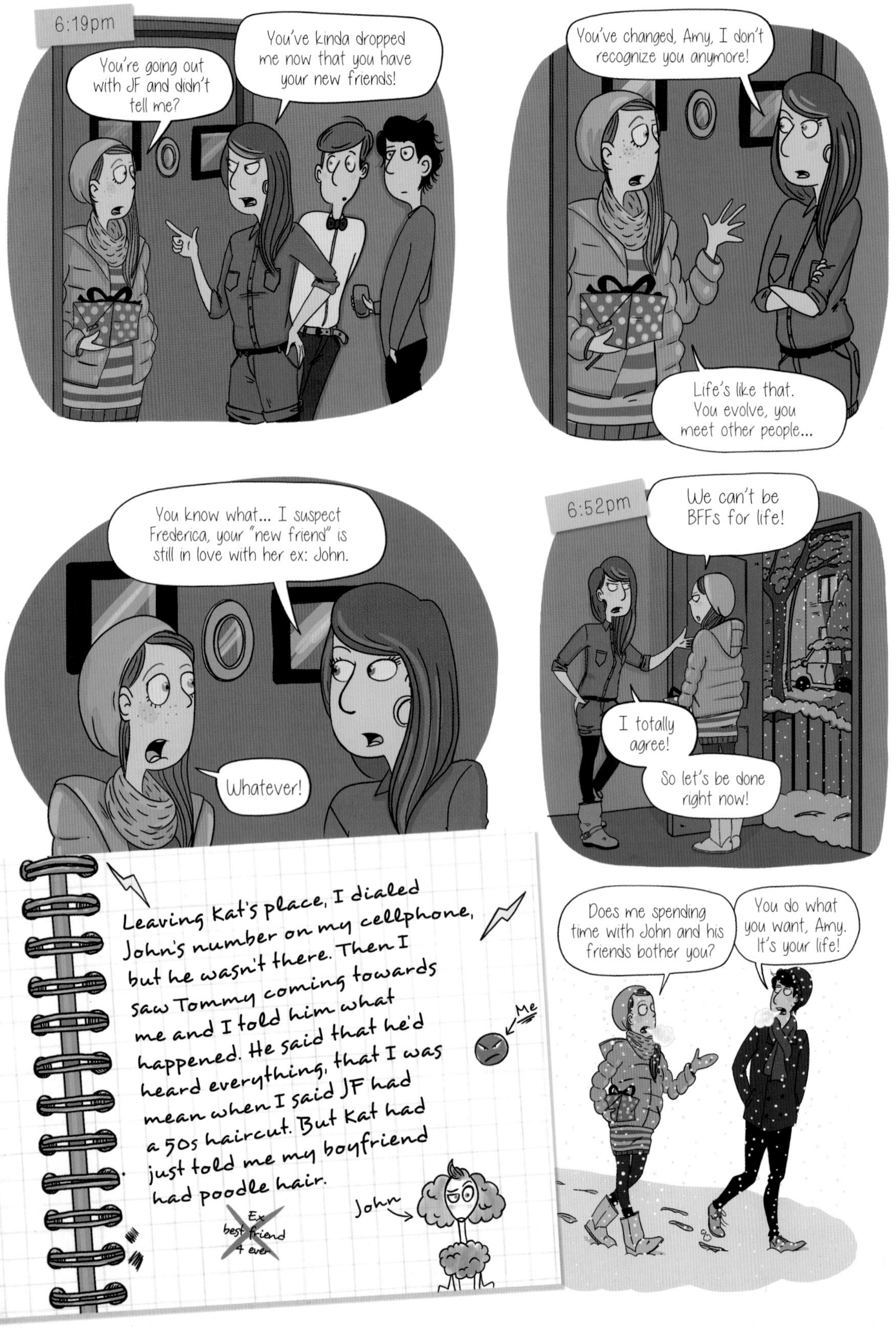
6:19pm
You're going out with JF and didn't tell me?
You've kinda dropped me now that you have your new friends!
You've changed, Amy, I don't recognize you anymore!
Life's like that. You evolve, you meet other people...
You know what... I suspect Frederica, your "new friend" is still in love with her ex: John.
Whatever!
6:52pm
We can't be BFFs for life!
I totally agree!
So let's be done right now!
Leaving Kat's place, I dialed John's number on my cellphone, but he wasn't there. Then I saw Tommy coming towards me and I told him what happened. He said that he'd heard everything, that I was mean when I said JF had a 50s haircut. But Kat had just told me my boyfriend had poodle hair.
Me
Ex best friend 4 ever
John
Does me spending time with John and his friends bother you?
You do what you want, Amy. It's your life!

APRIL
Perfect timing

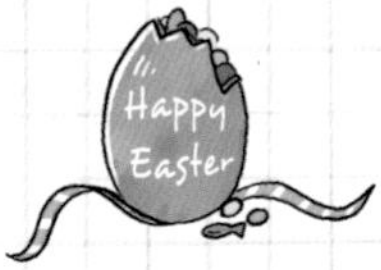
Happy
Easter

- Monday, April 2nd:

6:30pm:

Kat was right. Frederica's still totally in love with John. Whenever she looks at him, her eyes shine... I wonder if they haven't already kissed each other since their breakup, kind of like me with Nick. And they wouldn't have told me. And that would be the reason John didn't get mad when I told him about my kiss with Nick...

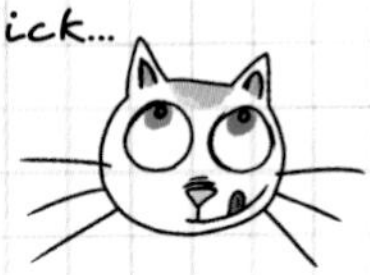

7:02pm:

I imagined my future with John.

1. I'd spend my time watching basketball games and/or soccer matches.
2. I'd spend my time with his friends because he doesn't want to leave his group to come see mine.
3. A life without peanut butter and without Sybil (because of his allergies).

I really like John, but I have the distinct impression there's NO room for me.

How long can a relationship go on once you discover it has no future?

8:10pm: **DRAMA!!!!!**

My mom broke up with Frank and quit her job (she works in Frank's company). She told me, (stuck to a box of Kleenex and pulling out tissue after tissue while crying), that her love for my father was still there. Frank would like things to progress between them, like, living together.
But my mom isn't ready, she told me (sniffling):
"How could I go any further since I still love someone else? Who isn't here anymore?..."
And I told her: "I'm probably going to break up with John, too..."

And then she took me in her arms and said: "I love you."

I miss Kat...

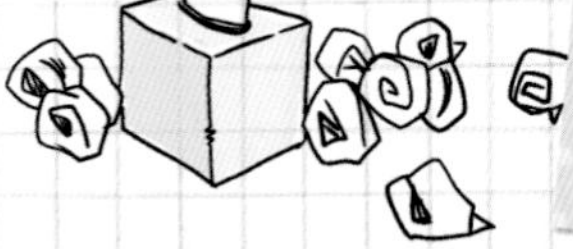

I've got a strong desire for chocolate. It's becoming an obsession.

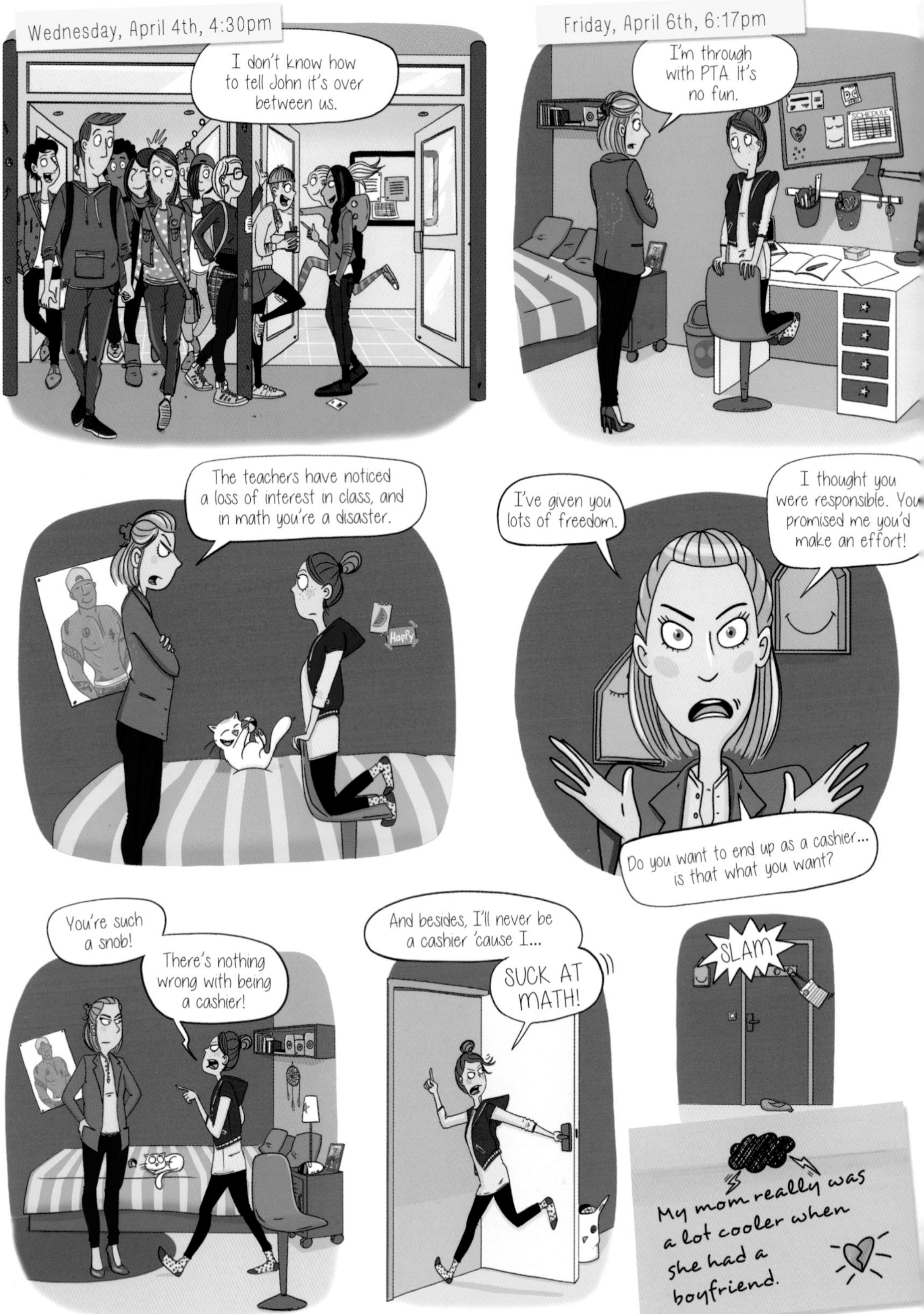

Wednesday, April 4th, 4:30pm
I don't know how to tell John it's over between us.
Friday, April 6th, 6:17pm
I'm through with PTA. It's no fun.
SCHEDULE
The teachers have noticed a loss of interest in class, and in math you're a disaster.
Happy
I've given you lots of freedom.
I thought you were responsible. You promised me you'd make an effort!
Do you want to end up as a cashier... is that what you want?
You're such a snob!
There's nothing wrong with being a cashier!
And besides, I'll never be a cashier 'cause I...
SUCK AT MATH!
SLAM
My mom really was a lot cooler when she had a boyfriend.

Poem

My friend for life

You were my friend
Now we're torn asunder
I'd love to talk to you
But you refuse to listen

Is there anything left of our friendship?
Or has it all been erased?
Have we become strangers?
Is our friendship forever lost?

I'm afraid an awkwardness has grown between us
And that things will never be the same
Living without each other hurts us
But we continue to ignore one another.

Who, in fact, is right?
What use is it asking that question?
Will it change anything, after all?
I just hope we'll be together again one day.

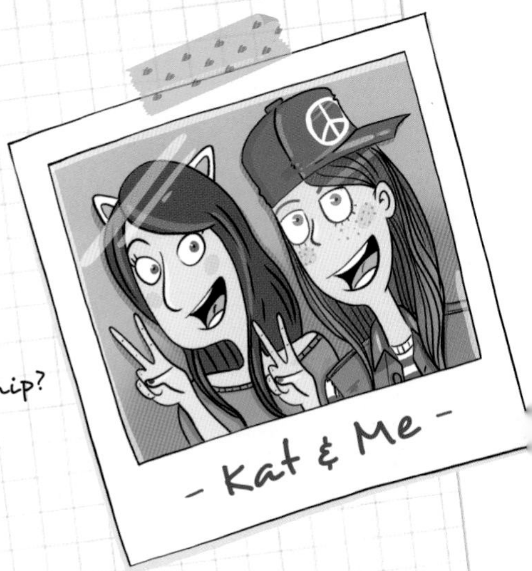

- Kat & Me -

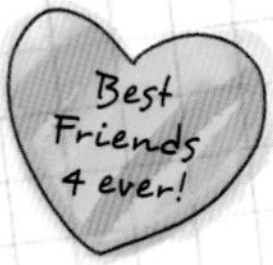

Best Friends 4 ever!

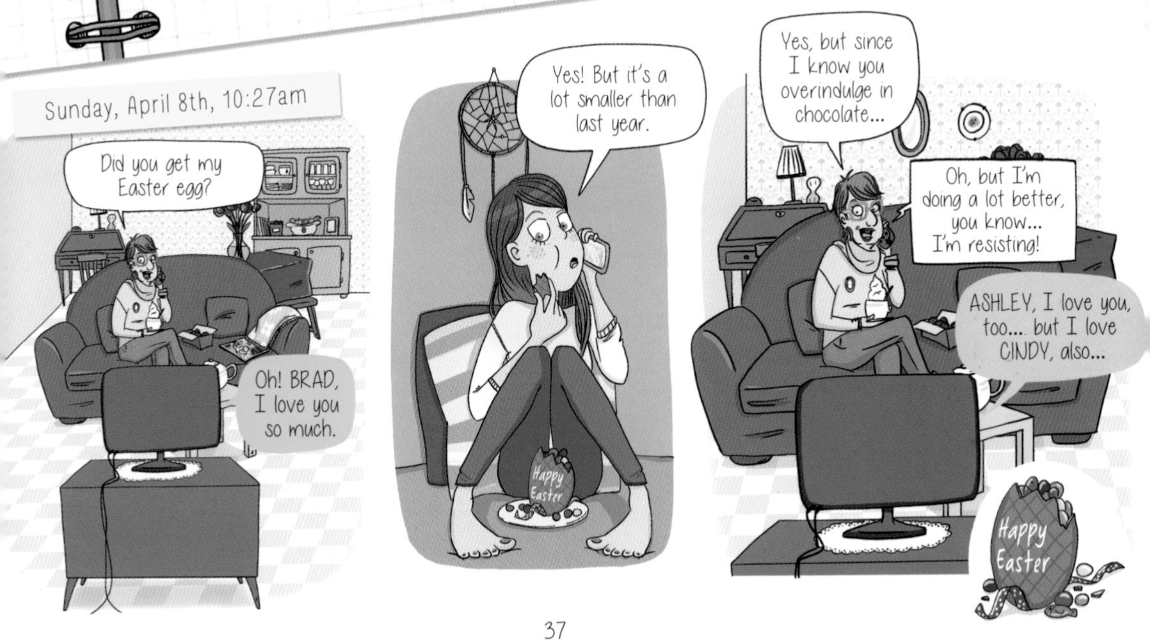

Sunday, April 8th, 10:27am
Did you get my Easter egg?
Oh! BRAD, I love you so much.
Yes! But it's a lot smaller than last year.
Happy Easter
Yes, but since I know you overindulge in chocolate...
Oh, but I'm doing a lot better, you know... I'm resisting!
ASHLEY, I love you, too... but I love CINDY, also...
Happy Easter

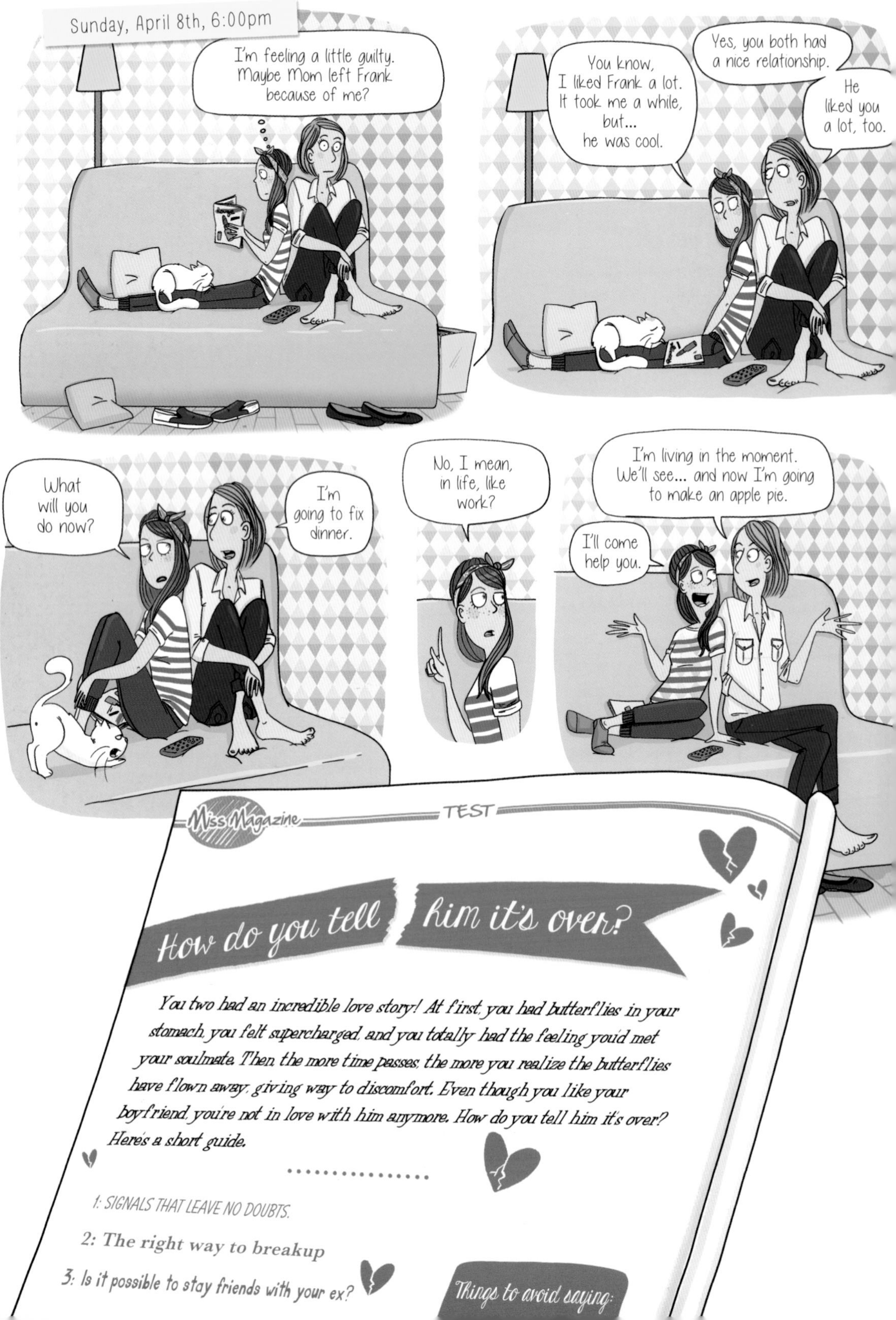

Sunday, April 8th, 6:00pm
I'm feeling a little guilty. Maybe Mom left Frank because of me?
You know, I liked Frank a lot. It took me a while, but... he was cool.
Yes, you both had a nice relationship.
He liked you a lot, too.
What will you do now?
I'm going to fix dinner.
No, I mean, in life, like work?
I'm living in the moment. We'll see... and now I'm going to make an apple pie.
I'll come help you.
Miss Magazine
TEST
How do you tell him it's over?
You two had an incredible love story! At first, you had butterflies in your stomach, you felt supercharged, and you totally had the feeling you'd met your soulmate. Then the more time passes, the more you realize the butterflies have flown away, giving way to discomfort. Even though you like your boyfriend, you're not in love with him anymore. How do you tell him it's over? Here's a short guide.
1: SIGNALS THAT LEAVE NO DOUBTS.
2: The right way to breakup
3: Is it possible to stay friends with your ex?
Things to avoid saying:

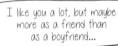

I'm leaving John today.

I like you a lot, but maybe more as a friend than as a boyfriend...

Yeah, I understand. I was thinking that, too.

5:30pm

In the end, it went really well, fast, like a lightning bolt.

5:35pm

Okay, now, I've got to go by Frank's office to tell him it's kind of my fault Mom left him.

6:10pm

You know, at first, I didn't really like you... but now, I do... and you're the only person who's brought any light to my mom's eyes since before my dad's death... I know she loves you...

If you still love her, you just have to tell her... in a romantic way!

So, it turns out you don't like me not being around anymore?

Ha ha ha!

Hee hee hee!

39

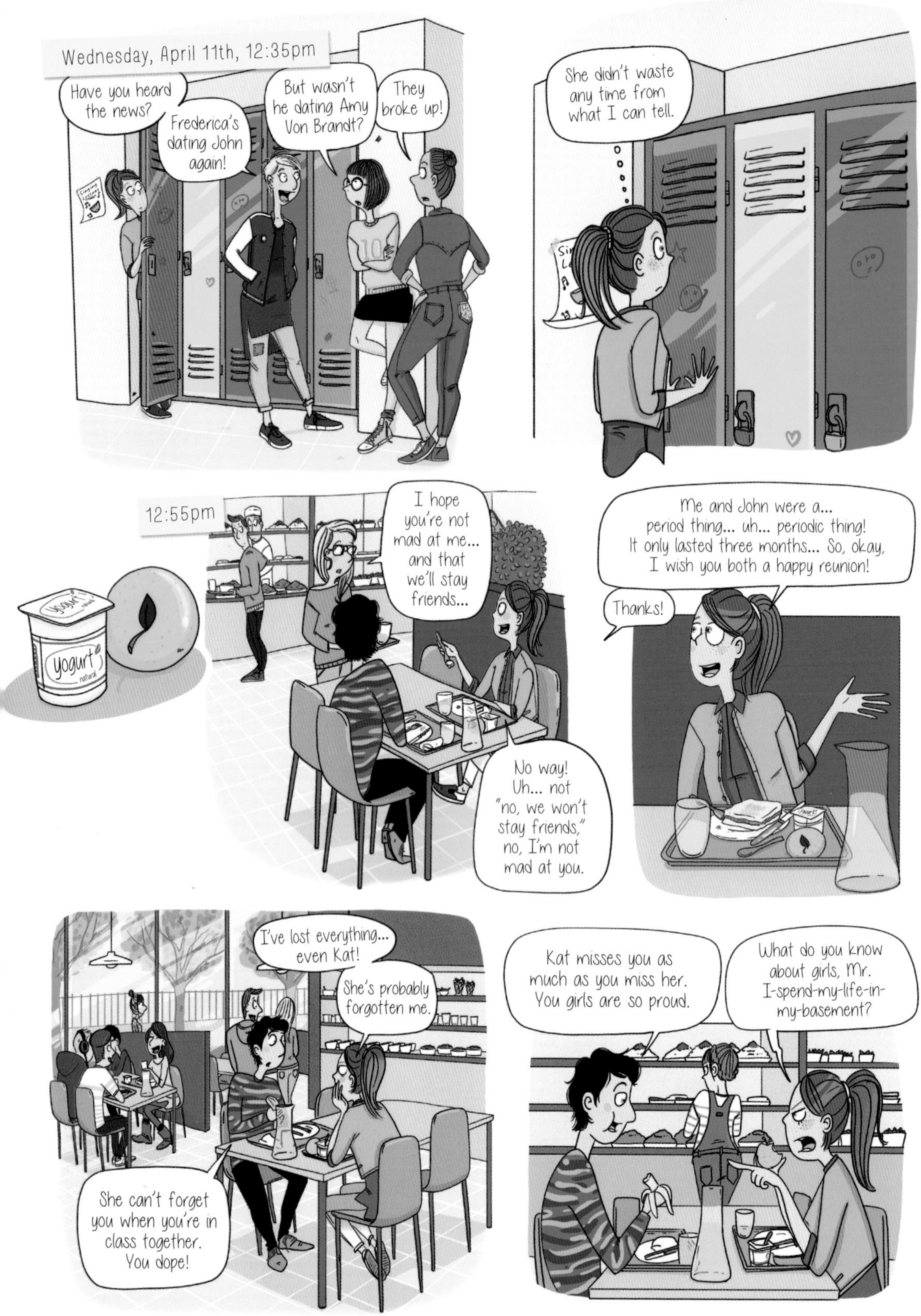
Wednesday, April 11th, 12:35pm
Have you heard the news?
Frederica's dating John again!
But wasn't he dating Amy Von Brandt?
They broke up!
She didn't waste any time from what I can tell.
12:55pm
I hope you're not mad at me... and that we'll stay friends...
No way! Uh... not "no, we won't stay friends," no, I'm not mad at you.
Me and John were a... period thing... uh... periodic thing! It only lasted three months... So, okay, I wish you both a happy reunion!
Thanks!
I've lost everything... even Kat!
She's probably forgotten me.
She can't forget you when you're in class together. You dope!
Kat misses you as much as you miss her. You girls are so proud.
What do you know about girls, Mr. I-spend-my-life-in-my-basement?

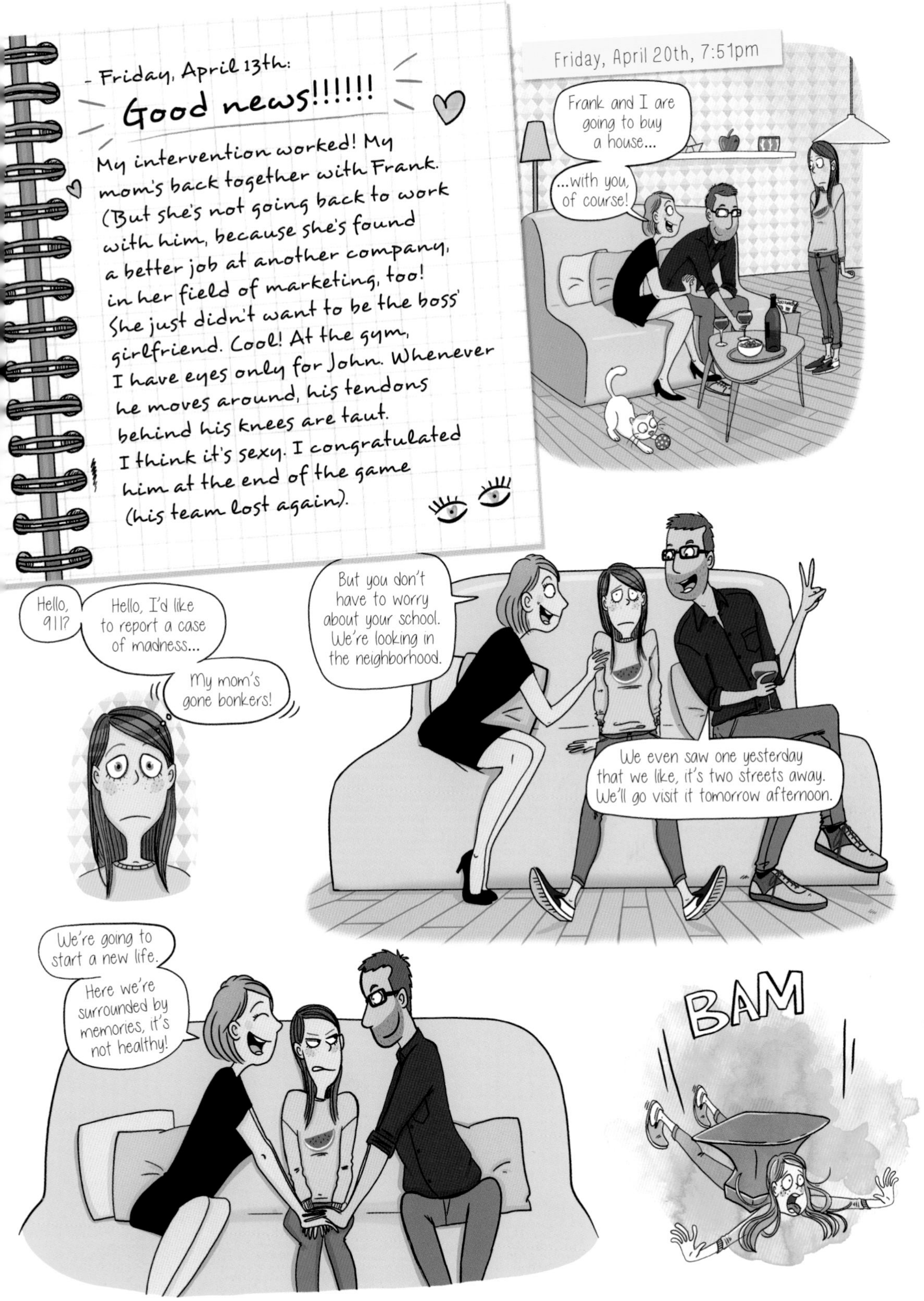
- Friday, April 13th:
Good news!!!!!!
My intervention worked! My mom's back together with Frank. (But she's not going back to work with him, because she's found a better job at another company, in her field of marketing, too! She just didn't want to be the boss' girlfriend. Cool! At the gym, I have eyes only for John. Whenever he moves around, his tendons behind his knees are taut. I think it's sexy. I congratulated him at the end of the game (his team lost again).
Friday, April 20th, 7:51pm
Frank and I are going to buy a house...
...with you, of course!
But you don't have to worry about your school. We're looking in the neighborhood.
We even saw one yesterday that we like, it's two streets away. We'll go visit it tomorrow afternoon.
Hello, 911?
Hello, I'd like to report a case of madness...
My mom's gone bonkers!
We're going to start a new life.
Here we're surrounded by memories, it's not healthy!
BAM

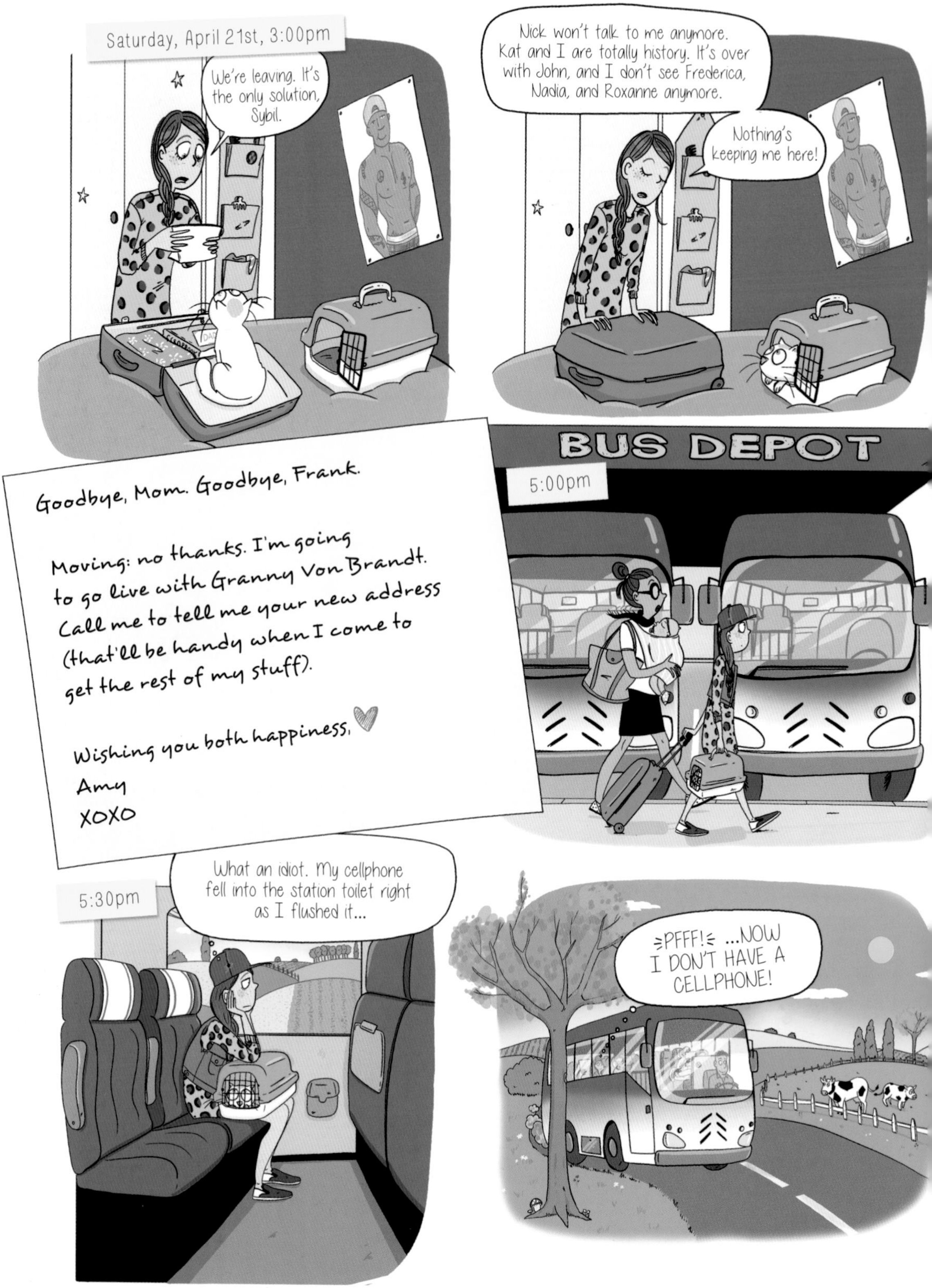
Saturday, April 21st, 3:00pm
We're leaving. It's the only solution, Sybil.
Nick won't talk to me anymore. Kat and I are totally history. It's over with John, and I don't see Frederica, Nadia, and Roxanne anymore.
Nothing's keeping me here!
Goodbye, Mom. Goodbye, Frank.
Moving: no thanks. I'm going to go live with Granny Von Brandt. Call me to tell me your new address (that'll be handy when I come to get the rest of my stuff).
Wishing you both happiness,
Amy
XOXO
BUS DEPOT
5:00pm
5:30pm
What an idiot. My cellphone fell into the station toilet right as I flushed it...
PFFF! ...NOW I DON'T HAVE A CELLPHONE!

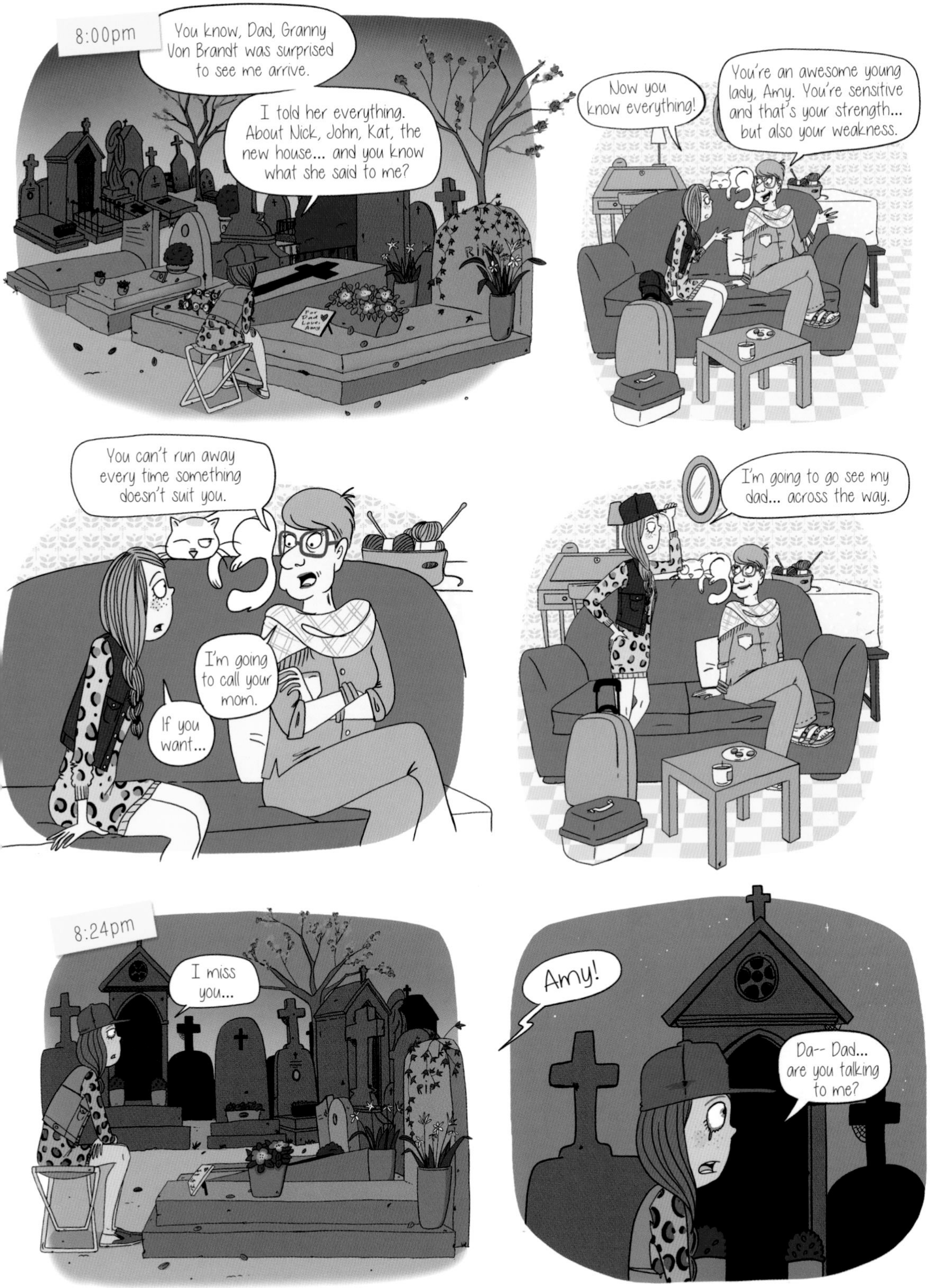
8:00pm
You know, Dad, Granny Von Brandt was surprised to see me arrive.
I told her everything. About Nick, John, Kat, the new house... and you know what she said to me?
Now you know everything!
You're an awesome young lady, Amy. You're sensitive and that's your strength... but also your weakness.
You can't run away every time something doesn't suit you.
I'm going to call your mom.
If you want...
I'm going to go see my dad... across the way.
8:24pm
I miss you...
Amy!
Da-- Dad... are you talking to me?

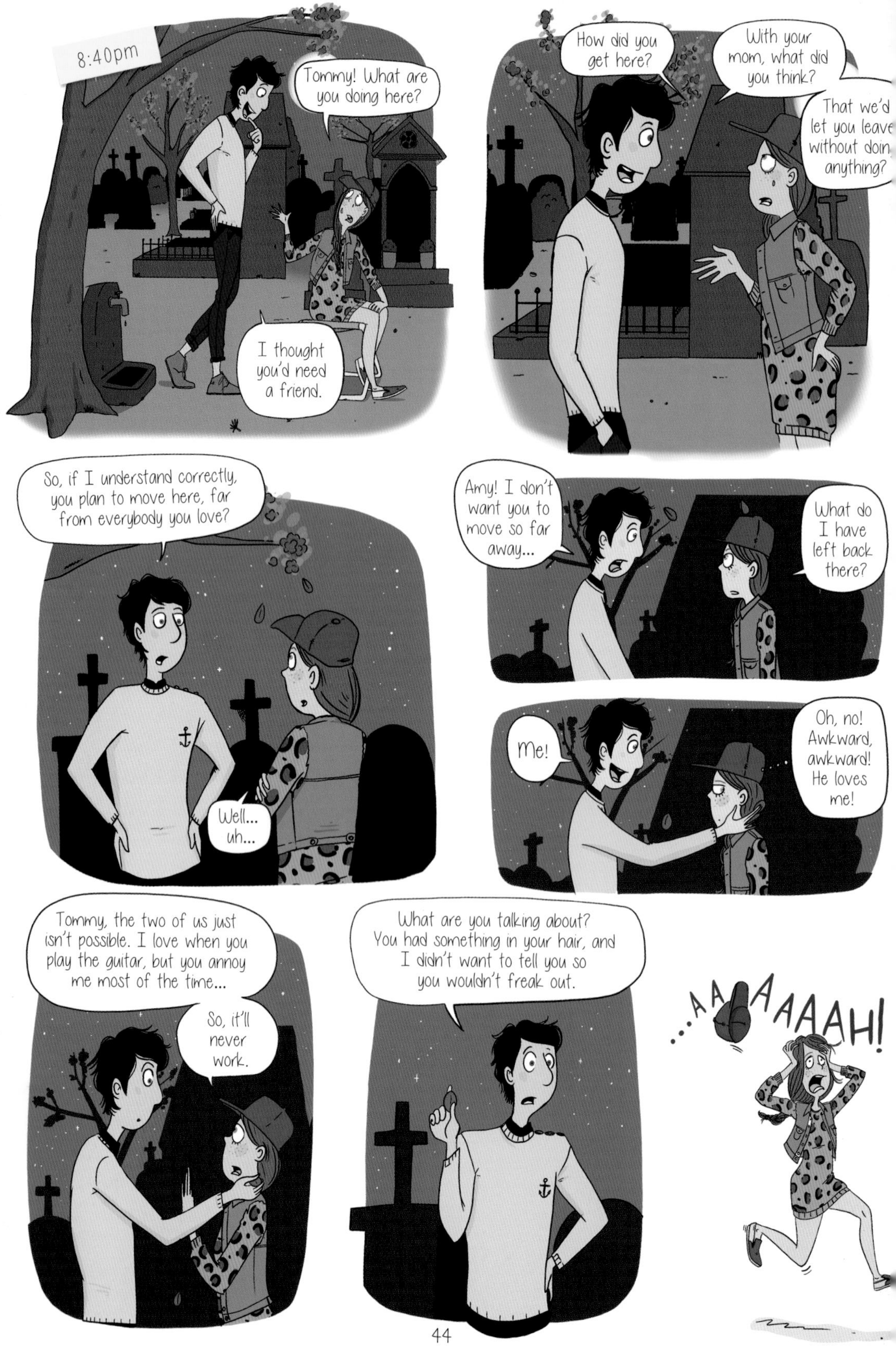
8:40pm
Tommy! What are you doing here?
I thought you'd need a friend.
How did you get here?
With your mom, what did you think?
That we'd let you leave without doin anything?
So, if I understand correctly, you plan to move here, far from everybody you love?
Well... uh...
Amy! I don't want you to move so far away...
What do I have left back there?
Me!
Oh, no! Awkward, awkward! He loves me!
Tommy, the two of us just isn't possible. I love when you play the guitar, but you annoy me most of the time...
So, it'll never work.
What are you talking about? You had something in your hair, and I didn't want to tell you so you wouldn't freak out.
...AAAAAAH!

MAY

Jumping for joy

Kat and me = BFF forever and ever and ever.

- Friday, May 4th:

6:09pm:

It's been a week since Kat and I made up. I went to see her with the poem I wrote for her about friendship. We hugged each other, we cried, we laughed, we apologized. And then we updated each other about our lives. She knew about my breakup with John (Tommy's the one who'd told her), she told me about JF. Things are cool with them. It's not passionate like with JD, it's a love based more on great friendship.

Everything's back to normal!!!!! Yeah!

I had the feeling, these past months, I was living somebody else's life and that I'd finally found my own again.

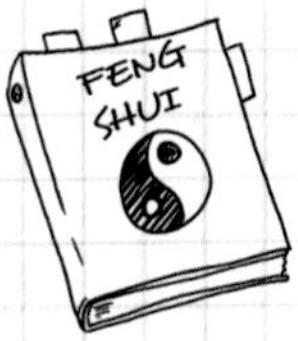
FENG SHUI

7:10pm:

I've seen the house Mom and Frank picked out. They did show it to me, however, before making the official purchase offer on it (what generosity!). It's nice. Nothing more. I'm not crazy about the colors. And I think the room layout isn't too feng shui. (I often go to the dentist's, and there's nothing but decorating magazines to read. I'm awesome in feng shui now!). So, the house isn't really my thing.

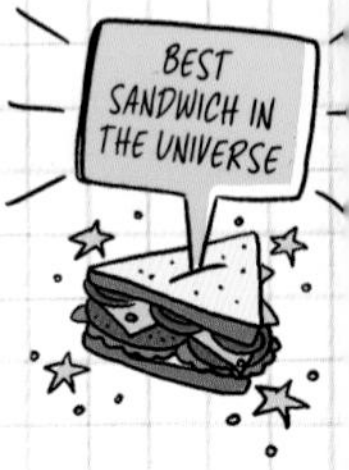
BEST SANDWICH IN THE UNIVERSE

- Saturday, May 5th, 8:20am:

Today I have a job interview at 9:45 at a restaurant where they make sandwiches. Not that I was particularly wanting to work; my mom's forcing me into this. Basically, she told me having a job would make me more independent and would let me buy whatever I want... she's not wrong!

If I work at a sandwich shop, maybe it'll become my gang's hangout. Like, everyone will come there and talk to me while I clean the counter. Maybe my bosses will even think I'm increasing their clientele.

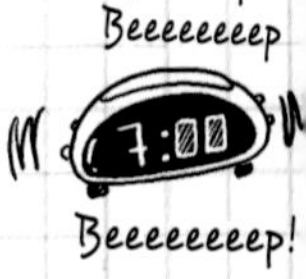
Beeeeep
Beeeeeeeep
7:00
Beeeeeeeep!

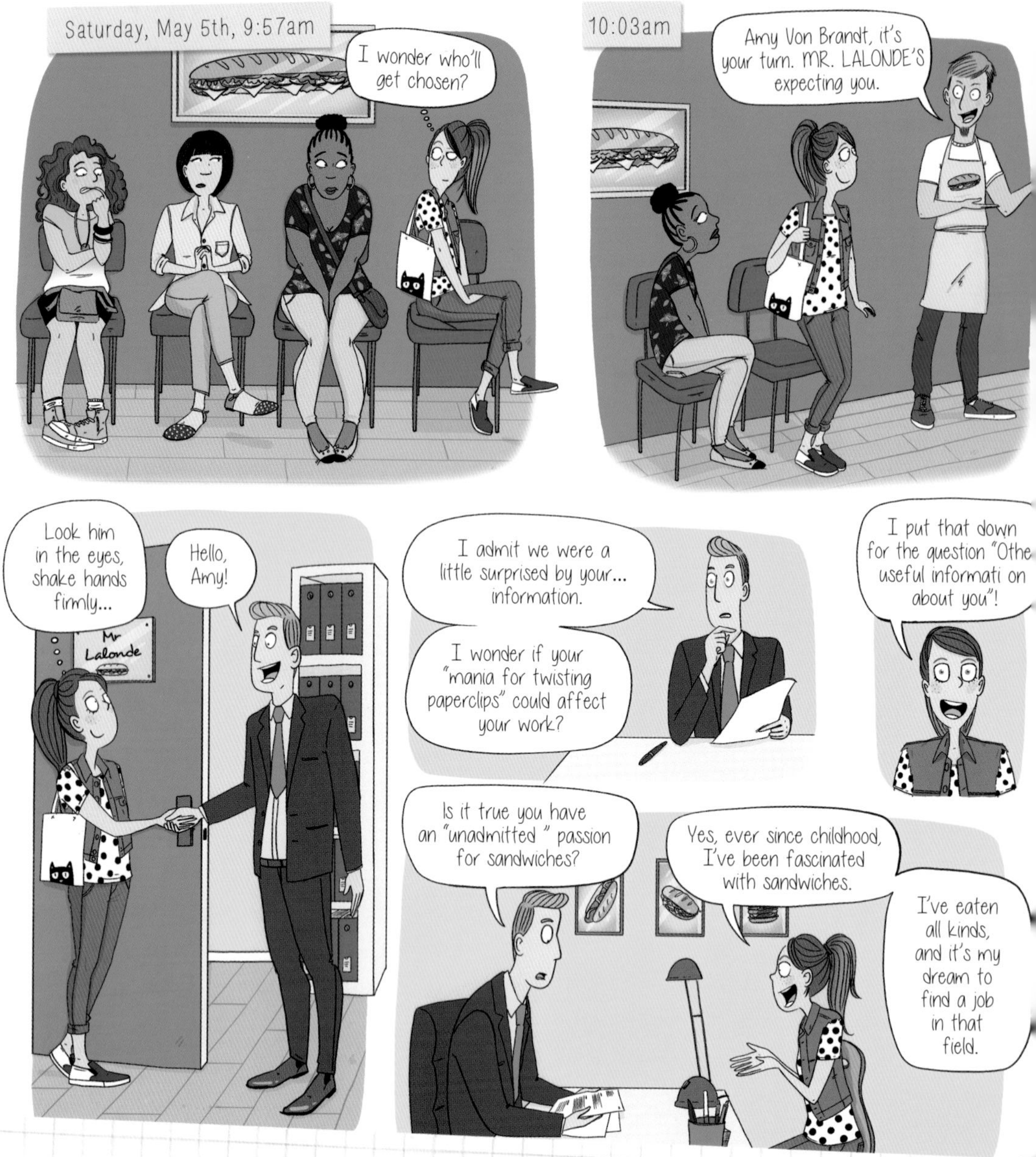
Saturday, May 5th, 9:57am
I wonder who'll get chosen?
10:03am
Amy Von Brandt, it's your turn. MR. LALONDE'S expecting you.
Look him in the eyes, shake hands firmly...
Mr Lalonde
Hello, Amy!
I admit we were a little surprised by your... information.
I wonder if your "mania for twisting paperclips" could affect your work?
I put that down for the question "Othe useful informati on about you"!
Is it true you have an "unadmitted" passion for sandwiches?
Yes, ever since childhood, I've been fascinated with sandwiches.
I've eaten all kinds, and it's my dream to find a job in that field.

I think that, overall, it went well. I left the office after shaking Mr. Lalonde's hand once more and his assistant's hand. Under the heading of "Other useful information about you," I'd put: I love to walk while dragging my feet on the street in the fall, when there are leaves that carpet the ground. I love to pop the bubbles in bubble wrap and I hate stepping on chewing gum. I did my best (even if I can't affirm beyond all doubt that's entirely pertinent for a job interview!).

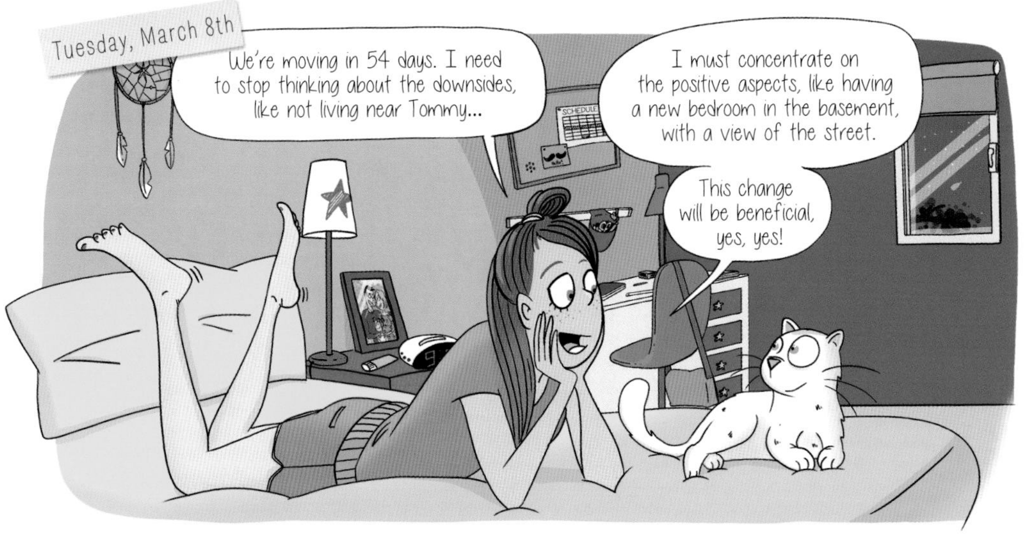
Tuesday, March 8th
We're moving in 54 days. I need to stop thinking about the downsides, like not living near Tommy...
I must concentrate on the positive aspects, like having a new bedroom in the basement, with a view of the street.
This change will be beneficial, yes, yes!
SCHEDULE

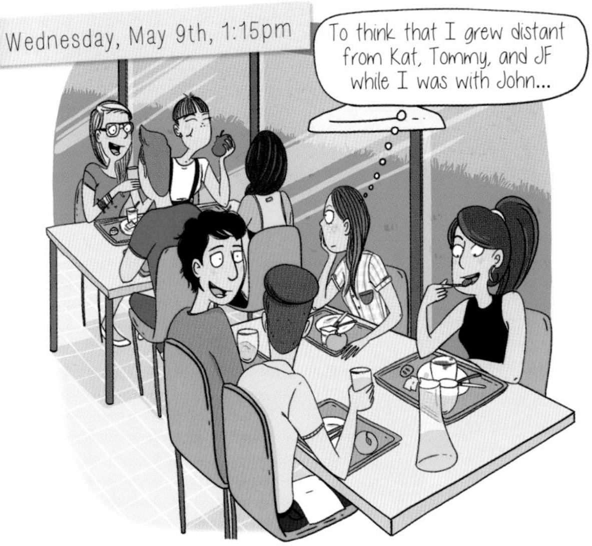
Wednesday, May 9th, 1:15pm
To think that I grew distant from Kat, Tommy, and JF while I was with John...

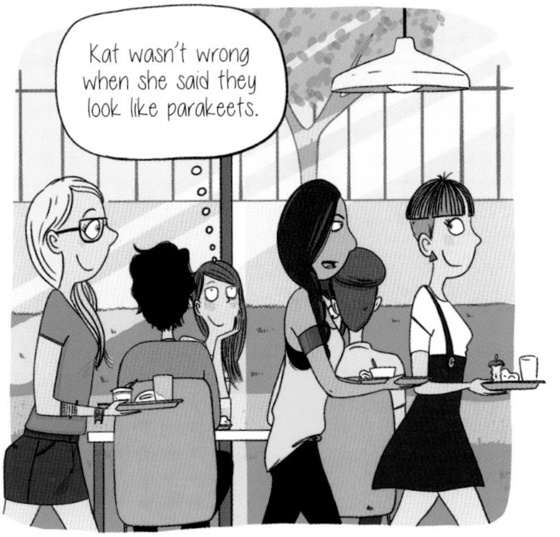
Kat wasn't wrong when she said they look like parakeets.

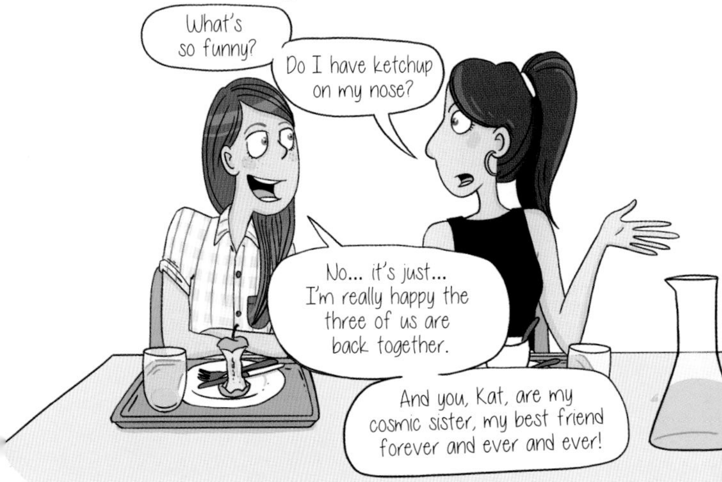
What's so funny?
Do I have ketchup on my nose?
No... it's just... I'm really happy the three of us are back together.
And you, Kat, are my cosmic sister, my best friend forever and ever and ever!

Rule #1:
Never get into arguments again (even if we make new friends).

Rule #2:
Never date a boy if he's a loser or if he doesn't like our bestie or if his friends don't like our bestie.

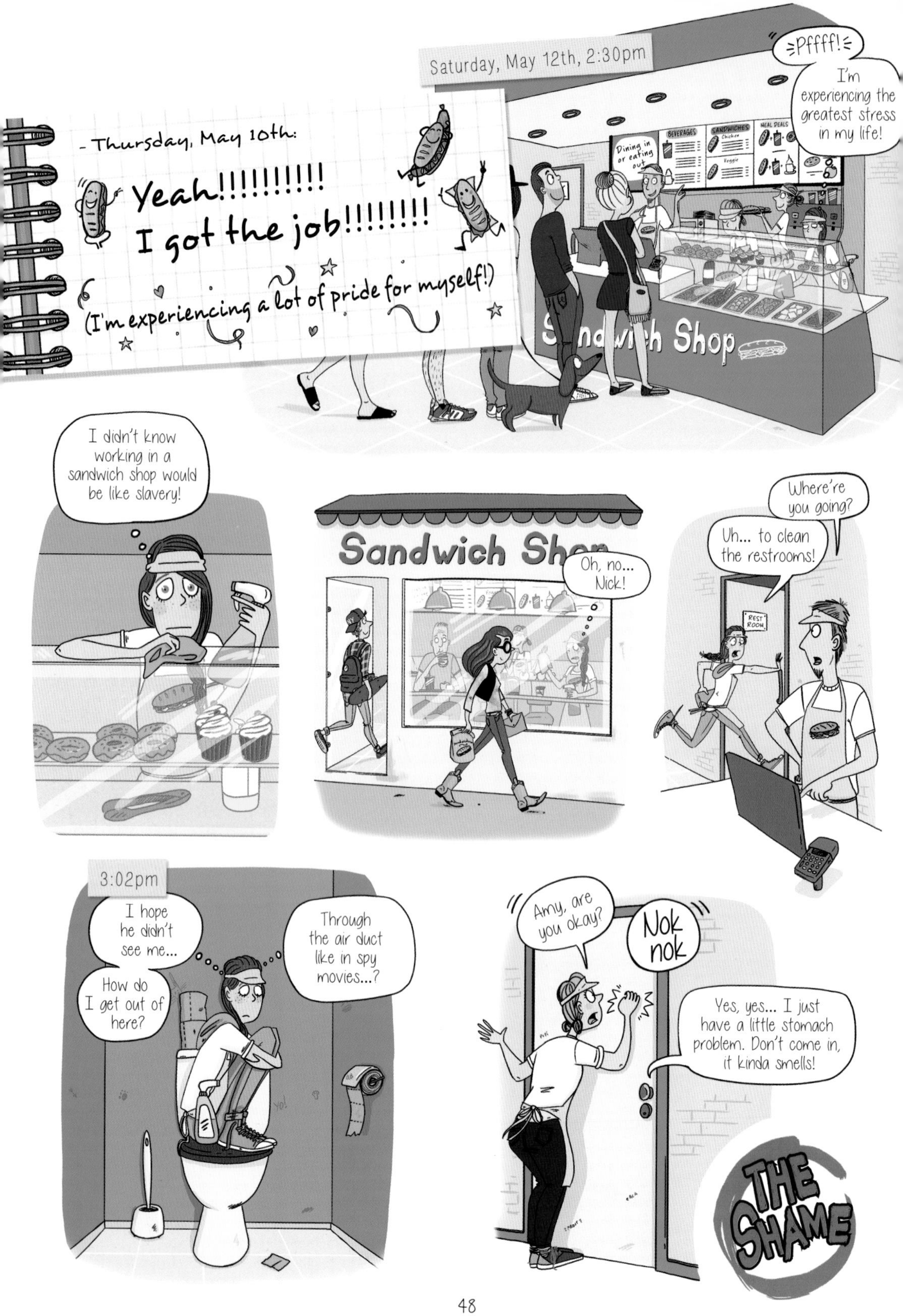
Saturday, May 12th, 2:30pm
- Thursday, May 10th:
Yeah!!!!!!!!!!
I got the job!!!!!!!!
(I'm experiencing a lot of pride for myself!)
Pffff!
I'm experiencing the greatest stress in my life!
Sandwich Shop
I didn't know working in a sandwich shop would be like slavery!
Sandwich Shop
Oh, no... Nick!
Where're you going?
Uh... to clean the restrooms!
REST ROOM
3:02pm
I hope he didn't see me...
How do I get out of here?
Through the air duct like in spy movies...?
Amy, are you okay?
Nok nok
Yes, yes... I just have a little stomach problem. Don't come in, it kinda smells!
THE SHAME

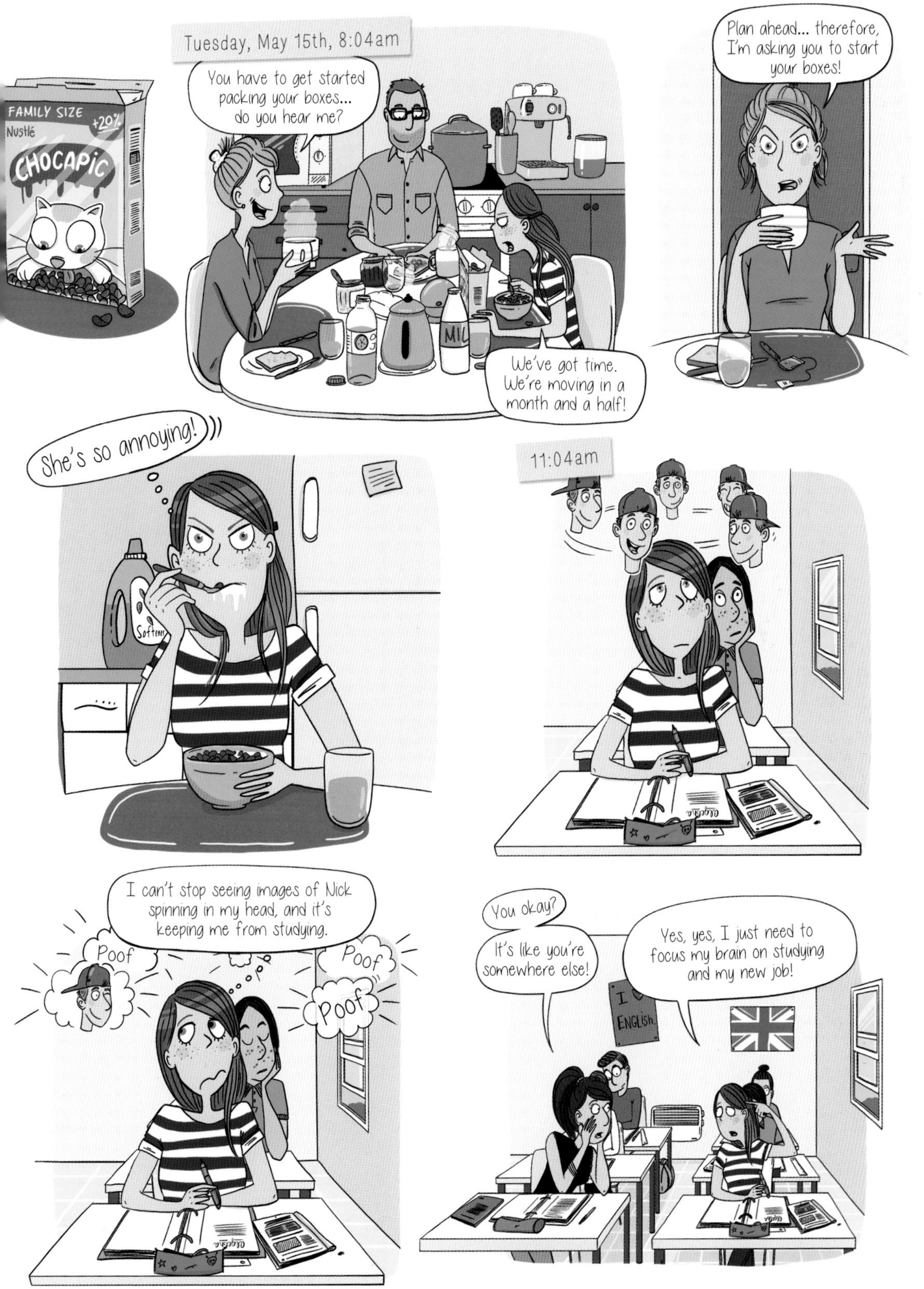
FAMILY SIZE
+20%
Nustlé
CHOCAPIC
Tuesday, May 15th, 8:04am
You have to get started packing your boxes... do you hear me?
We've got time. We're moving in a month and a half!
Plan ahead... therefore, I'm asking you to start your boxes!
She's so annoying!
Softener
11:04am
I can't stop seeing images of Nick spinning in my head, and it's keeping me from studying.
Poof
Poof
Poof
You okay?
It's like you're somewhere else!
Yes, yes, I just need to focus my brain on studying and my new job!
I ENGLISH

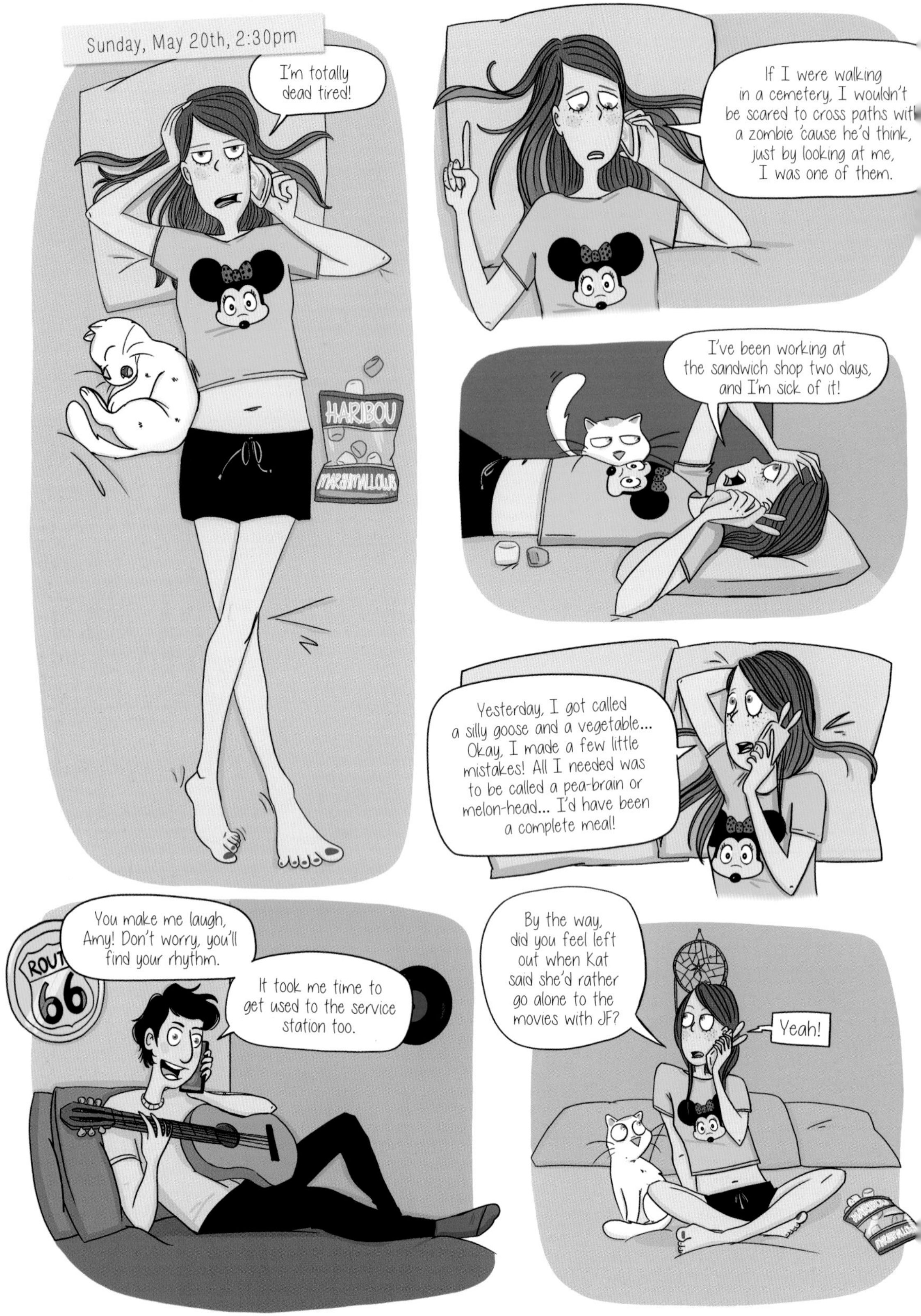
Sunday, May 20th, 2:30pm
I'm totally dead tired!
HARIBOU
MARSHMALLOWS
If I were walking in a cemetery, I wouldn't be scared to cross paths with a zombie 'cause he'd think, just by looking at me, I was one of them.
I've been working at the sandwich shop two days, and I'm sick of it!
Yesterday, I got called a silly goose and a vegetable... Okay, I made a few little mistakes! All I needed was to be called a pea-brain or melon-head... I'd have been a complete meal!
You make me laugh, Amy! Don't worry, you'll find your rhythm.
It took me time to get used to the service station too.
By the way, did you feel left out when Kat said she'd rather go alone to the movies with JF?
Yeah!

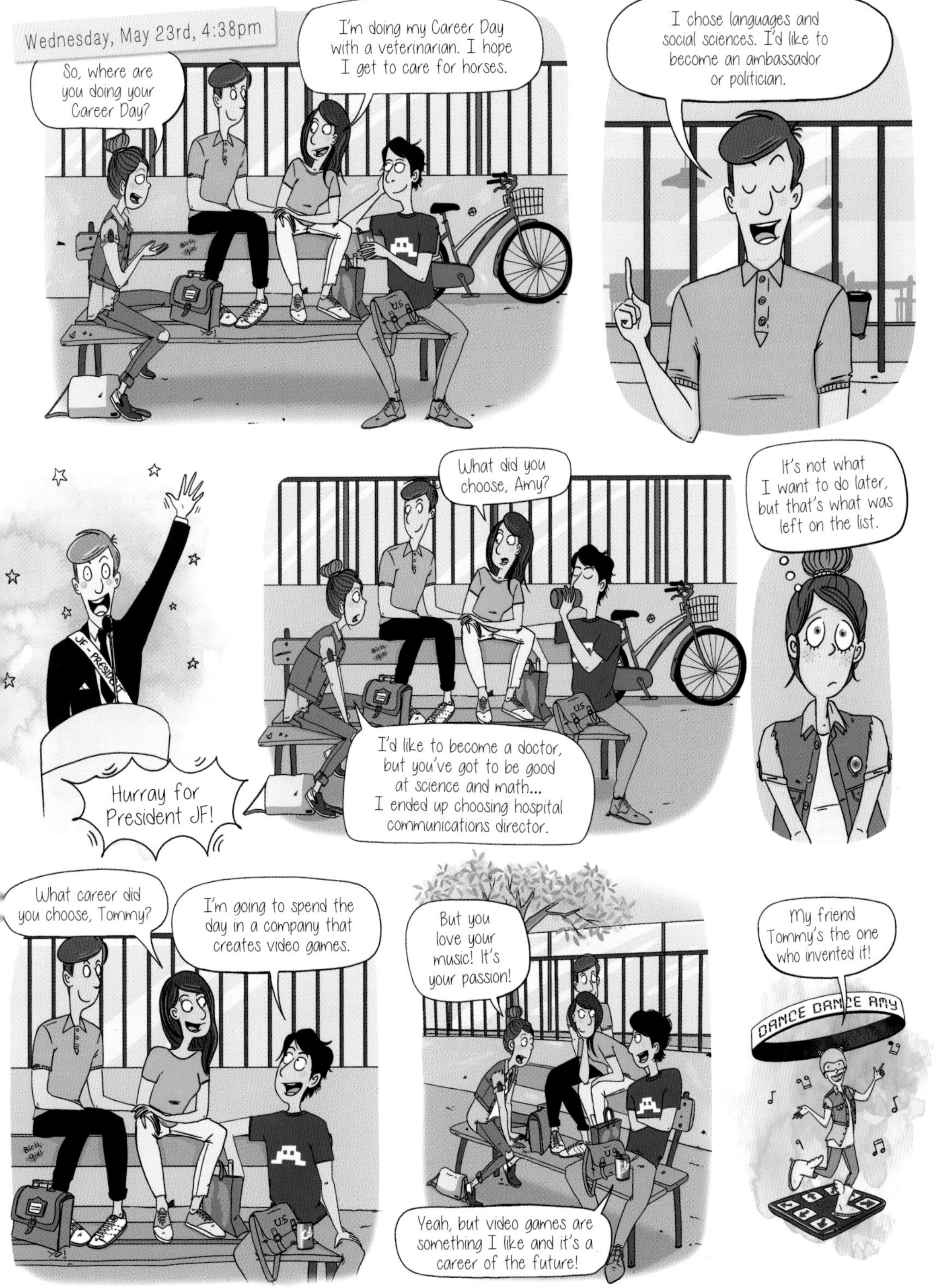

Wednesday, May 23rd, 4:38pm
So, where are you doing your Career Day?
I'm doing my Career Day with a veterinarian. I hope I get to care for horses.
I chose languages and social sciences. I'd like to become an ambassador or politician.
JF - PRESIDENT
Hurray for President JF!
What did you choose, Amy?
I'd like to become a doctor, but you've got to be good at science and math... I ended up choosing hospital communications director.
It's not what I want to do later, but that's what was left on the list.
What career did you choose, Tommy?
I'm going to spend the day in a company that creates video games.
But you love your music! It's your passion!
Yeah, but video games are something I like and it's a career of the future!
My friend Tommy's the one who invented it!
DANCE DANCE AMY

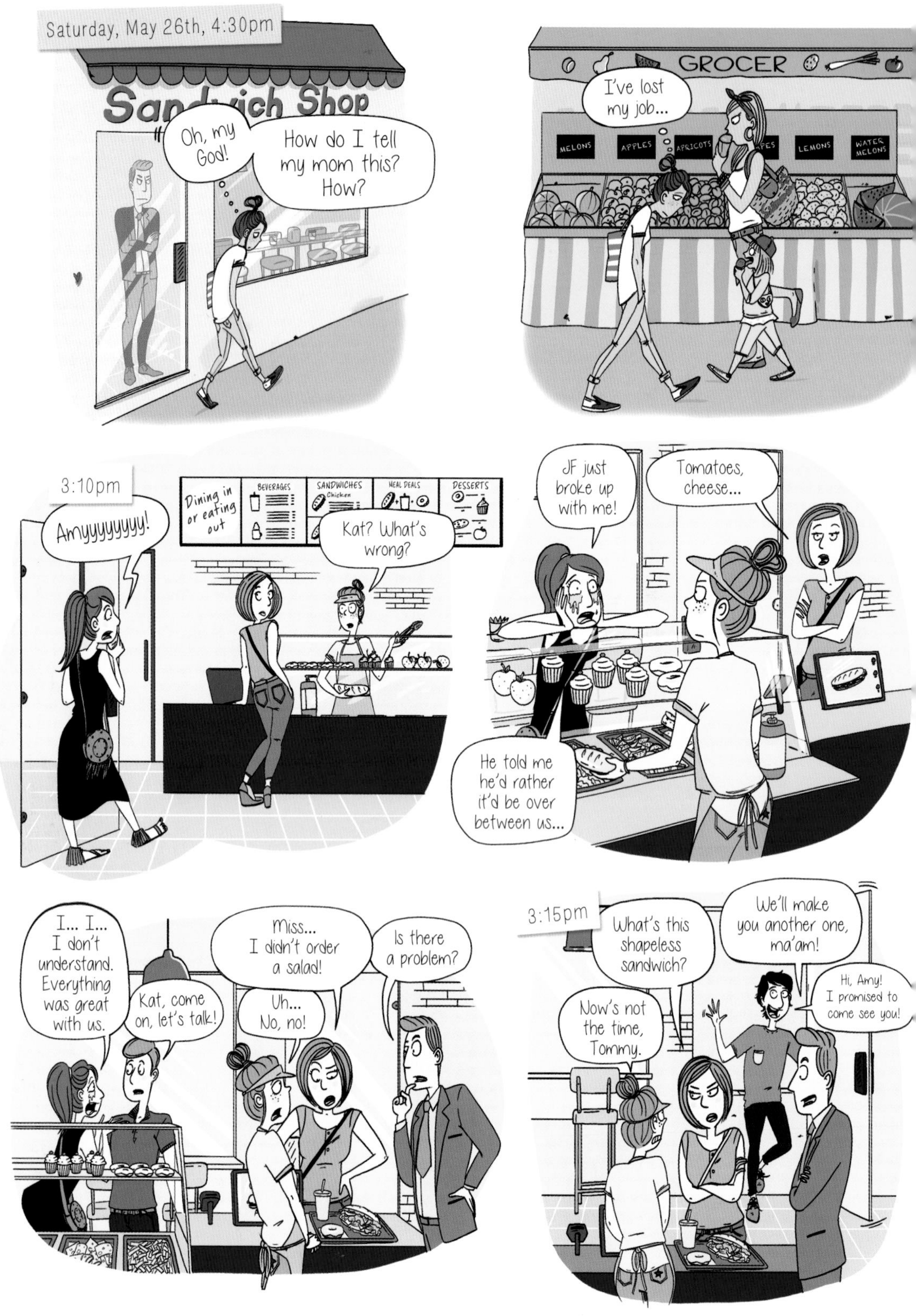
Saturday, May 26th, 4:30pm
Sandwich Shop
Oh, my God!
How do I tell my mom this? How?
GROCER
I've lost my job...
MELONS
APPLES
APRICOTS
LEMONS
WATER MELONS
3:10pm
Amyyyyyyyy!
Dining in or eating out
BEVERAGES
SANDWICHES
MEAL DEALS
DESSERTS
Kat? What's wrong?
JF just broke up with me!
Tomatoes, cheese...
He told me he'd rather it'd be over between us...
I... I... I don't understand. Everything was great with us.
Kat, come on, let's talk!
Miss... I didn't order a salad!
Uh... No, no!
Is there a problem?
3:15pm
What's this shapeless sandwich?
We'll make you another one, ma'am!
Now's not the time, Tommy.
Hi, Amy! I promised to come see you!

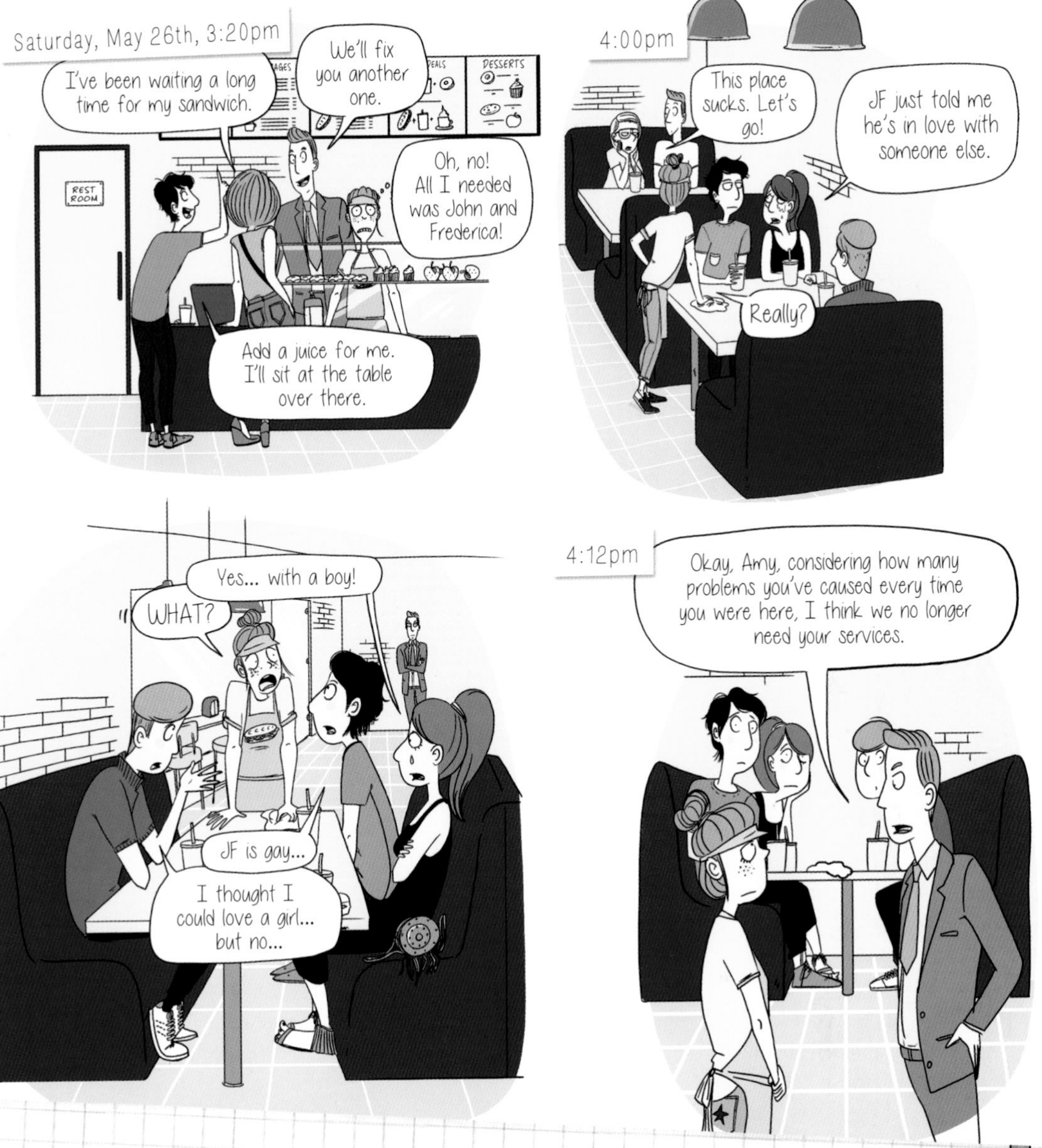
Saturday, May 26th, 3:20pm
I've been waiting a long time for my sandwich.
We'll fix you another one.
DESSERTS
REST ROOM
Oh, no! All I needed was John and Frederica!
Add a juice for me. I'll sit at the table over there.
4:00pm
This place sucks. Let's go!
JF just told me he's in love with someone else.
Really?
Yes... with a boy!
WHAT?
JF is gay...
I thought I could love a girl... but no...
4:12pm
Okay, Amy, considering how many problems you've caused every time you were here, I think we no longer need your services.

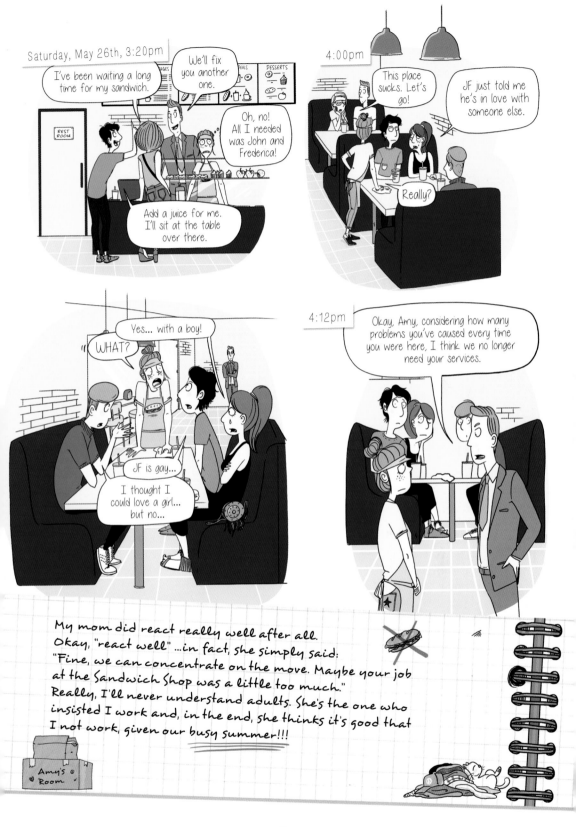

My mom did react really well after all.
Okay, "react well" ...in fact, she simply said:
"Fine, we can concentrate on the move. Maybe your job at the Sandwich Shop was a little too much."
Really, I'll never understand adults. She's the one who insisted I work and, in the end, she thinks it's good that I not work, given our busy summer!!!

Amy's Room

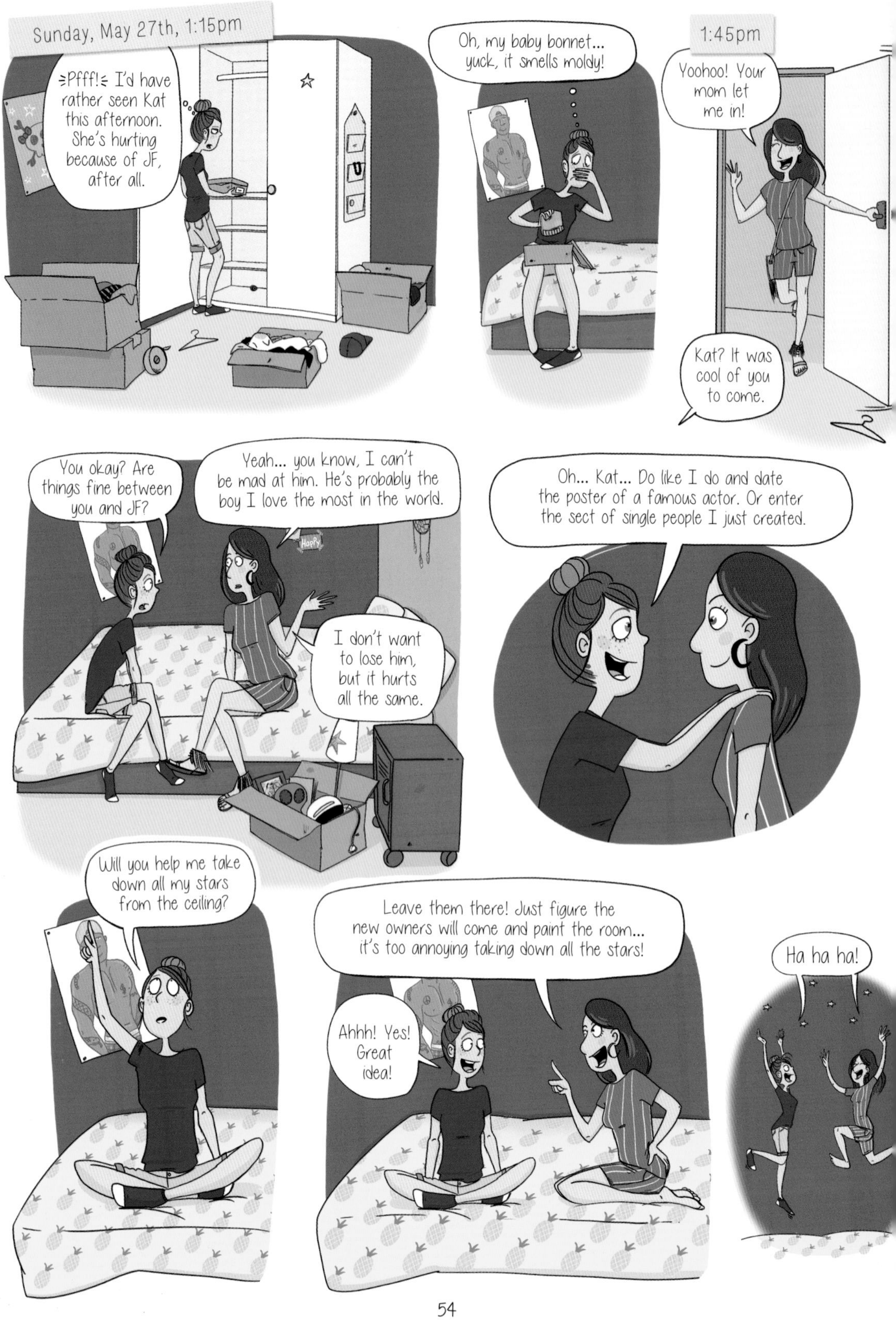
Sunday, May 27th, 1:15pm
≶Pfff!≶ I'd have rather seen Kat this afternoon. She's hurting because of JF, after all.
Oh, my baby bonnet... yuck, it smells moldy!
1:45pm
Yoohoo! Your mom let me in!
Kat? It was cool of you to come.
You okay? Are things fine between you and JF?
Yeah... you know, I can't be mad at him. He's probably the boy I love the most in the world.
Happy
I don't want to lose him, but it hurts all the same.
Oh... Kat... Do like I do and date the poster of a famous actor. Or enter the sect of single people I just created.
Will you help me take down all my stars from the ceiling?
Leave them there! Just figure the new owners will come and paint the room... it's too annoying taking down all the stars!
Ahhh! Yes! Great idea!
Ha ha ha!

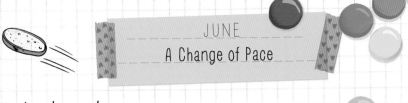

JUNE
A Change of Pace

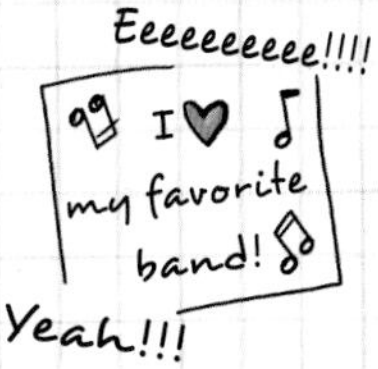
Eeeeeeeeee!!!!
I ♥ my favorite band!
Yeah!!!

- Friday, June 1st:

6:03pm:
I can really feel the end of the school year coming! Everyone's a little excited in anticipation. Summer's just around the corner, even though it's overcast and rainy. It's like a lull, just before the exam week, when you already almost feel like you're on vacation and when you forget you have big-time studying to do.

6:08pm:
Kat and JF are stuck together like never before. There's no awkwardness between them. It was a shock at first, but she's happy JF's being honest with himself. The ONLY problem is that Frederica heard the conversation in the Sandwich Shop, and I think she told a few people, because JF's getting weird looks at school. But since he's quick-witted (he is!), he stands up for himself. We talked a lot with JF, it drew all four of us closer together. He explained to us he really did feel in love with Kat. That he feels like she's his soulmate. But his nature caught up with him. And that it wasn't his fault.

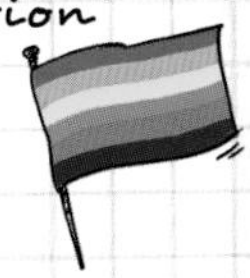

6:35pm:
I'm going to miss my friends... everyone's going their separate ways for summer vacation. Kat's spending several weeks at her horse-riding camp. JF's going on a trip with his parents, and Tommy's going to his mom's...

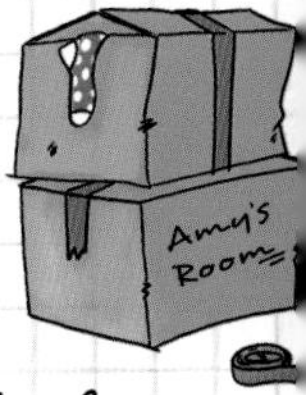
Amy's Room

Several endings are approaching. The end of the school year. The end of spring. The end of my life in MY house. The end of the world, too, perhaps? Naaah, I'm kidding!

I don't really want to move!!!!!!

7:00pm:
Yesterday, we had a food fight in the cafeteria. While leaning over to pick up a few pieces of bread on the ground, I bumped heads with someone else... Nick. I suddenly felt out of breath, my heart started throbbing. But I think it was because of the food fight that had exhausted me and for saying stupid things in Nick's presence such as:
"Sorry... Oops... Uh-oh..."

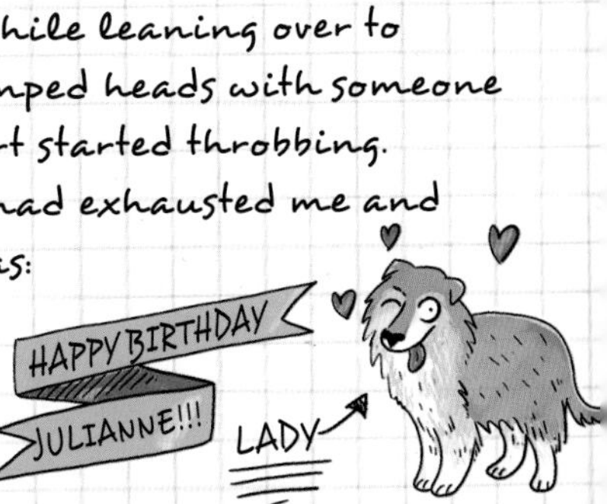
HAPPY BIRTHDAY
JULIANNE!!!
LADY

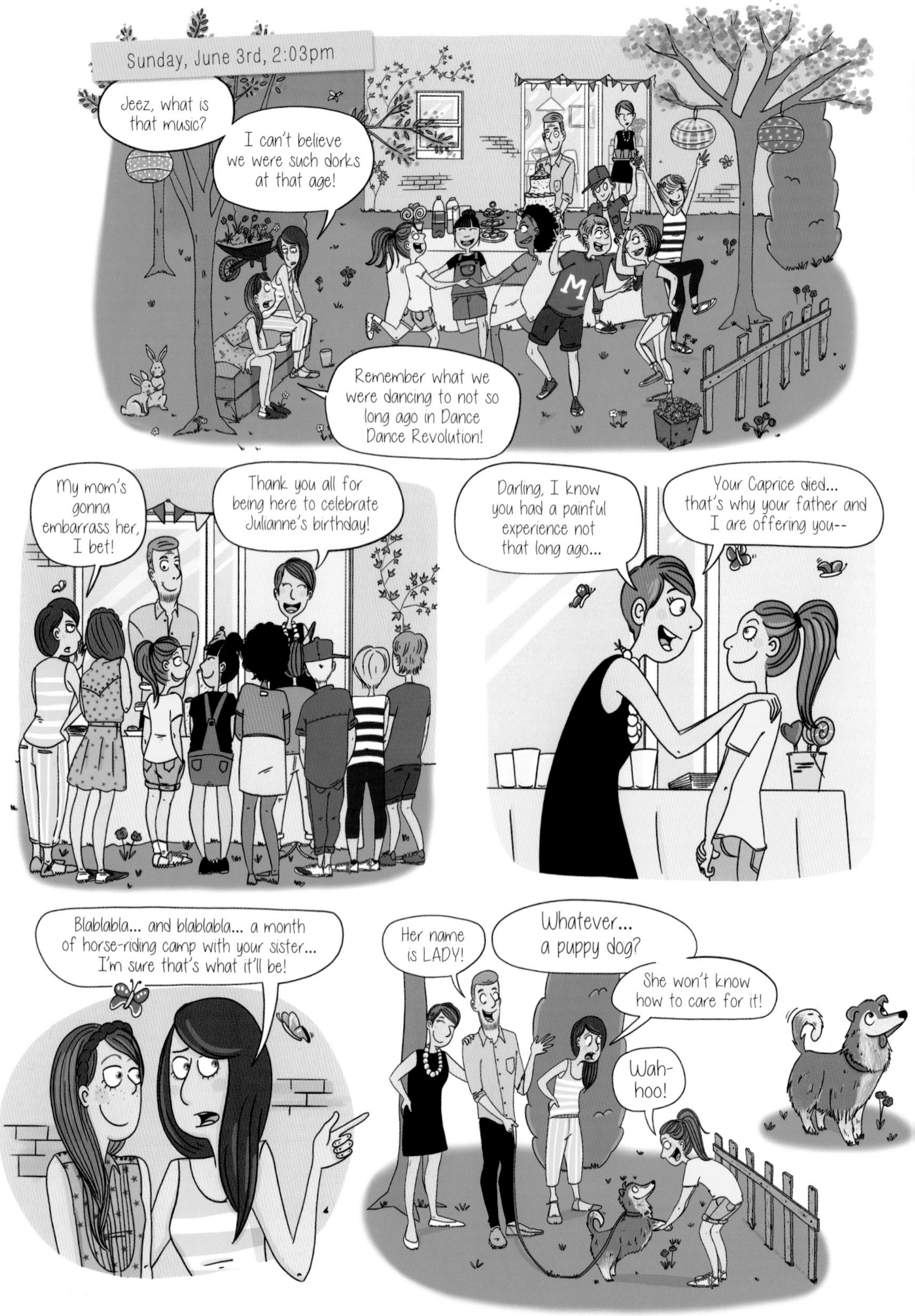
Sunday, June 3rd, 2:03pm
Jeez, what is that music?
I can't believe we were such dorks at that age!
Remember what we were dancing to not so long ago in Dance Dance Revolution!
My mom's gonna embarrass her, I bet!
Thank you all for being here to celebrate Julianne's birthday!
Darling, I know you had a painful experience not that long ago...
Your Caprice died... that's why your father and I are offering you--
Blablabla... and blablabla... a month of horse-riding camp with your sister... I'm sure that's what it'll be!
Her name is LADY!
Whatever... a puppy dog?
She won't know how to care for it!
Wah-hoo!

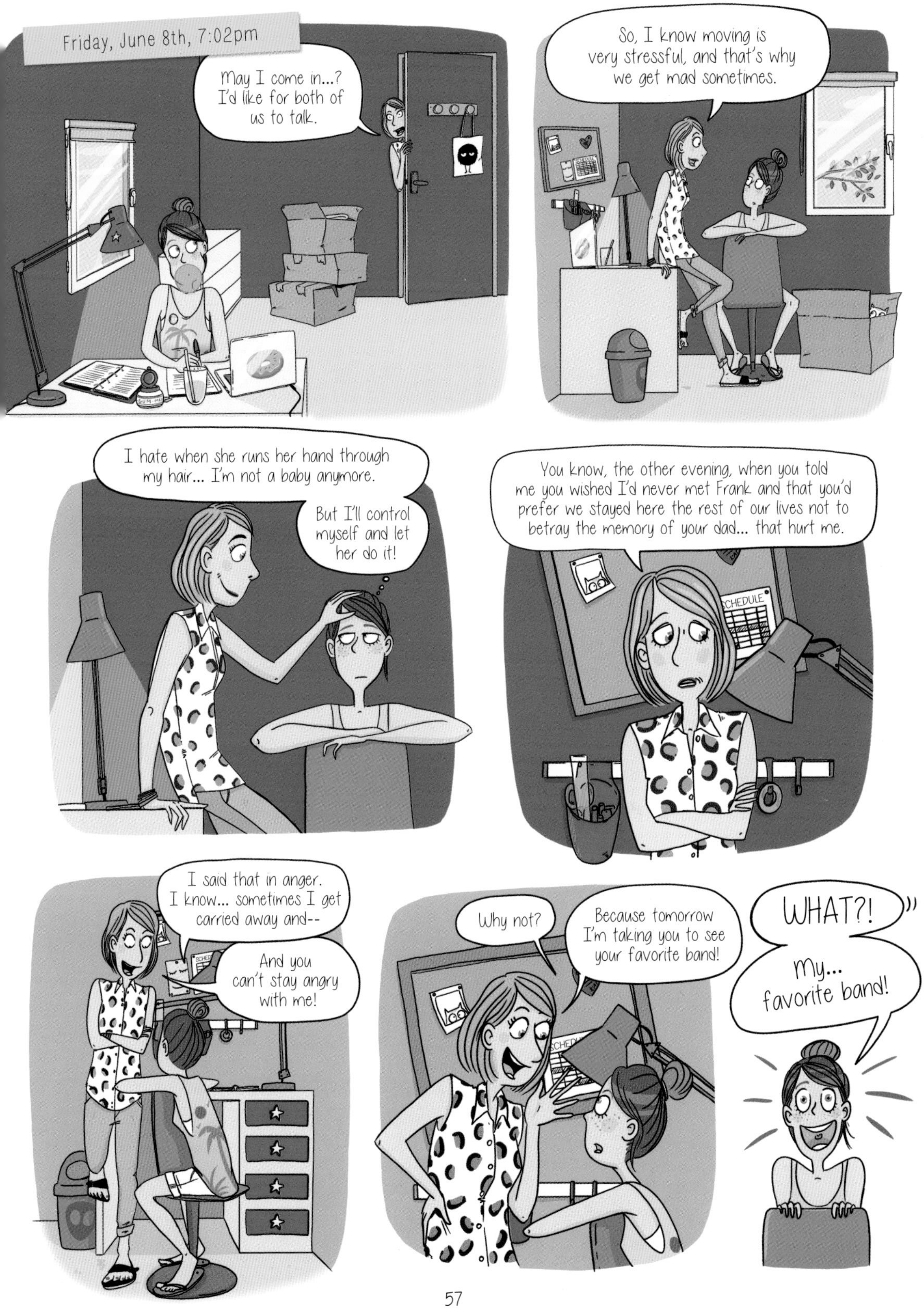
Friday, June 8th, 7:02pm
May I come in...? I'd like for both of us to talk.
So, I know moving is very stressful, and that's why we get mad sometimes.
I hate when she runs her hand through my hair... I'm not a baby anymore.
But I'll control myself and let her do it!
You know, the other evening, when you told me you wished I'd never met Frank and that you'd prefer we stayed here the rest of our lives not to betray the memory of your dad... that hurt me.
SCHEDULE
I said that in anger. I know... sometimes I get carried away and--
And you can't stay angry with me!
Why not?
Because tomorrow I'm taking you to see your favorite band!
WHAT?!
My... favorite band!

- Saturday, June 9th: I ♥ the singer

Oh, God, I'm going to die. I'm suffocating, I can't catch my breath. My head's about to explode. I'm going to faint! My favorite band is signing autographs in a bookstore. When my mom told me that yesterday, I thought I'd pass out. You have to admit, she knows how to make me forget our "slight" differences.

☺ ← Me

My Favorite Band

Dedication

ROCK

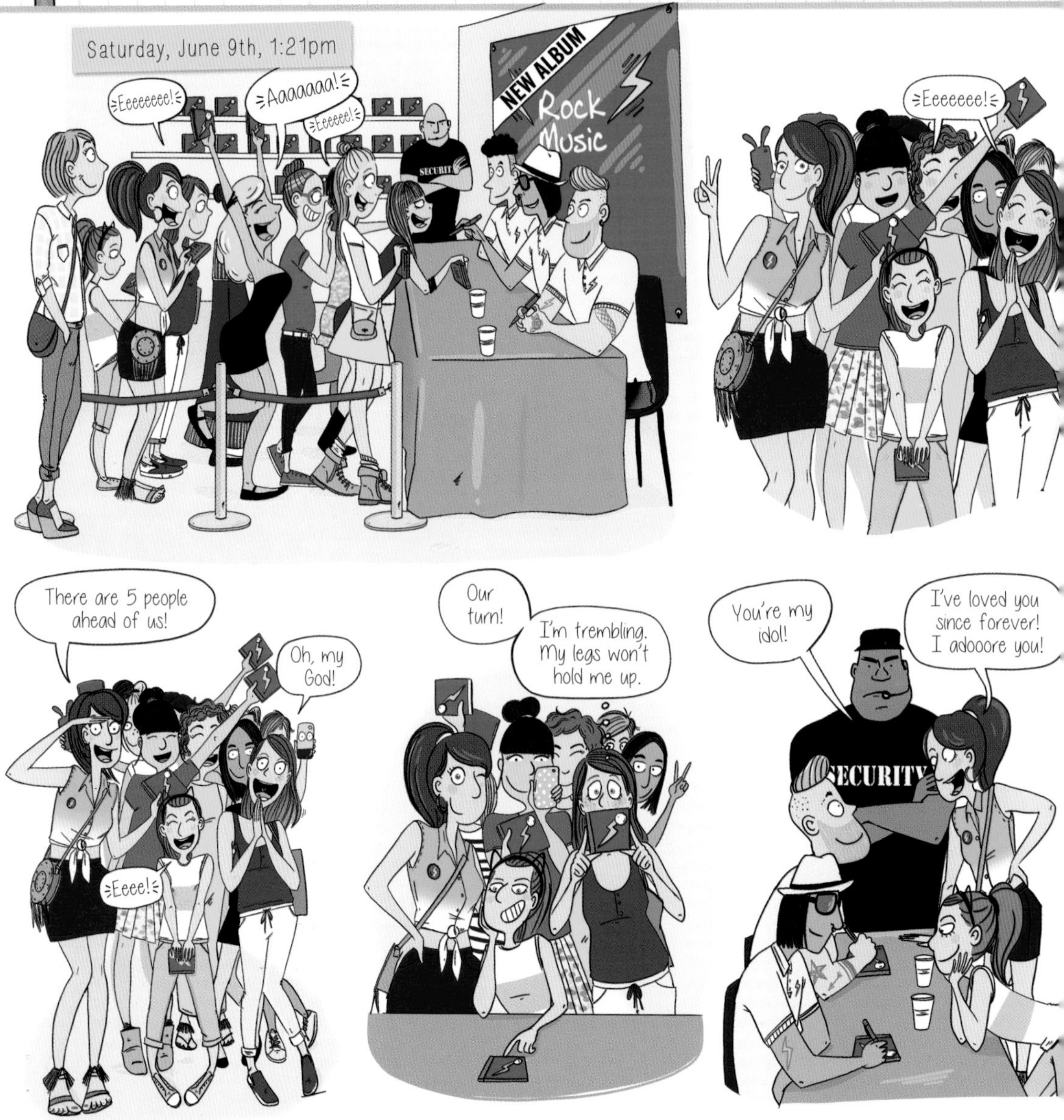

Saturday, June 9th, 1:21pm
Eeeeeee!
Aaaaaaa!
Eeeeee!
NEW ALBUM
Rock Music
SECURIT
Eeeeeee!
There are 5 people ahead of us!
Oh, my God!
Eeee!
Our turn!
I'm trembling. My legs won't hold me up.
You're my idol!
I've loved you since forever! I adooore you!
SECURITY

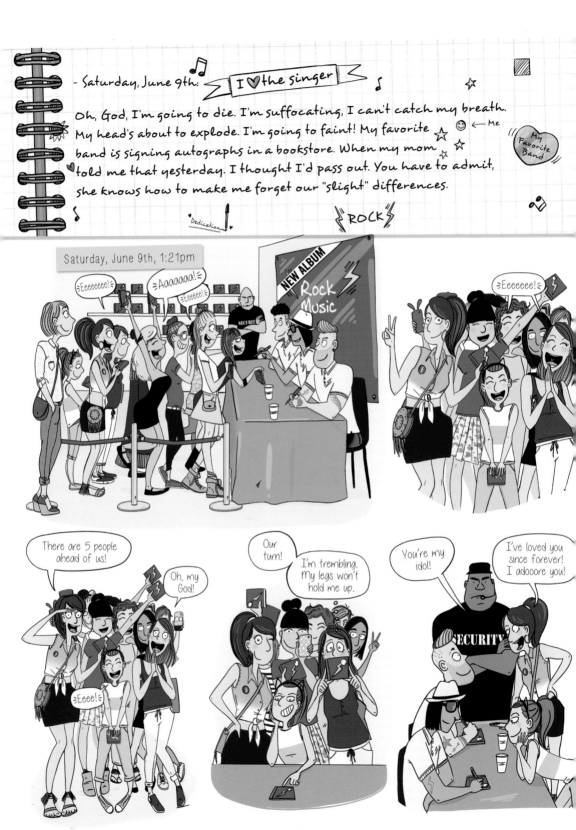

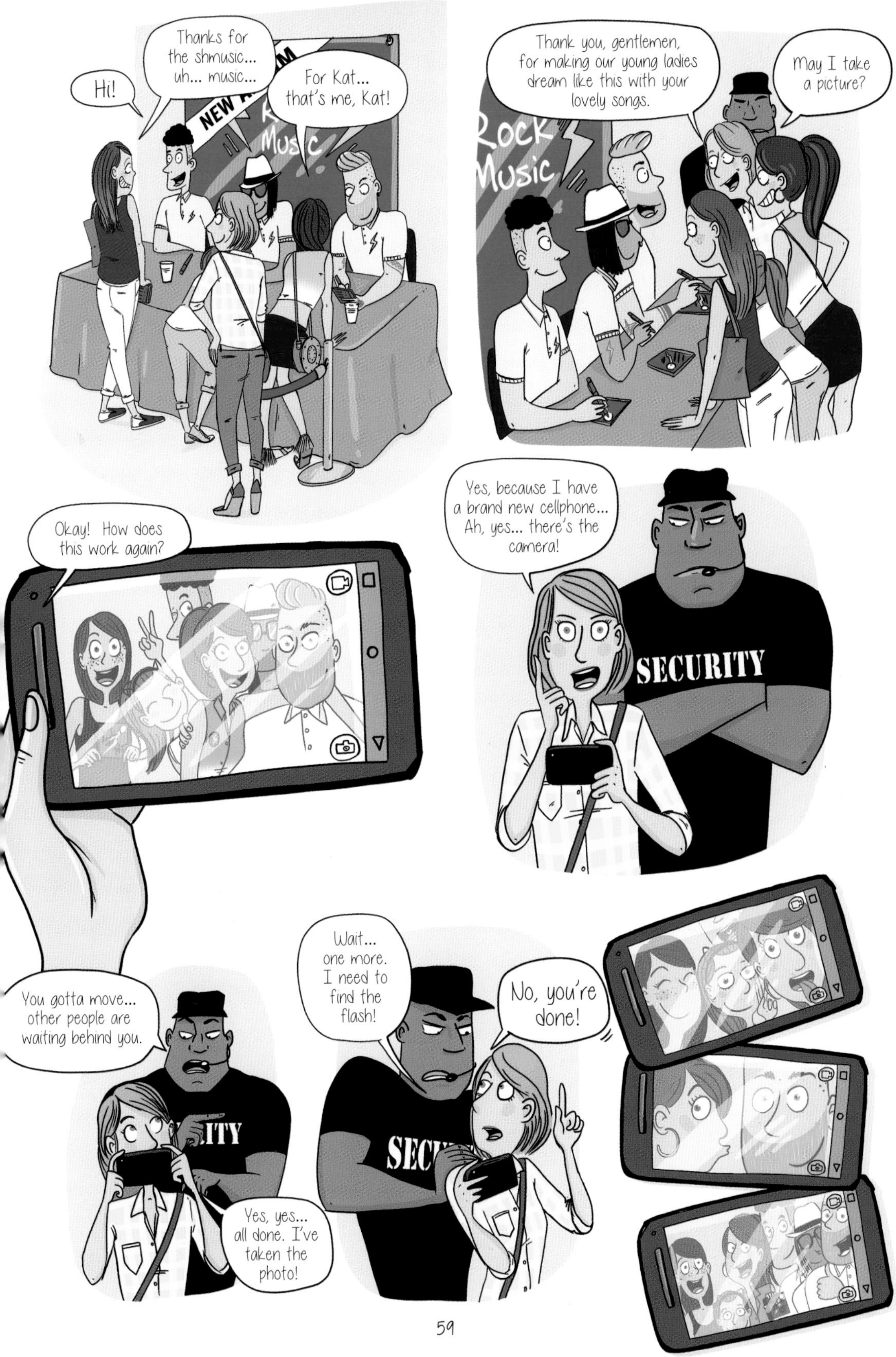

Hi!
Thanks for the shmusic... uh... music...
For Kat... that's me, Kat!
NEW
Rock Music
Thank you, gentlemen, for making our young ladies dream like this with your lovely songs.
May I take a picture?
Okay! How does this work again?
Yes, because I have a brand new cellphone... Ah, yes... there's the camera!
SECURITY
You gotta move... other people are waiting behind you.
Yes, yes... all done. I've taken the photo!
Wait... one more. I need to find the flash!
No, you're done!

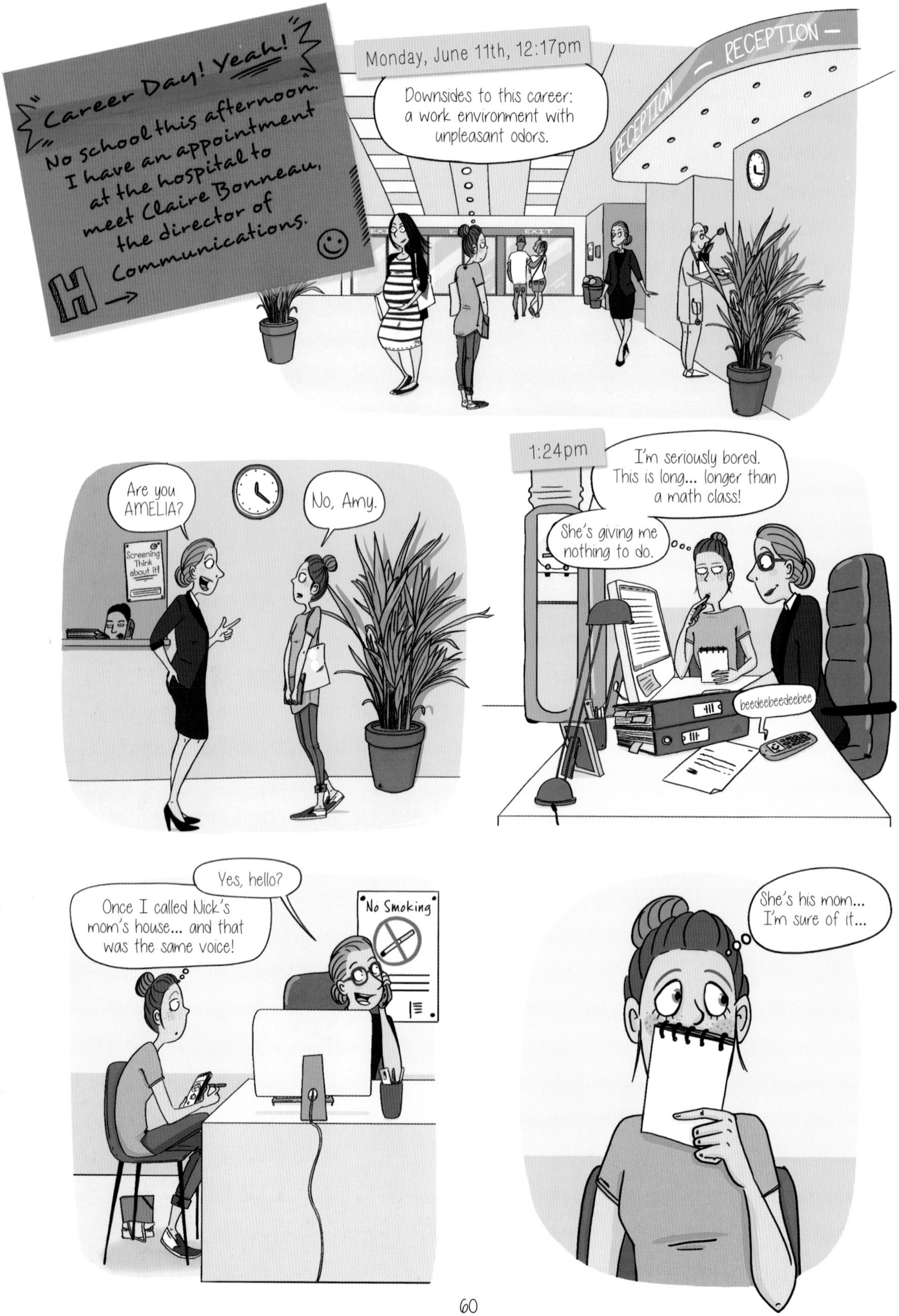

Career Day! Yeah!
No school this afternoon. I have an appointment at the hospital to meet Claire Bonneau, the director of Communications.
Monday, June 11th, 12:17pm
Downsides to this career: a work environment with unpleasant odors.
RECEPTION
EXIT
Are you AMELIA?
No, Amy.
Screening Think about it!
1:24pm
I'm seriously bored. This is long... longer than a math class!
She's giving me nothing to do.
beedeebeedeebee
Once I called Nick's mom's house... and that was the same voice!
Yes, hello?
No Smoking
She's his mom... I'm sure of it...

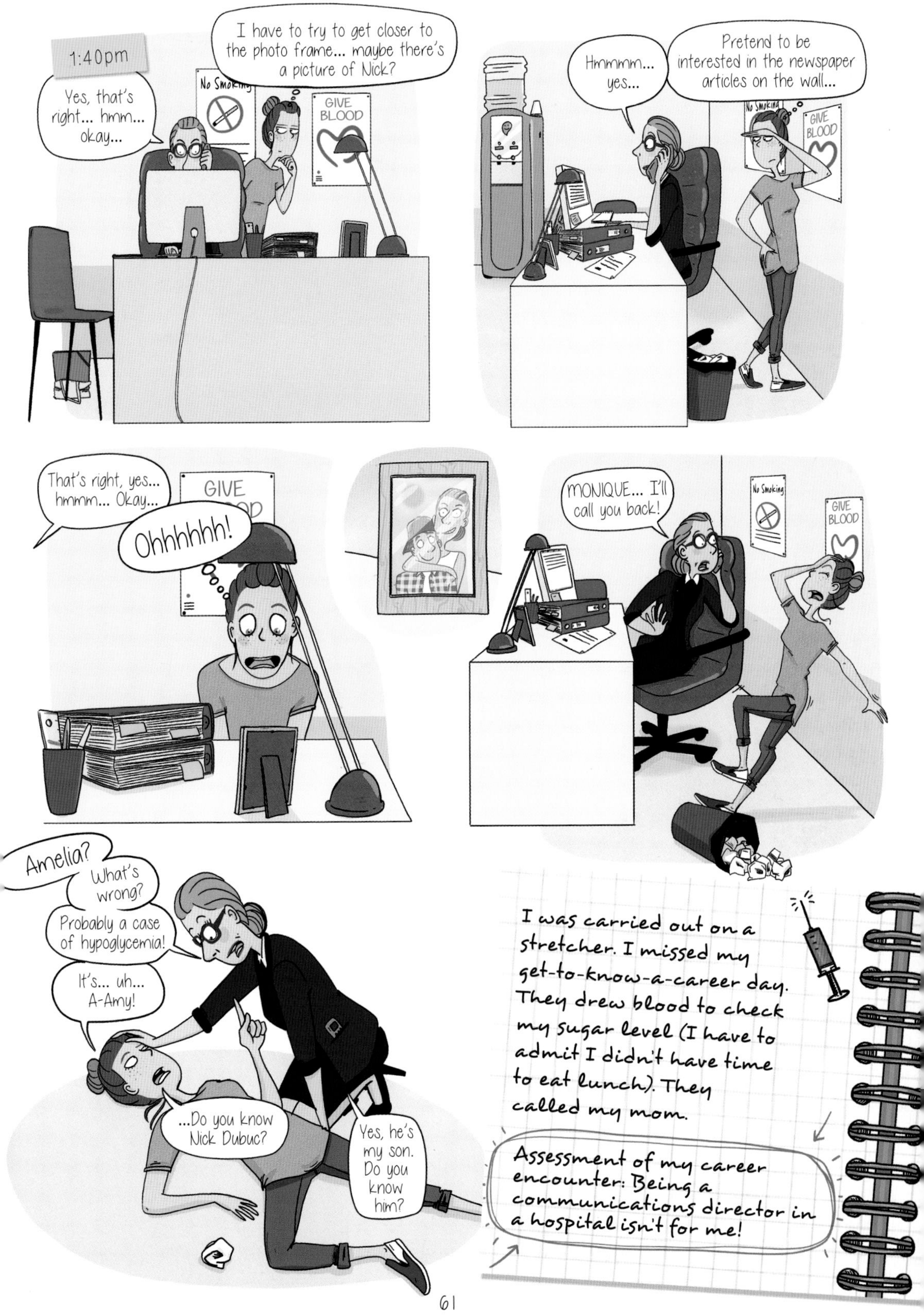
1:40pm
Yes, that's right... hmm... okay...
I have to try to get closer to the photo frame... maybe there's a picture of Nick?
No Smoking
GIVE BLOOD
Hmmmm... yes...
Pretend to be interested in the newspaper articles on the wall...
No Smoking
GIVE BLOOD
That's right, yes... hmmm... Okay...
Ohhhhhh!
MONIQUE... I'll call you back!
No Smoking
GIVE BLOOD
Amelia?
What's wrong?
Probably a case of hypoglycemia!
It's... uh... A-Amy!
...Do you know Nick Dubuc?
Yes, he's my son. Do you know him?
I was carried out on a stretcher. I missed my get-to-know-a-career day. They drew blood to check my sugar level (I have to admit I didn't have time to eat lunch). They called my mom.
Assessment of my career encounter: Being a communications director in a hospital isn't for me!

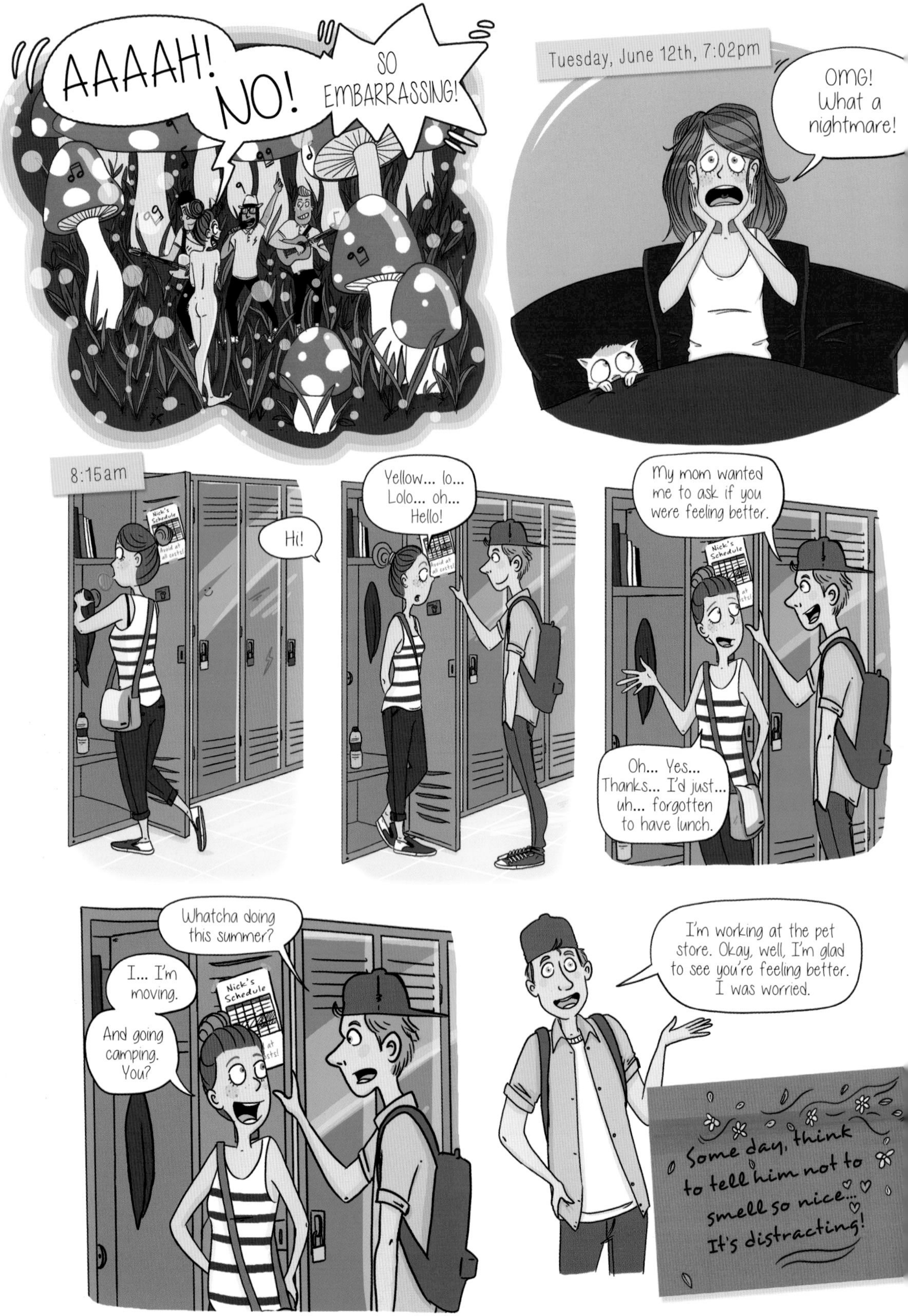
AAAAH! NO!
SO EMBARRASSING!
Tuesday, June 12th, 7:02pm
OMG! What a nightmare!
8:15am
Nick's Schedule
Avoid at all costs!
Hi!
Yellow... lo... Lolo... oh... Hello!
My mom wanted me to ask if you were feeling better.
Oh... Yes... Thanks... I'd just... uh... forgotten to have lunch.
Whatcha doing this summer?
I... I'm moving.
And going camping. You?
Nick's Schedule
I'm working at the pet store. Okay, well, I'm glad to see you're feeling better. I was worried.
Some day, think to tell him not to smell so nice... It's distracting!

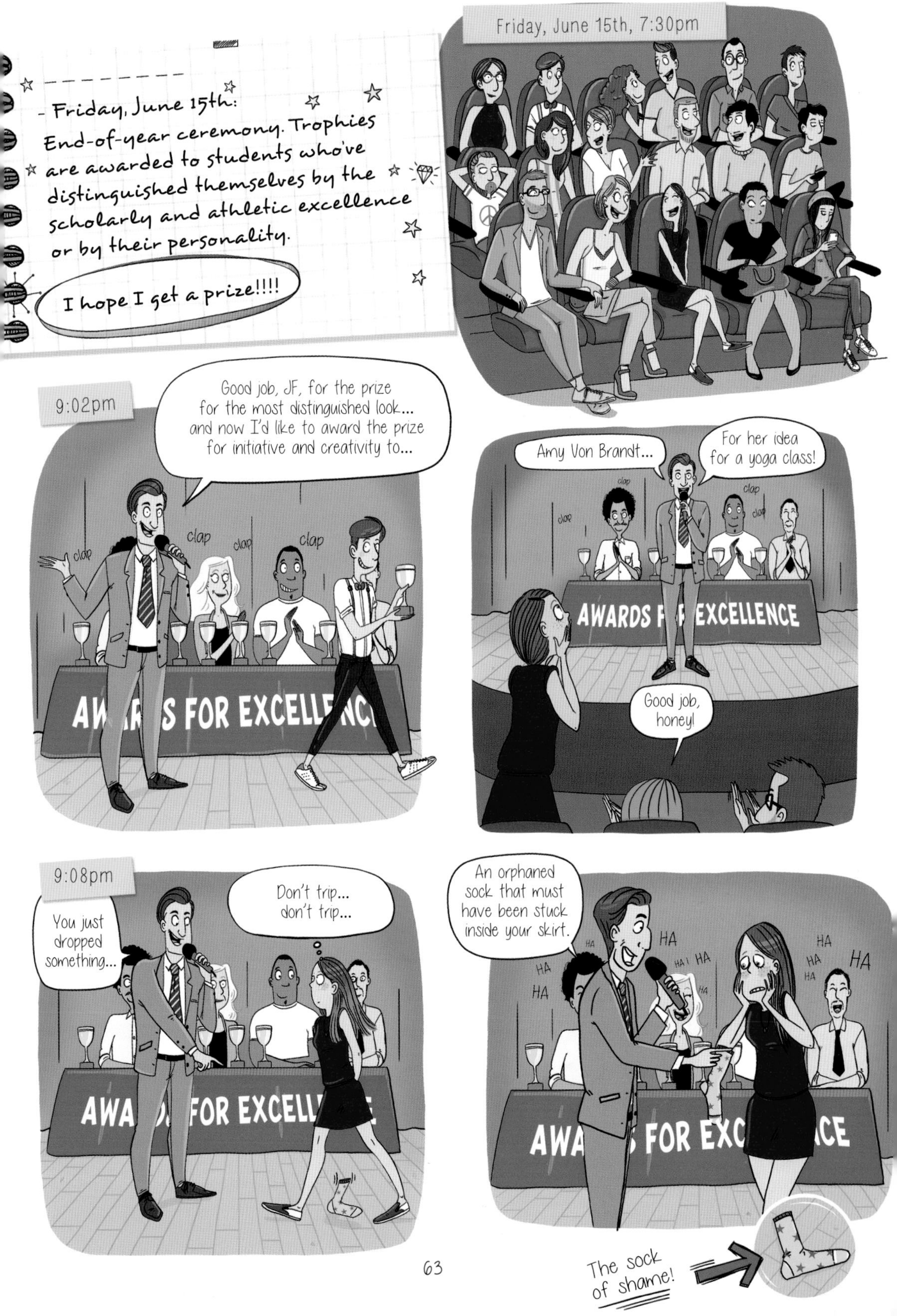
- Friday, June 15th:
End-of-year ceremony. Trophies are awarded to students who've distinguished themselves by the scholarly and athletic excellence or by their personality.
I hope I get a prize!!!!
Friday, June 15th, 7:30pm
9:02pm
Good job, JF, for the prize for the most distinguished look... and now I'd like to award the prize for initiative and creativity to...
clap clap clap clap
AWARDS FOR EXCELLENCE
Amy Von Brandt...
For her idea for a yoga class!
clap clap clap clap
AWARDS FOR EXCELLENCE
Good job, honey!
9:08pm
You just dropped something...
Don't trip... don't trip...
AWARDS FOR EXCELLENCE
An orphaned sock that must have been stuck inside your skirt.
HA HA HA HA HA HA HA HA HA HA HA
AWARDS FOR EXCELLENCE
The sock of shame!

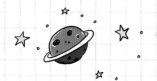

JULY

Blending into the Background

- Sunday, July 1st :

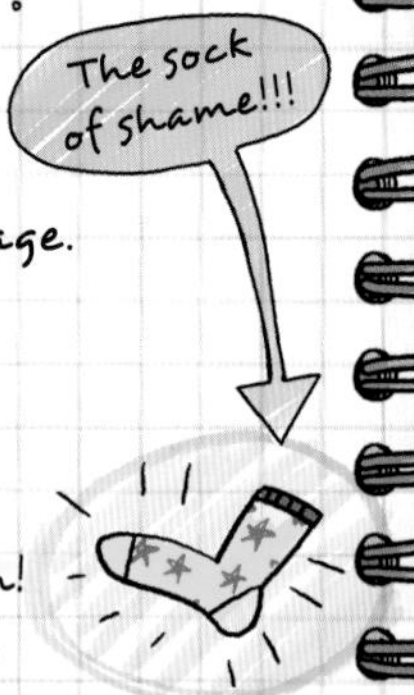
The sock of shame!!!

Lots of things happened after the episode of the fallen sock on stage.
But okay, I came out of it all right! It let me solve an enigma:
Now I know there's no ghost in the washing machine...
It's just static electricity making the clothes stick together.

Okay, I really did get embarrassed in front of everyone!

Weeteepeewoopeedoowooahhhhhh! School's over!!!!!

My last night in my house... was last night. I finished packing my last box at 9:52pm exactly. Tommy came over to help me. I felt a little sad... I had tears in my eyes looking at the stars on the ceiling...
I thought back to everything I'd experienced in my house... important details about my dad. The other day, my mom told me he had hair in his ears and, in my memories, he didn't have any. (Maybe it was a single hair, maybe in her memory, she added some... How can I trust my mom's memory?).

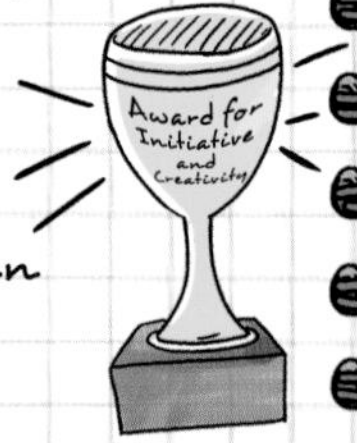
Award for Initiative and Creativity

That's what will happen to me with my home. I'll forget. And certain memories I'd sometimes have, flashbacks that came to me just because I was in the house, will maybe no longer come to mind.
Moving means forgetting my dad even more.

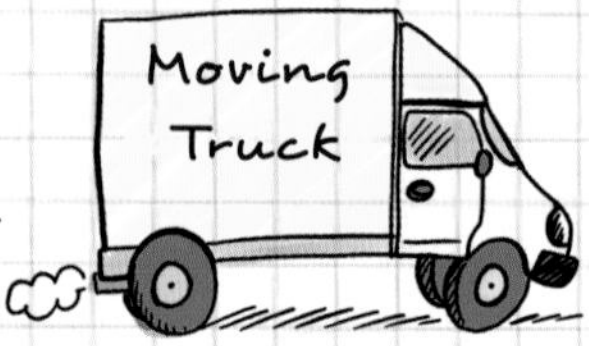
Moving Truck

8:23am:
This morning, the huge moving truck arrived. Then everything was emptied from my home.

And I watched that huge truck drive off with all of our stuff.
And then I felt like my home, empty, wasn't really my home anymore.

10:30am:

That's it, I'm in Frank's car, Sybil's cage on my lap, boxes beside me...
I'm having trouble breathing. I swore I wouldn't look back or look at Tommy, who's waving at me.

Okay, I'm moving two streets away... it's not the far side of the world, after all! But starting now, nothing will ever be like it was before.

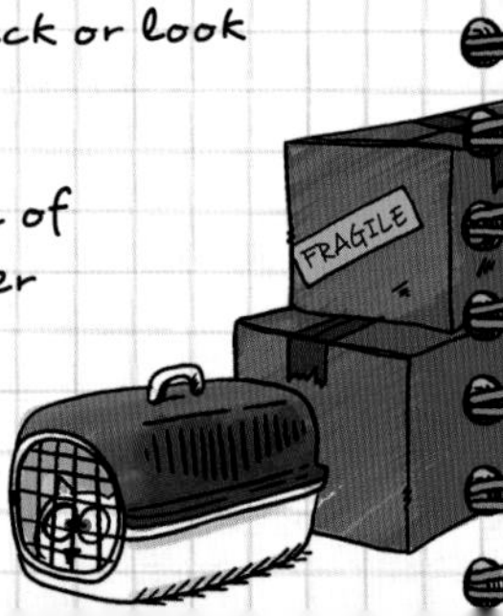
FRAGILE

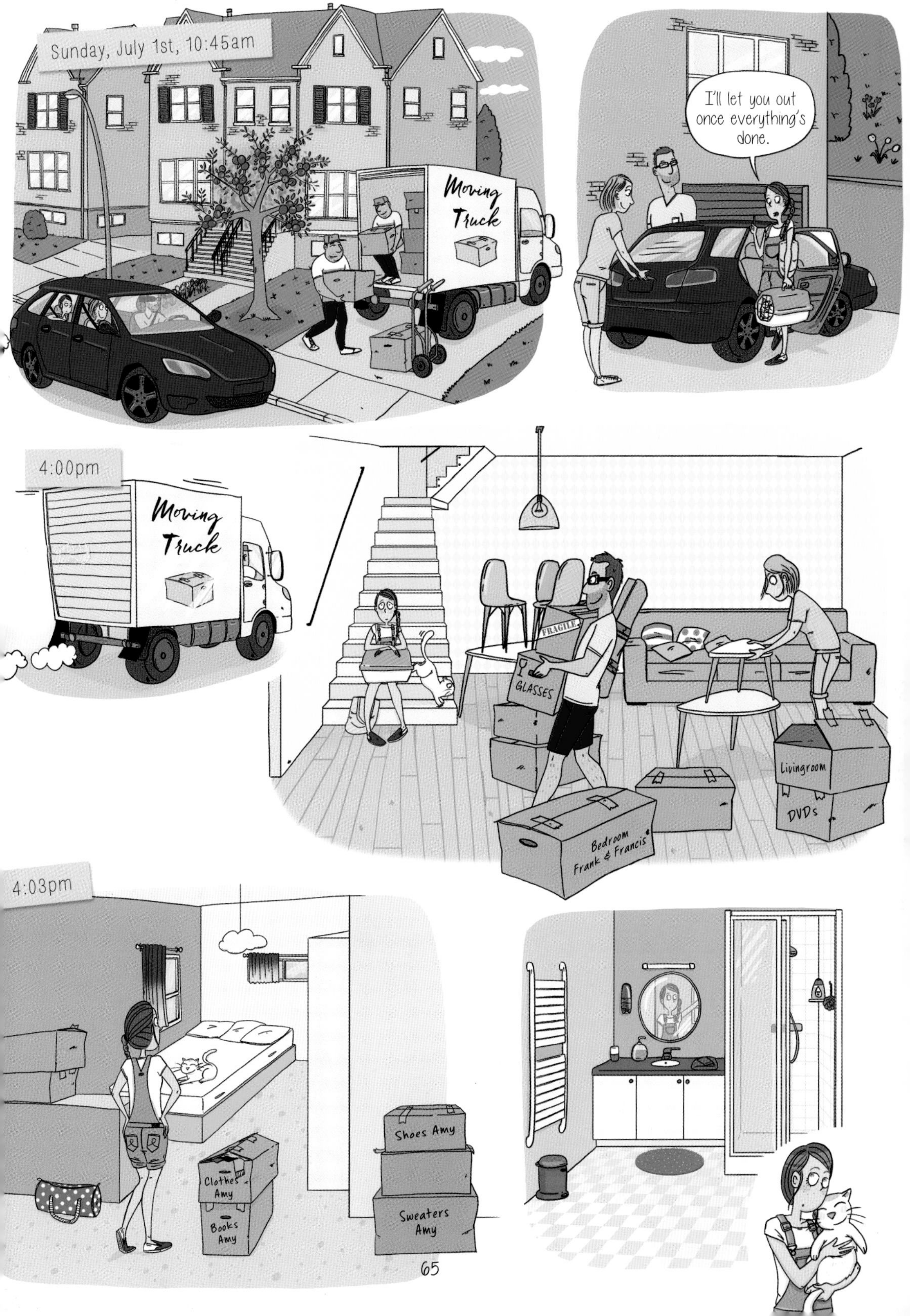
Sunday, July 1st, 10:45am
Moving Truck
I'll let you out once everything's done.
4:00pm
Moving Truck
FRAGILE
GLASSES
Livingroom
DVDs
Bedroom Frank & Francis
4:03pm
Clothes Amy
Books Amy
Shoes Amy
Sweaters Amy

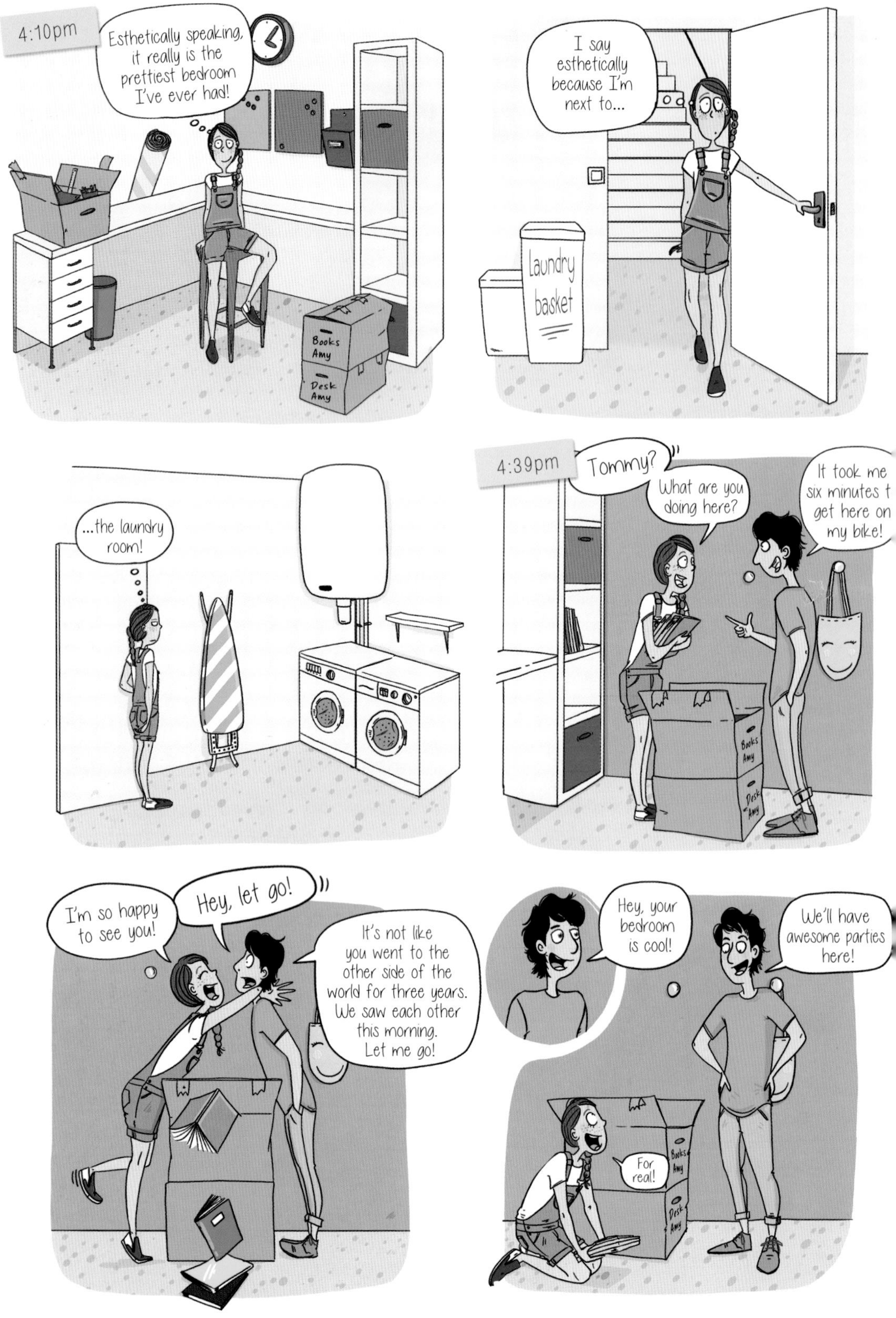
4:10pm
Esthetically speaking, it really is the prettiest bedroom I've ever had!
Books Amy
Desk Amy
I say esthetically because I'm next to...
Laundry basket
...the laundry room!
4:39pm
Tommy?
What are you doing here?
It took me six minutes t get here on my bike!
Books Amy
Desk Amy
I'm so happy to see you!
Hey, let go!
It's not like you went to the other side of the world for three years. We saw each other this morning. Let me go!
Hey, your bedroom is cool!
We'll have awesome parties here!
For real!
Books Amy
Desk Amy

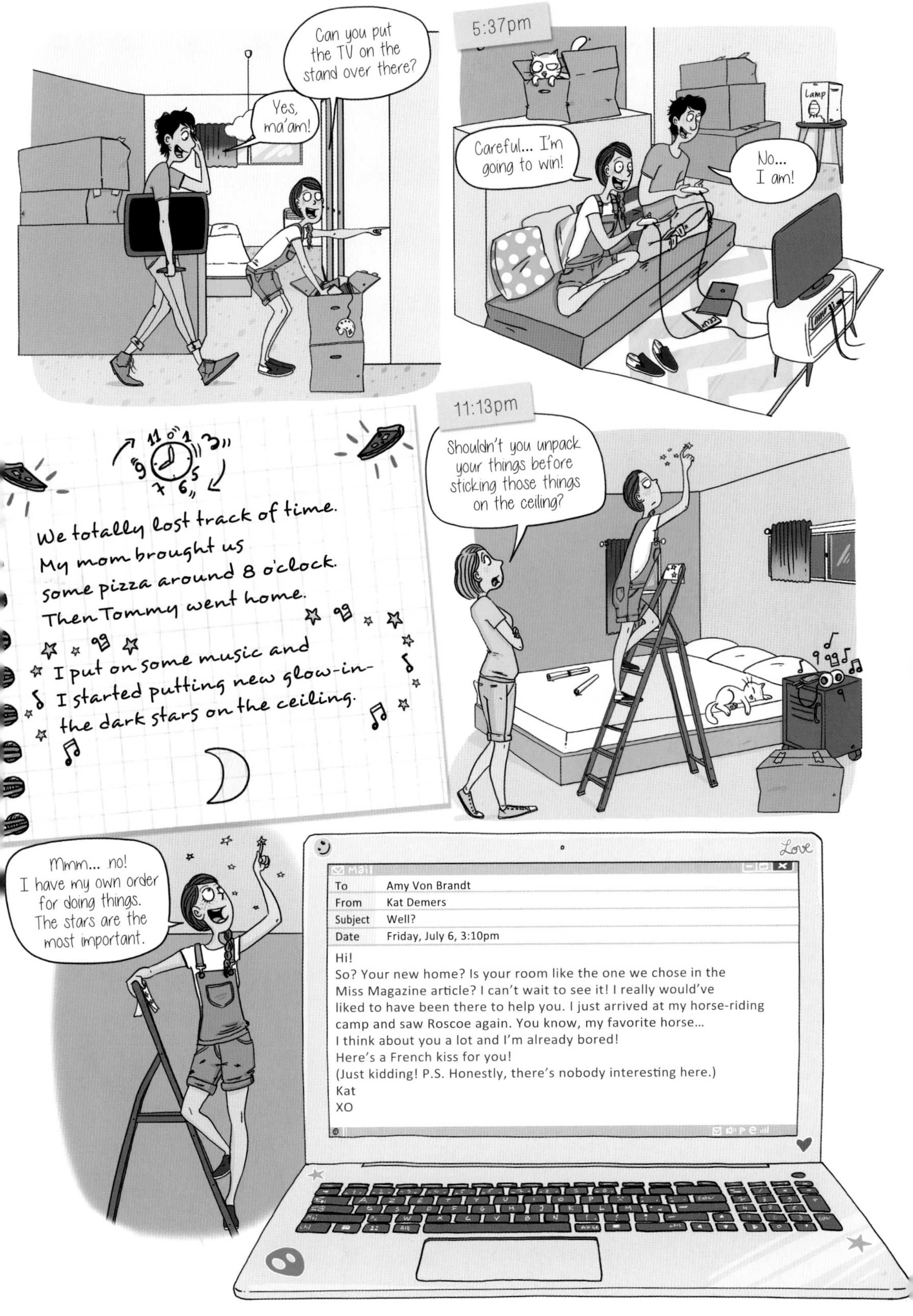
Can you put the TV on the stand over there?
Yes, ma'am!
5:37pm
Lamp
Careful... I'm going to win!
No... I am!
We totally lost track of time. My mom brought us some pizza around 8 o'clock. Then Tommy went home.
I put on some music and I started putting new glow-in-the dark stars on the ceiling.
11:13pm
Shouldn't you unpack your things before sticking those things on the ceiling?
Mmm... no! I have my own order for doing things. The stars are the most important.
Love
Mail
To Amy Von Brandt
From Kat Demers
Subject Well?
Date Friday, July 6, 3:10pm
Hi!
So? Your new home? Is your room like the one we chose in the Miss Magazine article? I can't wait to see it! I really would've liked to have been there to help you. I just arrived at my horse-riding camp and saw Roscoe again. You know, my favorite horse...
I think about you a lot and I'm already bored!
Here's a French kiss for you!
(Just kidding! P.S. Honestly, there's nobody interesting here.)
Kat
XO

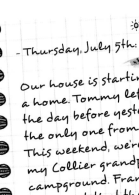

- Thursday, July 5th:

Our house is starting to feel like a home. Tommy left for vacation the day before yesterday, so I'm the only one from our group here. This weekend, we're going to see my Collier grandparents at the campground. Frank decided we'd camp out, that there was no way we'd sleep in my grandparents RV. I don't really like camping out... that means there'll be critters... littles one, big ones...

Mom, your breakfast was yummy!

Okay, let's go into the forest to set up our tent.

3:01pm

Is it far away?

Here... it's perfect for putting up the tent.

3:35pm

What do we do now?

It's an adventure! We're not slaves to time here.

Enjoy it and breath in the fresh air

68

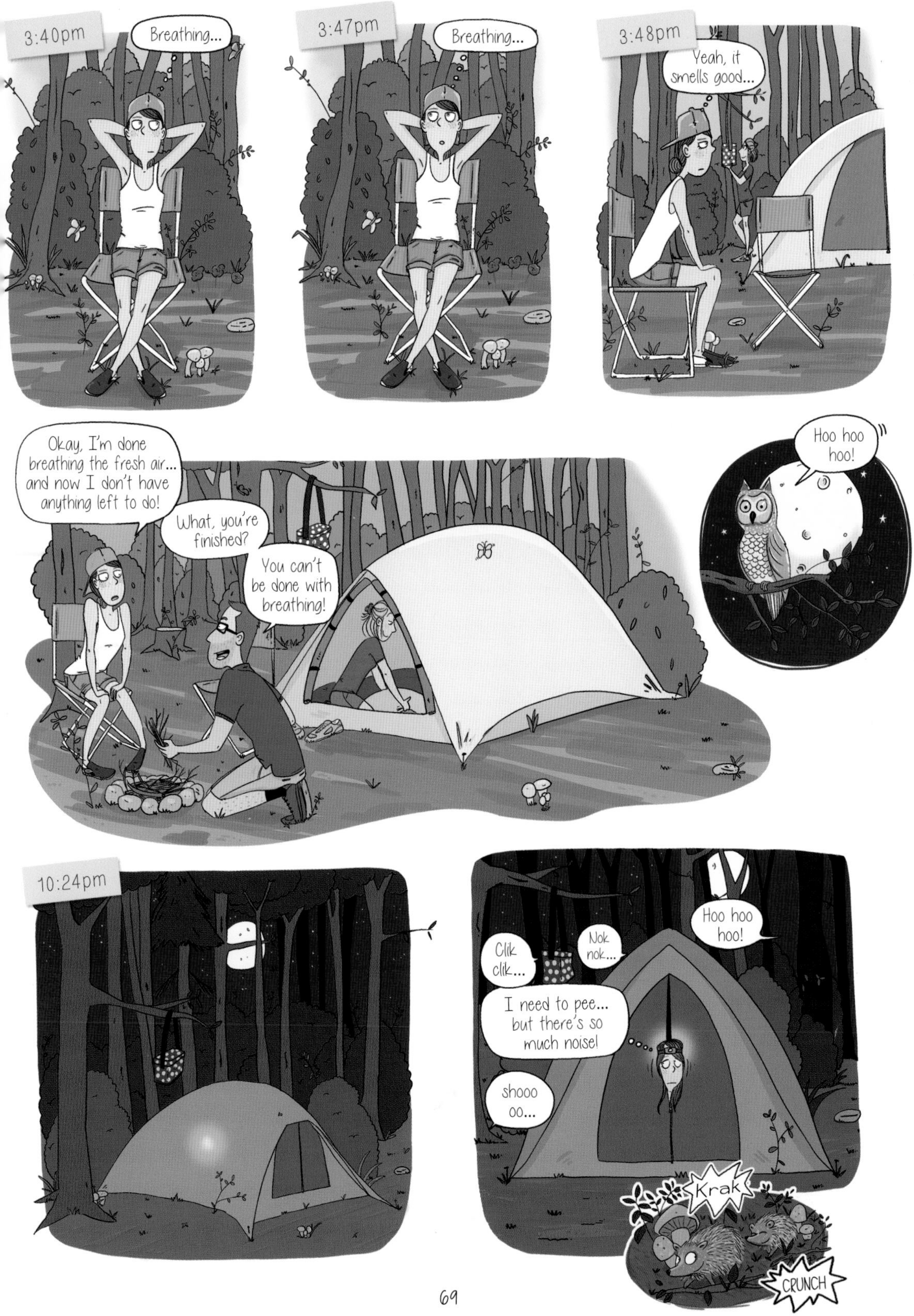
3:40pm
Breathing...
3:47pm
Breathing...
3:48pm
Yeah, it smells good...
Okay, I'm done breathing the fresh air... and now I don't have anything left to do!
What, you're finished?
You can't be done with breathing!
Hoo hoo hoo!
10:24pm
Clik clik...
Nok nok...
Hoo hoo hoo!
I need to pee... but there's so much noise!
shooo oo...
Krak
CRUNCH

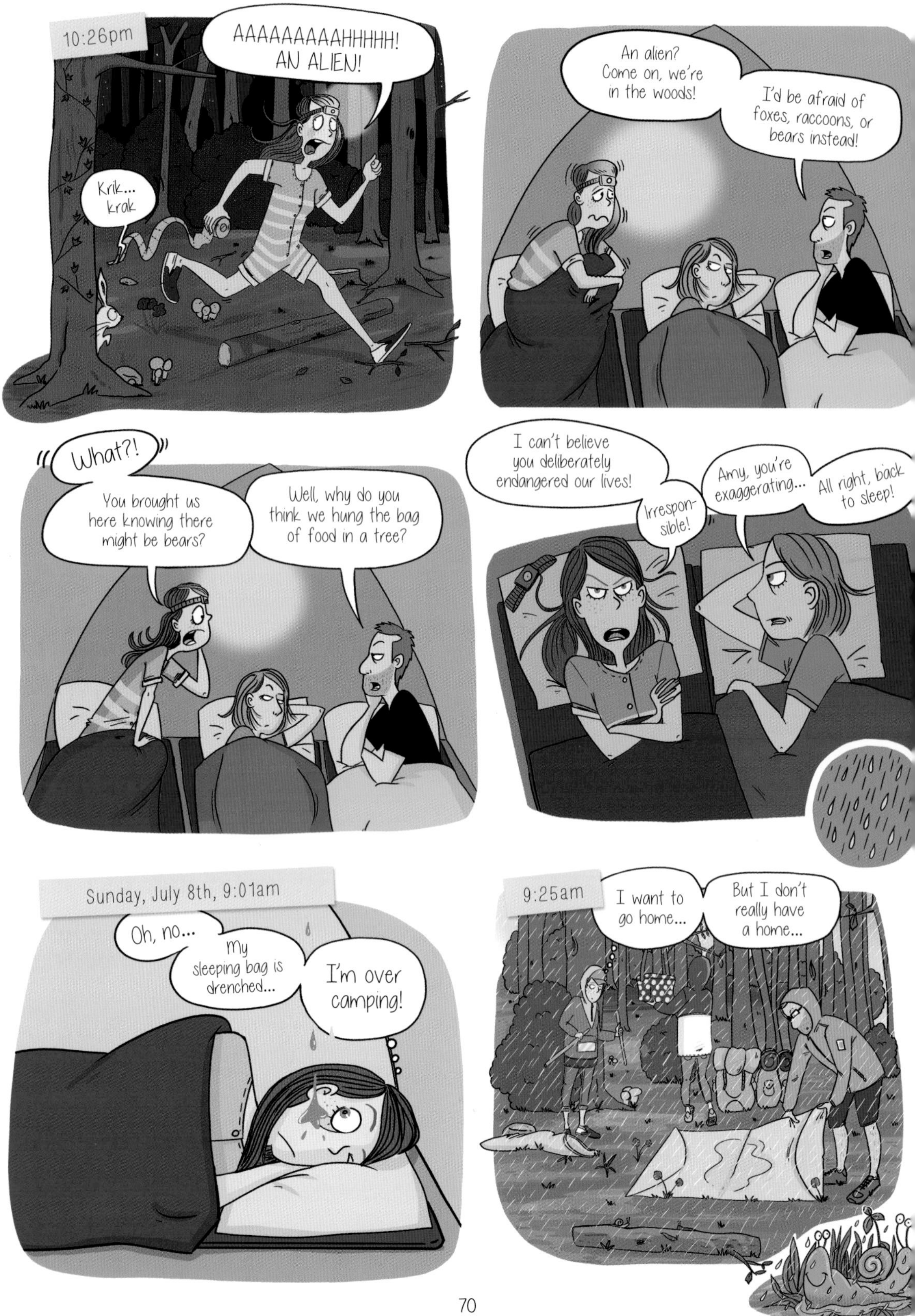

10:26pm
AAAAAAAAAHHHHH! AN ALIEN!
Krik... krak
An alien? Come on, we're in the woods!
I'd be afraid of foxes, raccoons, or bears instead!
What?!
You brought us here knowing there might be bears?
Well, why do you think we hung the bag of food in a tree?
I can't believe you deliberately endangered our lives!
Irrespon-sible!
Amy, you're exaggerating...
All right, back to sleep!
Sunday, July 8th, 9:01am
Oh, no...
My sleeping bag is drenched...
I'm over camping!
9:25am
I want to go home...
But I don't really have a home...

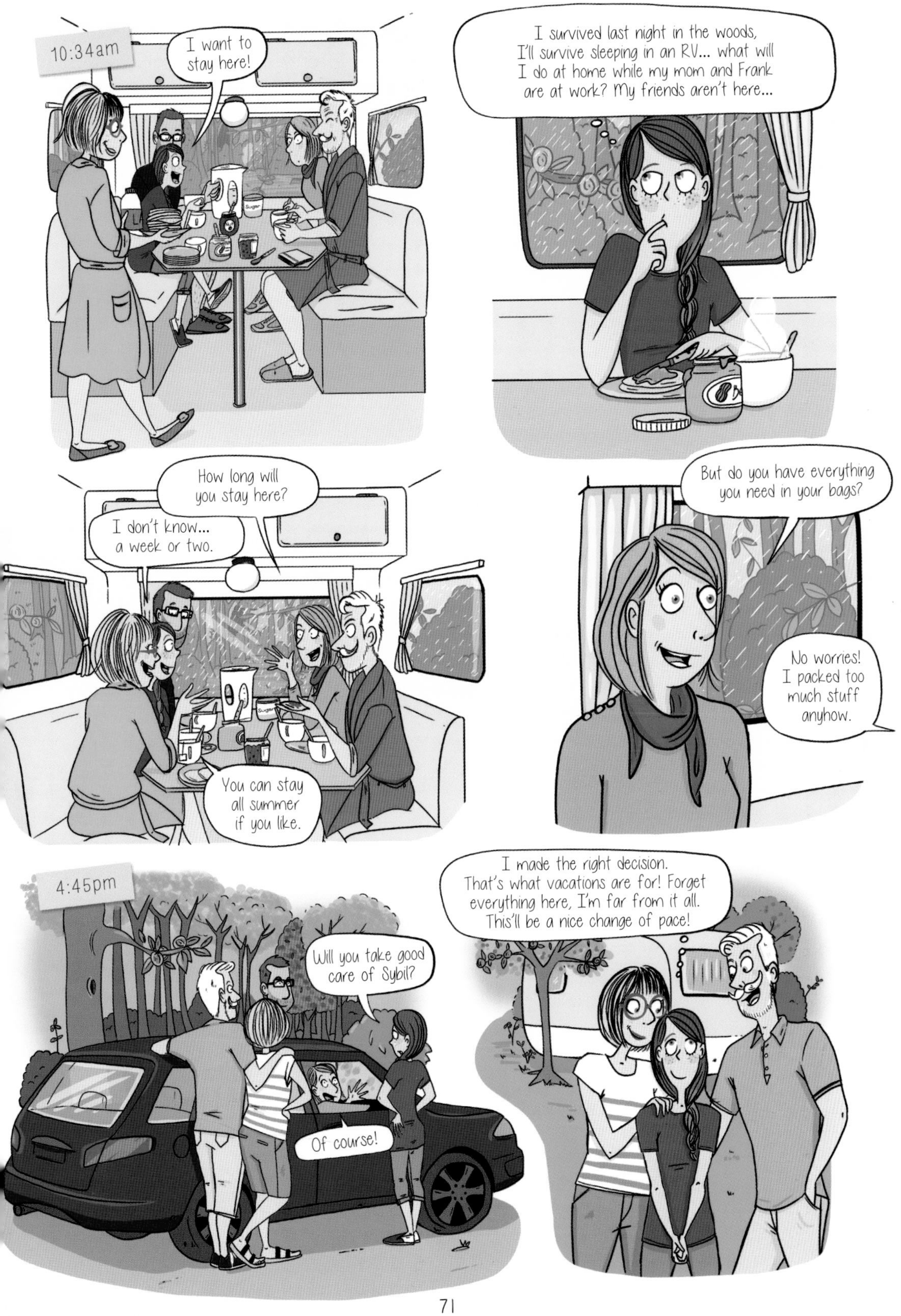
10:34am
I want to stay here!
I survived last night in the woods, I'll survive sleeping in an RV... what will I do at home while my mom and Frank are at work? My friends aren't here...
How long will you stay here?
I don't know... a week or two.
You can stay all summer if you like.
But do you have everything you need in your bags?
No worries! I packed too much stuff anyhow.
4:45pm
Will you take good care of Sybil?
Of course!
I made the right decision. That's what vacations are for! Forget everything here, I'm far from it all. This'll be a nice change of pace!

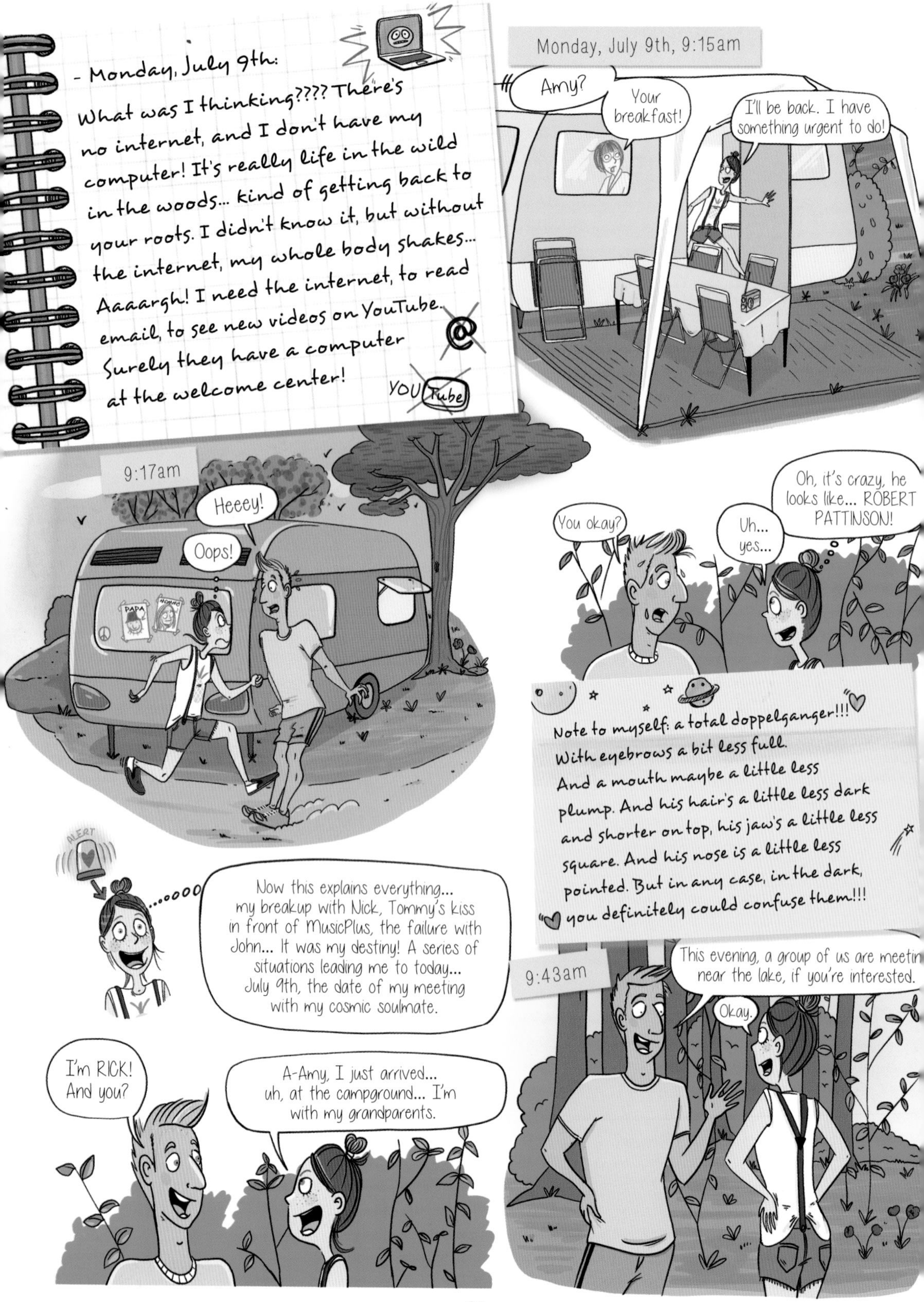

- Monday, July 9th:
What was I thinking???? There's
no internet, and I don't have my
computer! It's really life in the wild
in the woods... kind of getting back to
your roots. I didn't know it, but without
the internet, my whole body shakes...
Aaaargh! I need the internet, to read
email, to see new videos on YouTube.
Surely they have a computer
at the welcome center!
@
YOU Tube
Monday, July 9th, 9:15am
Amy?
Your breakfast!
I'll be back. I have something urgent to do!
9:17am
Heeey!
Oops!
PAPA
MOMMO
Now this explains everything... my breakup with Nick, Tommy's kiss in front of MusicPlus, the failure with John... It was my destiny! A series of situations leading me to today... July 9th, the date of my meeting with my cosmic soulmate.
ALERT
...oooo
I'm RICK! And you?
A-Amy, I just arrived... uh, at the campground... I'm with my grandparents.
You okay?
Uh... yes...
Oh, it's crazy, he looks like... ROBERT PATTINSON!
Note to myself: a total doppelganger!!!
With eyebrows a bit less full.
And a mouth maybe a little less
plump. And his hair's a little less dark
and shorter on top, his jaw's a little less
square. And his nose is a little less
pointed. But in any case, in the dark,
you definitely could confuse them!!!
9:43am
This evening, a group of us are meetin near the lake, if you're interested.
Okay.

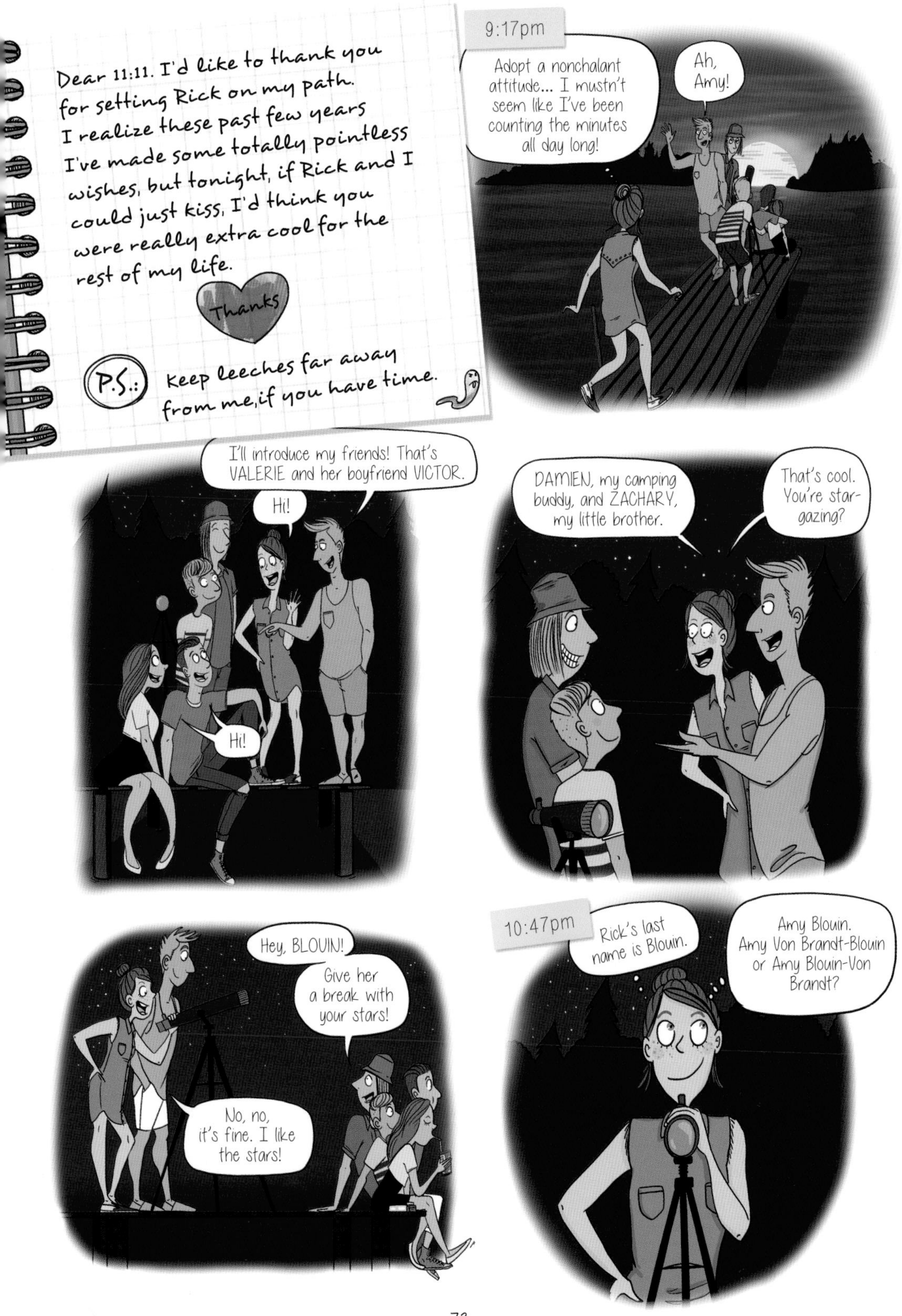

Dear 11:11. I'd like to thank you for setting Rick on my path. I realize these past few years I've made some totally pointless wishes, but tonight, if Rick and I could just kiss, I'd think you were really extra cool for the rest of my life.
Thanks
P.S.: Keep leeches far away from me, if you have time.
9:17pm
Adopt a nonchalant attitude... I mustn't seem like I've been counting the minutes all day long!
Ah, Amy!
I'll introduce my friends! That's VALERIE and her boyfriend VICTOR.
Hi!
Hi!
DAMIEN, my camping buddy, and ZACHARY, my little brother.
That's cool. You're star-gazing?
Hey, BLOUIN!
Give her a break with your stars!
No, no, it's fine. I like the stars!
10:47pm
Rick's last name is Blouin.
Amy Blouin. Amy Von Brandt-Blouin or Amy Blouin-Von Brandt?

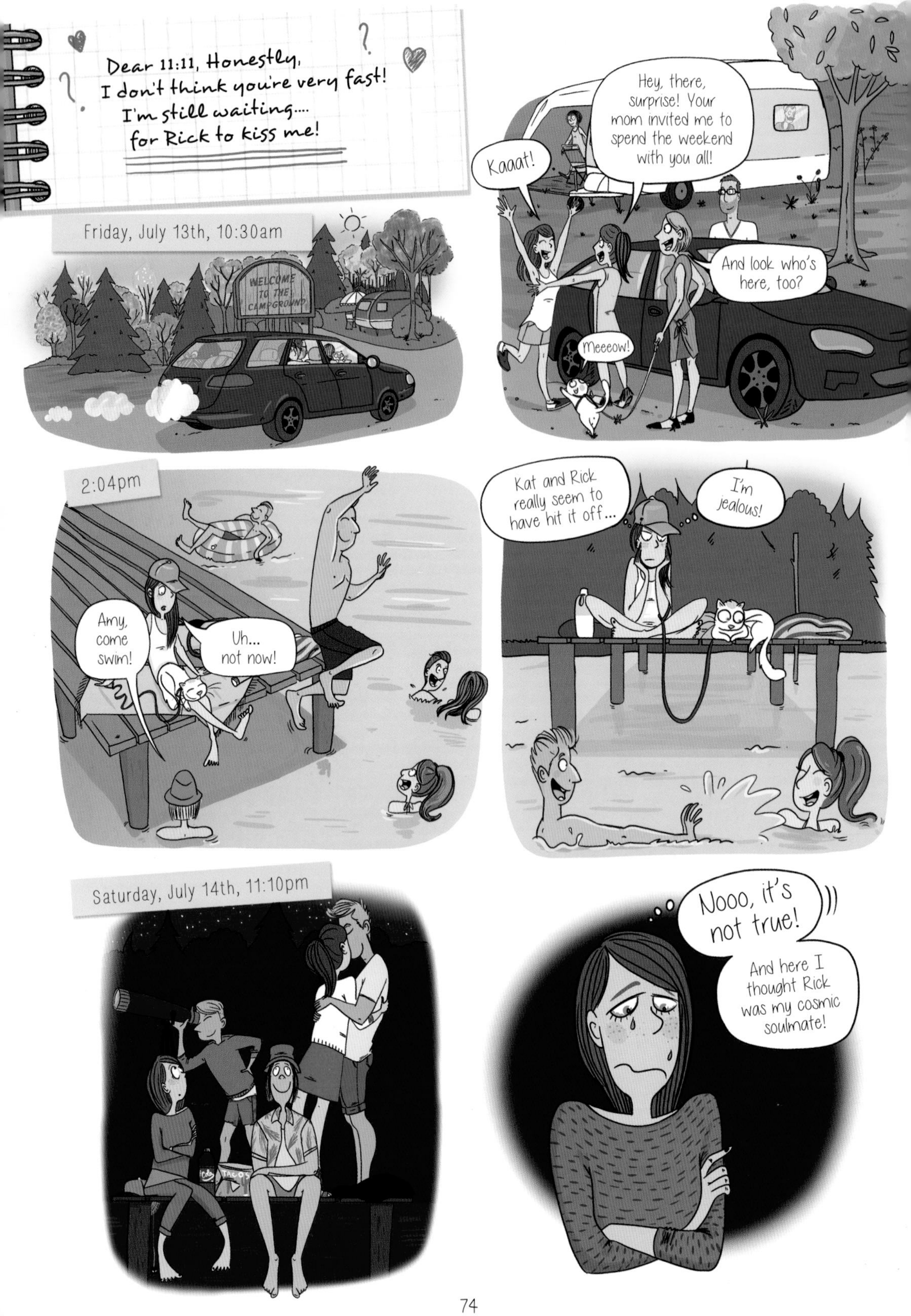
Dear 11:11, Honestly, I don't think you're very fast! I'm still waiting.... for Rick to kiss me!
Kaaat!
Hey, there, surprise! Your mom invited me to spend the weekend with you all!
And look who's here, too?
Meeeow!
Friday, July 13th, 10:30am
WELCOME TO THE CAMPGROUND
2:04pm
Amy, come swim!
Uh... not now!
Kat and Rick really seem to have hit it off...
I'm jealous!
Saturday, July 14th, 11:10pm
TACOS
Nooo, it's not true!
And here I thought Rick was my cosmic soulmate!

AUGUST

Save the Furniture

- Friday, August 3rd:

9:05pm:
The end of my vacation at the campground really sucked! When I saw Kat kissing Rick... I don't know what got into me, surely out of spite... I kissed Damien. When I think back on it, it gives me spasms of fright. I kissed him and it really was totally disgusting! (I still get the shivers)... He had a doughy mouth and bad breath (it almost tasted like the smell of manure).

I'm trying to forget that moment which has been on a loop in my mind for days and makes me gag.

And that evening, in the RV, Kat confided to me that Rick had told her: "I'm Amy's cosmic soulmate, but I'm in love with you by mistake, Kat!" No, he didn't say that. She simply told me that no boy had ever had that effect on her. That no boy had ever kissed her like that!

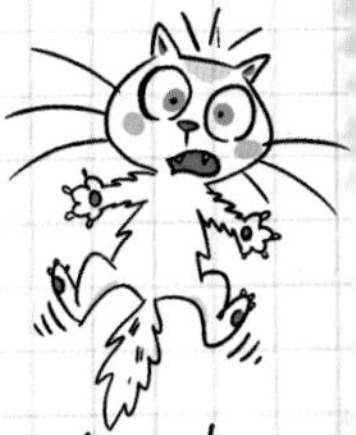

I'm jealous of my friend and I'm mad at myself!

We celebrated my birthday on July 17th at the campground. But my heart wasn't in it! Okay, I did get a bicycle as a gift! The only nice thing: Tommy sang a song to me over the phone. My mom told me she wanted to organize a surprise party with my friends... and then she gave up because it was too difficult to invite my friends to the campground. Then we came home on July 20th.

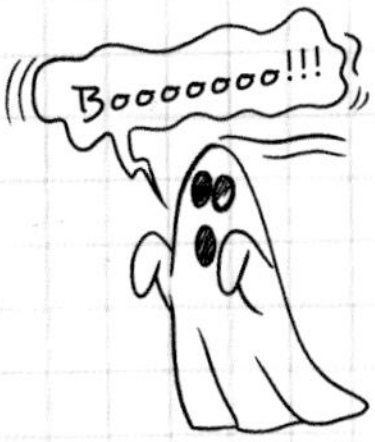
Boooooooo!!!

- Saturday, August 4th, 2:30pm:
I woke up this morning with a start. A frightened Sybil had jumped on me.

I don't really like sleeping in the basement... I realize that now. I think that if ghosts existed, they'd live in the basement. Not only because of the laundry room, but because it's a chilly, humid, terrifying place... and there are spiders there, too.

It's decided, I don't want to sleep here anymore!

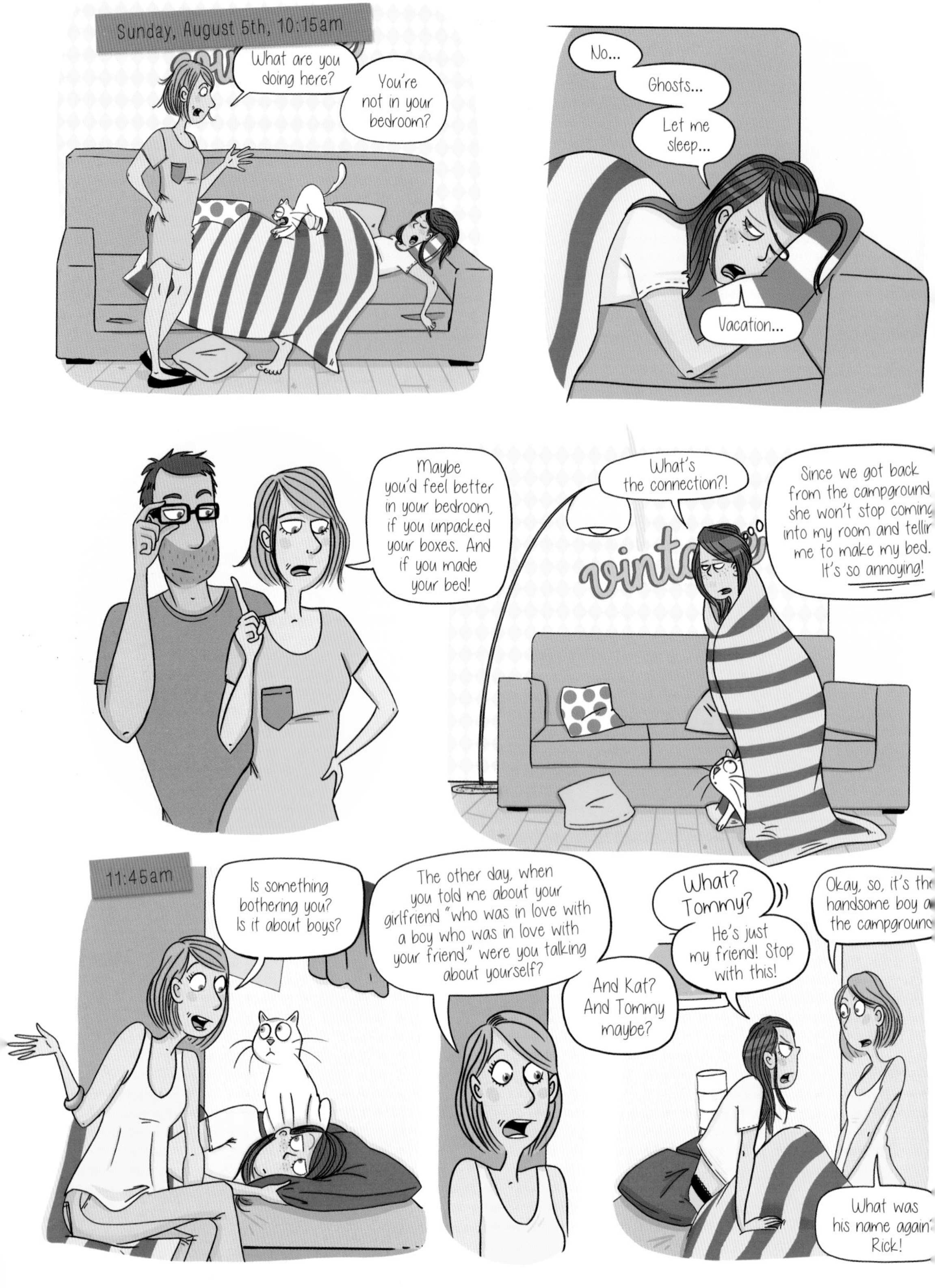
Sunday, August 5th, 10:15am
What are you doing here?
You're not in your bedroom?
No...
Ghosts...
Let me sleep...
Vacation...
Maybe you'd feel better in your bedroom, if you unpacked your boxes. And if you made your bed!
What's the connection?!
Since we got back from the campground she won't stop coming into my room and tellin me to make my bed. It's so annoying!
vintage
11:45am
Is something bothering you? Is it about boys?
The other day, when you told me about your girlfriend "who was in love with a boy who was in love with your friend," were you talking about yourself?
And Kat? And Tommy maybe?
What? Tommy?
He's just my friend! Stop with this!
Okay, so, it's the handsome boy at the campground
What was his name again? Rick!

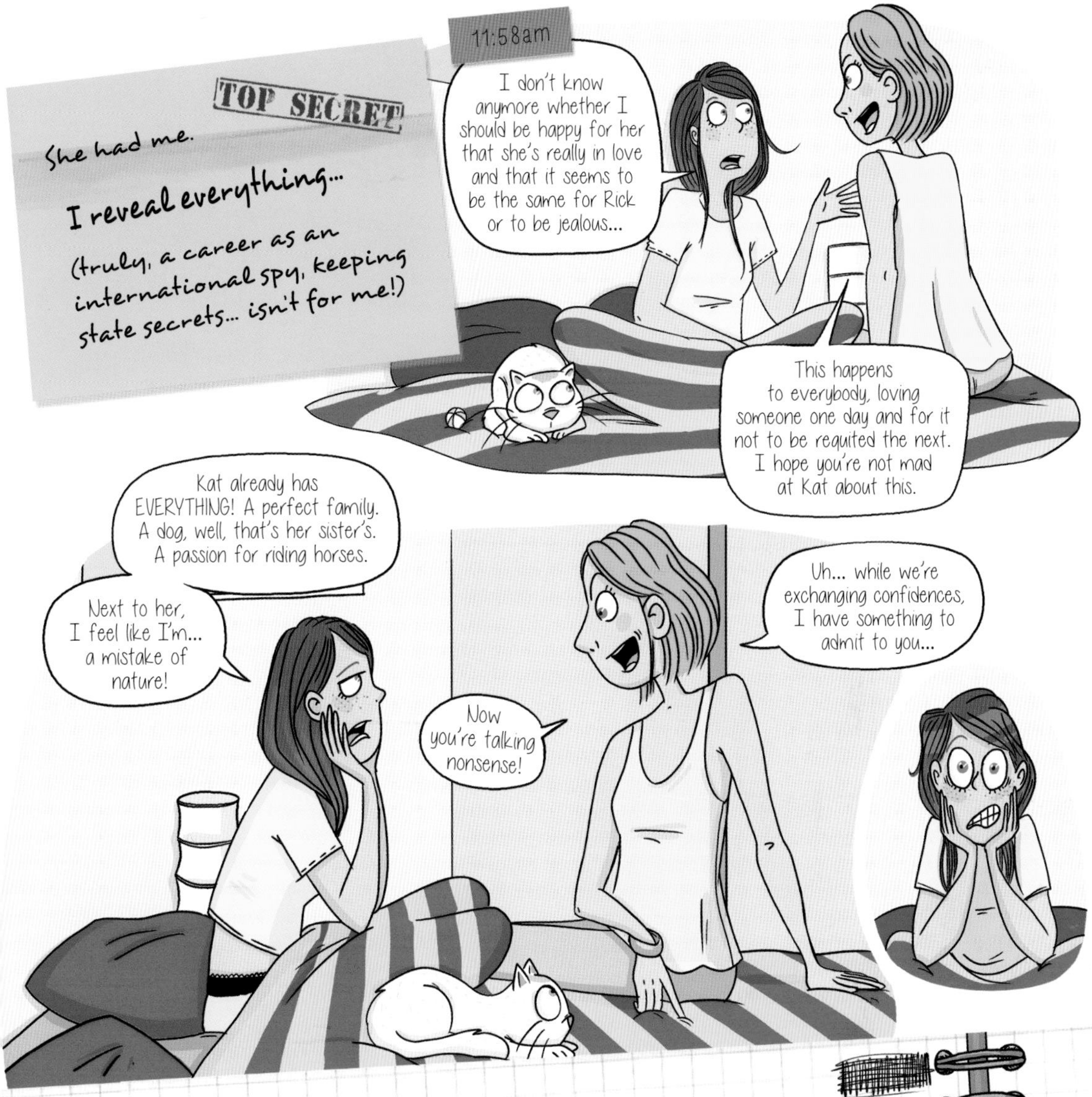
TOP SECRET
She had me.
I reveal everything...
(truly, a career as an international spy, keeping state secrets... isn't for me!)
11:58am
I don't know anymore whether I should be happy for her that she's really in love and that it seems to be the same for Rick or to be jealous...
This happens to everybody, loving someone one day and for it not to be requited the next. I hope you're not mad at Kat about this.
Kat already has EVERYTHING! A perfect family. A dog, well, that's her sister's. A passion for riding horses.
Next to her, I feel like I'm... a mistake of nature!
Now you're talking nonsense!
Uh... while we're exchanging confidences, I have something to admit to you...

- Sunday, August 5th, 1:00pm:

AAAAARRRRGGGGHHHHH! ALERT! IT'S HORRIBLE!!!

For my surprise birthday (that only happened with Kat), my mom got my address book, which is in my computer, and she called NICK! To invite him... and he couldn't come (luckily!)... NO WAY! I was starting to think she was cool and she admits she CALLED NICK!

LET A TORNADO CARRY ME FAR FROM HERE AND MAKE ME DISAPPEAR BECAUSE I'VE NEVER BEEN SO EMBARRASSED IN MY LIFE!

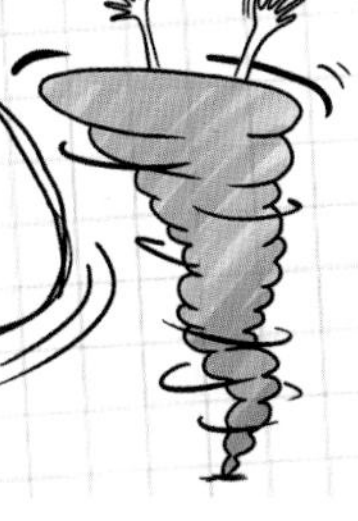

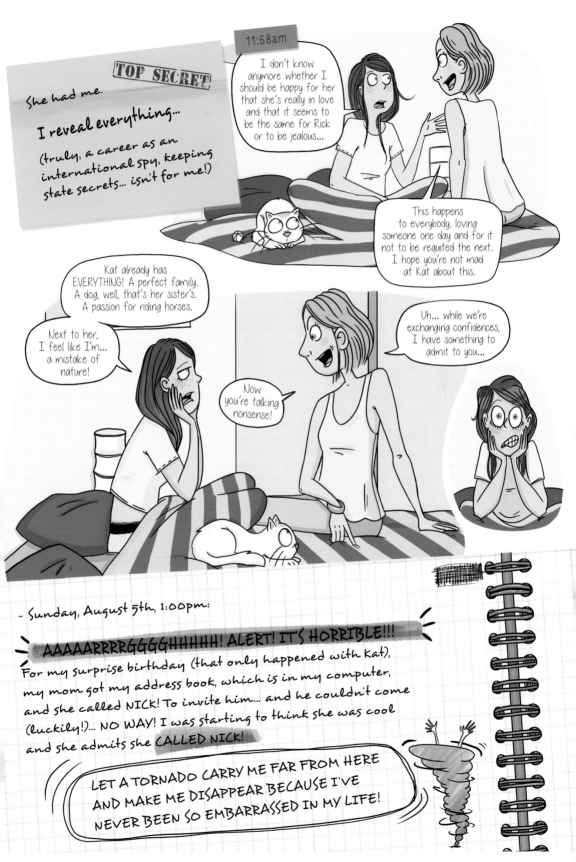

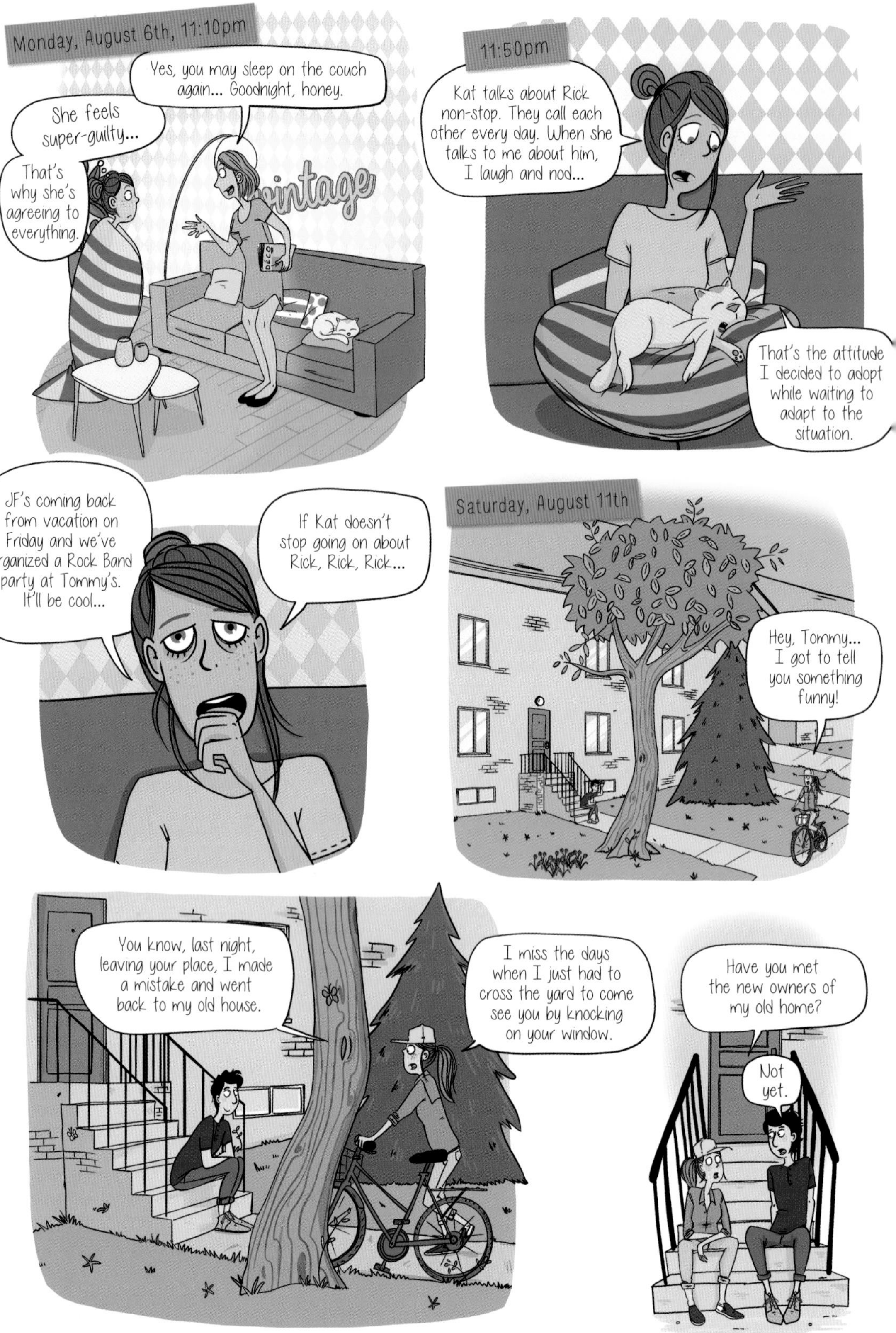

Monday, August 6th, 11:10pm
She feels super-guilty...
That's why she's agreeing to everything.
Yes, you may sleep on the couch again... Goodnight, honey.
vintage
11:50pm
Kat talks about Rick non-stop. They call each other every day. When she talks to me about him, I laugh and nod...
That's the attitude I decided to adopt while waiting to adapt to the situation.
JF's coming back from vacation on Friday and we've organized a Rock Band party at Tommy's. It'll be cool...
If Kat doesn't stop going on about Rick, Rick, Rick...
Saturday, August 11th
Hey, Tommy... I got to tell you something funny!
You know, last night, leaving your place, I made a mistake and went back to my old house.
I miss the days when I just had to cross the yard to come see you by knocking on your window.
Have you met the new owners of my old home?
Not yet.

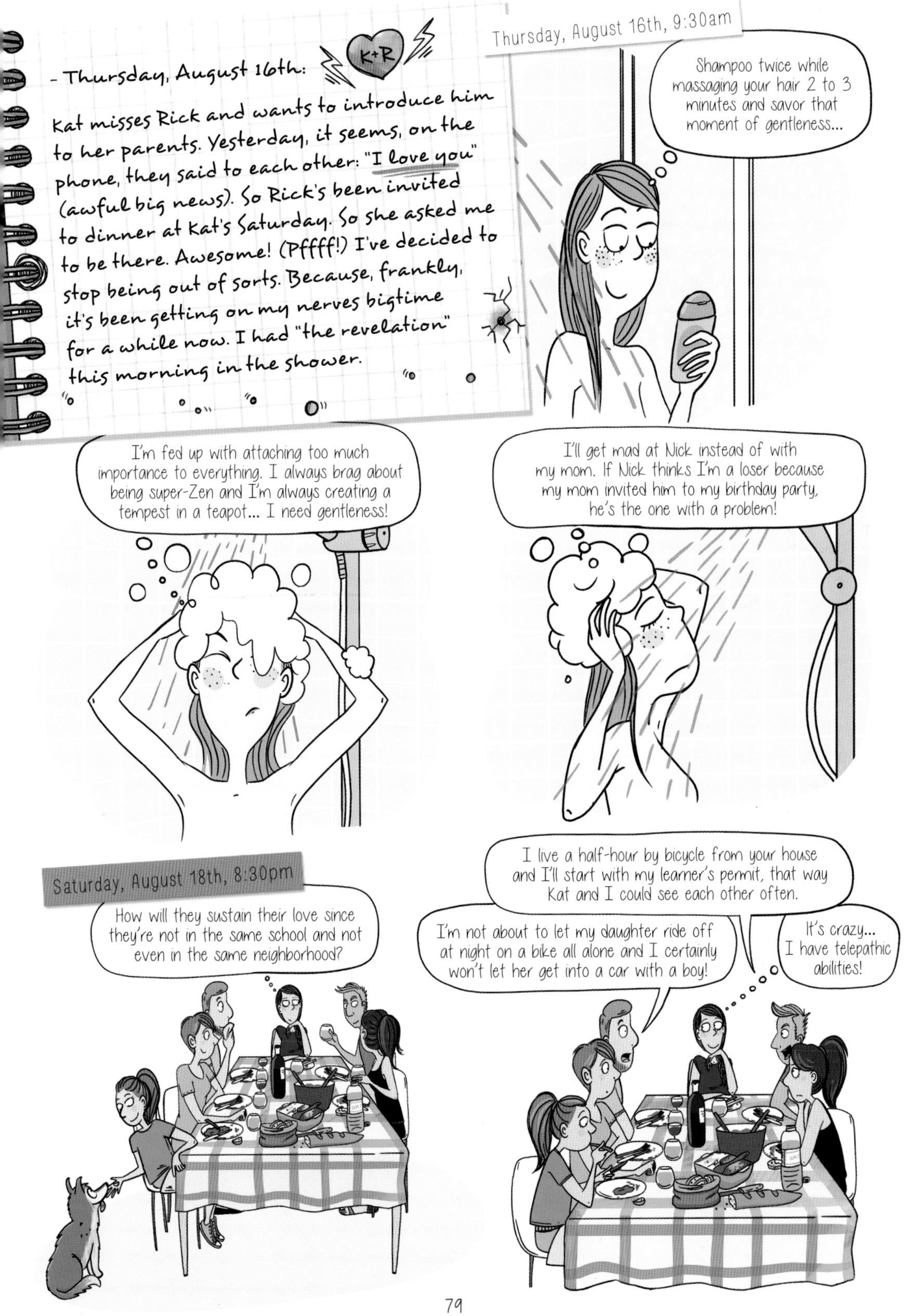
- Thursday, August 16th:
K+R
Kat misses Rick and wants to introduce him to her parents. Yesterday, it seems, on the phone, they said to each other: "I love you" (awful big news). So Rick's been invited to dinner at Kat's Saturday. So she asked me to be there. Awesome! (Pffff!) I've decided to stop being out of sorts. Because, frankly, it's been getting on my nerves bigtime for a while now. I had "the revelation" this morning in the shower.
Thursday, August 16th, 9:30am
Shampoo twice while massaging your hair 2 to 3 minutes and savor that moment of gentleness...
I'm fed up with attaching too much importance to everything. I always brag about being super-Zen and I'm always creating a tempest in a teapot... I need gentleness!
I'll get mad at Nick instead of with my mom. If Nick thinks I'm a loser because my mom invited him to my birthday party, he's the one with a problem!
Saturday, August 18th, 8:30pm
How will they sustain their love since they're not in the same school and not even in the same neighborhood?
I live a half-hour by bicycle from your house and I'll start with my learner's permit, that way Kat and I could see each other often.
I'm not about to let my daughter ride off at night on a bike all alone and I certainly won't let her get into a car with a boy!
It's crazy... I have telepathic abilities!

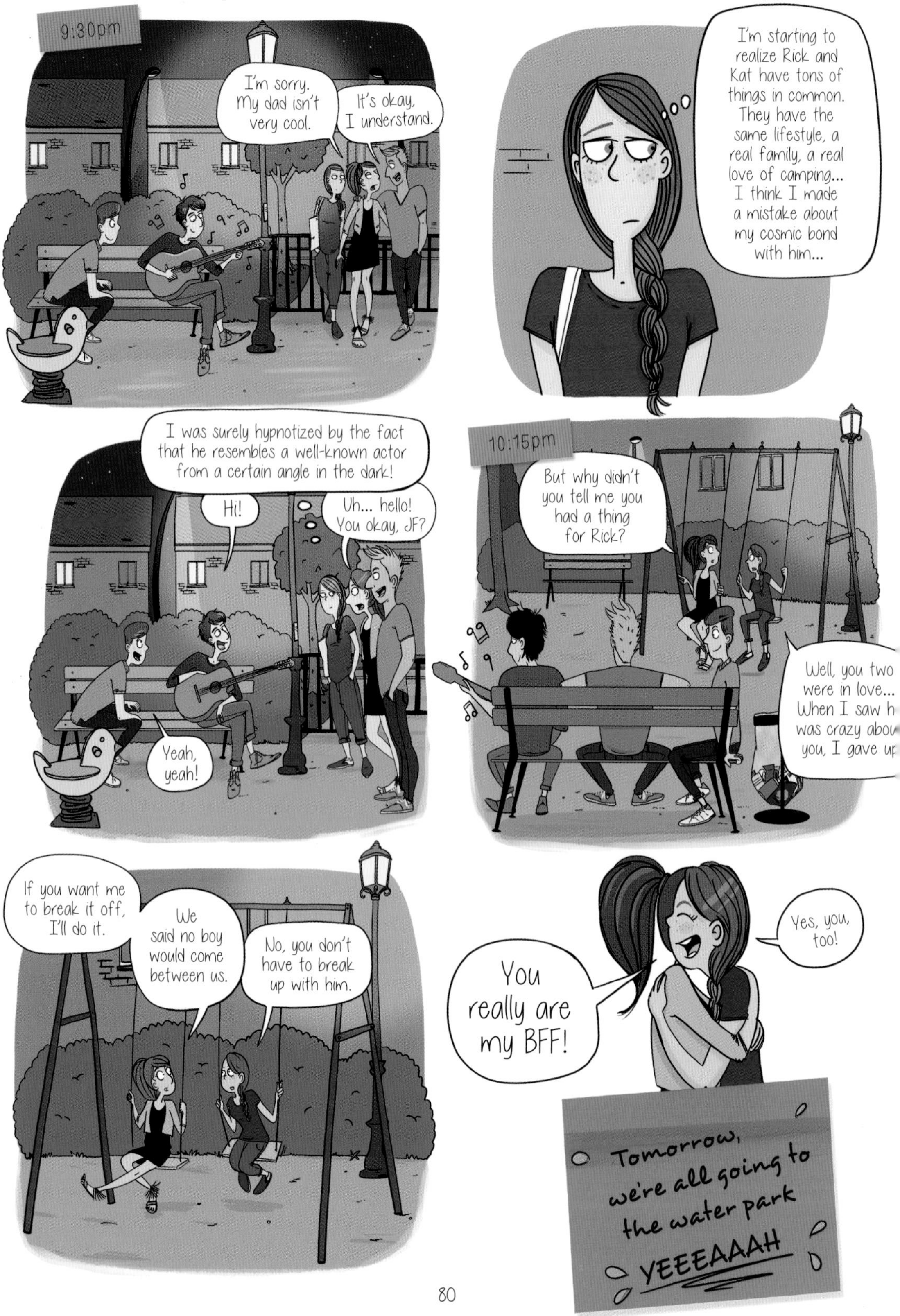
9:30pm
I'm sorry. My dad isn't very cool.
It's okay, I understand.
I'm starting to realize Rick and Kat have tons of things in common. They have the same lifestyle, a real family, a real love of camping... I think I made a mistake about my cosmic bond with him...
I was surely hypnotized by the fact that he resembles a well-known actor from a certain angle in the dark!
Hi!
Uh... hello! You okay, JF?
Yeah, yeah!
10:15pm
But why didn't you tell me you had a thing for Rick?
If you want me to break it off, I'll do it.
We said no boy would come between us.
No, you don't have to break up with him.
You really are my BFF!
Yes, you, too!
Tomorrow, we're all going to the water park YEEEAAAH

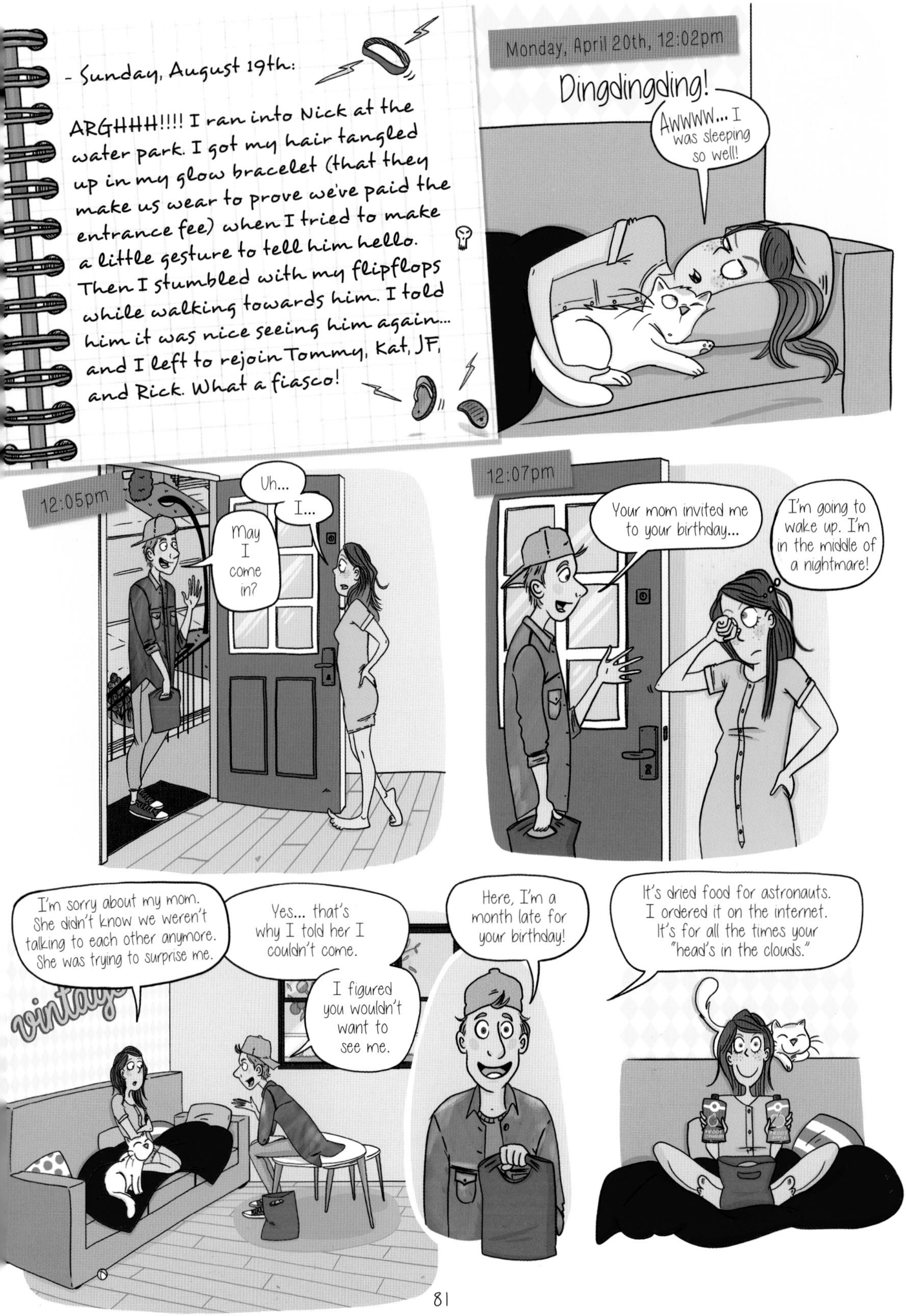
- Sunday, August 19th:
ARGHHH!!!! I ran into Nick at the water park. I got my hair tangled up in my glow bracelet (that they make us wear to prove we've paid the entrance fee) when I tried to make a little gesture to tell him hello. Then I stumbled with my flipflops while walking towards him. I told him it was nice seeing him again... and I left to rejoin Tommy, Kat, JF, and Rick. What a fiasco!
Monday, April 20th, 12:02pm
Dingdingding!
Awwww... I was sleeping so well!
12:05pm
May I come in?
Uh...
I...
12:07pm
Your mom invited me to your birthday...
I'm going to wake up. I'm in the middle of a nightmare!
I'm sorry about my mom. She didn't know we weren't talking to each other anymore. She was trying to surprise me.
Yes... that's why I told her I couldn't come.
I figured you wouldn't want to see me.
Here, I'm a month late for your birthday!
It's dried food for astronauts. I ordered it on the internet. It's for all the times your "head's in the clouds."

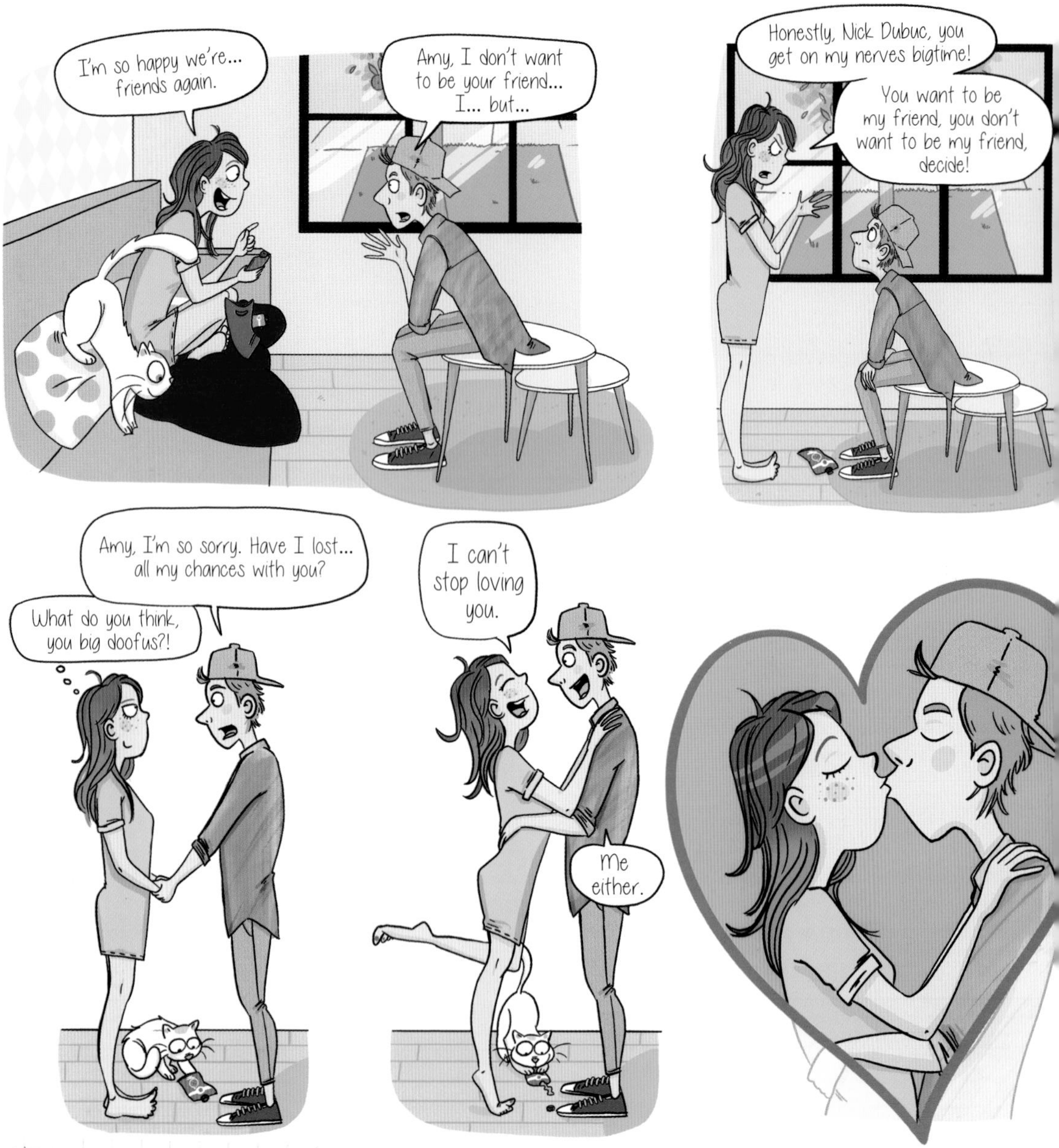
I'm so happy we're... friends again.
Amy, I don't want to be your friend... I... but...
Honestly, Nick Dubuc, you get on my nerves bigtime!
You want to be my friend, you don't want to be my friend, decide!
Amy, I'm so sorry. Have I lost... all my chances with you?
What do you think, you big doofus?!
I can't stop loving you.
Me either.

In a few days, I'll start my final year in high school... I don't really know what awaits me afterwards. Maybe I just have to stop fearing the unknown and let myself be surprised, to manage the present. Sometimes, I feel like everything's always starting over. As though I were always rebuilding foundations atop ruins and that, time after time, storms were blowing away my work. But through everything I've experienced, I've understood one thing: regardless of what I do to struggle against it, my heart will always be stronger than me.

charmz chat™

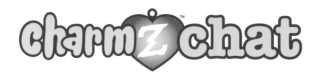

Welcome to AMY'S DIARY #3 "Moving On," based on the novels by India Desjardins, adapted by Véronique Grisseaux, writer, and Laëtitia Aynié, artist. Unlike many long-running comicbook characters, Amy Von Brandt is growing older with each and every volume of this graphic novel series. How could she not? This series is based upon her diaries, after all. We get to see Amy's life unfold, and we witness all of her ups and downs, her smart decisions and her mistakes. It's a fascinating look at the life of a teenage girl just trying to lead as happy a life as possible, despite certain problems.

In AMY'S DIARY #1 "Space Alien…Almost?" it was revealed that Amy copes with perhaps her greatest problem, the loss of her father, by imagining that he's "not gone, but an extraterrestrial who returned to his planet." Obviously, Amy knows that's not really true, but a fiction she's telling herself to cope with her tragic loss. But what if it was true? What if AMY'S DIARY was a science fiction series, and we found out what did happen to her father? Well, Charmz happens to be an imprint of Papercutz, which also has another imprint called Super Genius. There's a graphic novel series published by Papercutz and one by Super Genius that may explore that kind of territory.

THE HIT SERIES THE ONLY LIVING BOY CONTINUES IN...
THE ONLY LIVING GIRL
THE ISLAND AT THE EDGE OF INFINITY

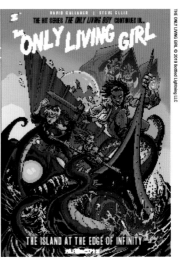

First there's Zandra Parfitt, THE ONLY LIVING GIRL, co-created by writer, David Gallaher, and artist, Steve Ellis. Zee, as she's usually called, first appeared in THE ONLY LIVING BOY, the Harvey Award-nominated series by Gallaher and Ellis, which has been collected by Papercutz into a beautiful OMNIBUS edition. The ONLY LIVING GIRL series stars Zee, who after years of being in suspended animation, has woken up on a strange new world and is now haunted by memories of her past. As the only living girl she must redeem her lost father's legacy, while trying to survive life on this strange planet. If Amy was aware of what Zee was going through, she'd probably want to rethink the whole my-father-was-taken-by-aliens scenario. Just take a look at the preview pages starting on the next page, for a taste of exactly what Zee is going through (and some hints at exactly why she needs to redeem her father's legacy).

JESSICA ABEL
TRISH TRASH
ROLLERGIRL OF MARS

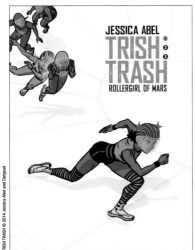

Then there's Patricia "Trish Trash" Nupindju, who was actually born on Mars—200 years in the future. Her parents weren't exactly taken away by aliens, but by something far more sinister. Trish is seven and a half in Martian years, which is 15 in Earth years. She dreams of becoming the biggest hoverderby star on Mars, as it seems the only way to escape a future of poverty and hard labor on her family's moisture farm in Candor Chasma. But even if she could make the team, she's too young to get a pro hoverderby contract. What's a girl to do? Trish's whole story was told in three great Eisner Award-nominated graphic novels, TRISH TRASH ROLLERGIRL OF MARS by writer/artist Jessica Abel. All three graphic novels are available separately or in one big COLLECTED EDITION from Super Genius. Check out the short preview starting right after THE ONLY LIVING GIRL preview. Life on Mars is certainly not something we imagine Amy would want to experience.

Meanwhile back on Earth, Amy continues her unique journey and hopes you'll pick up AMY'S DIARY #4 "Secret Plan," coming soon to your favorite bookseller or library. While she may not want anyone else to read her diary, she's willing to make an exception for you. Sorry, but AMY'S DIARY is currently unavailable on Mars.

Thanks,

JIM
Editor-in-Chief

STAY IN TOUCH!

EMAIL:	salicrup@papercutz.com
WEB:	Papercutz.com
TWITTER:	@papercutzgn
INSTAGRAM:	@papercutzgn
FACEBOOK:	PAPERCUTZGRAPHICNOVELS
FANMAIL:	Charmz, 160 Broadway, Suite 700, East Wing, New York, NY 10038

Special Preview of THE ONLY LIVING GIRL #1

"The Island at the Edge of Infinity"

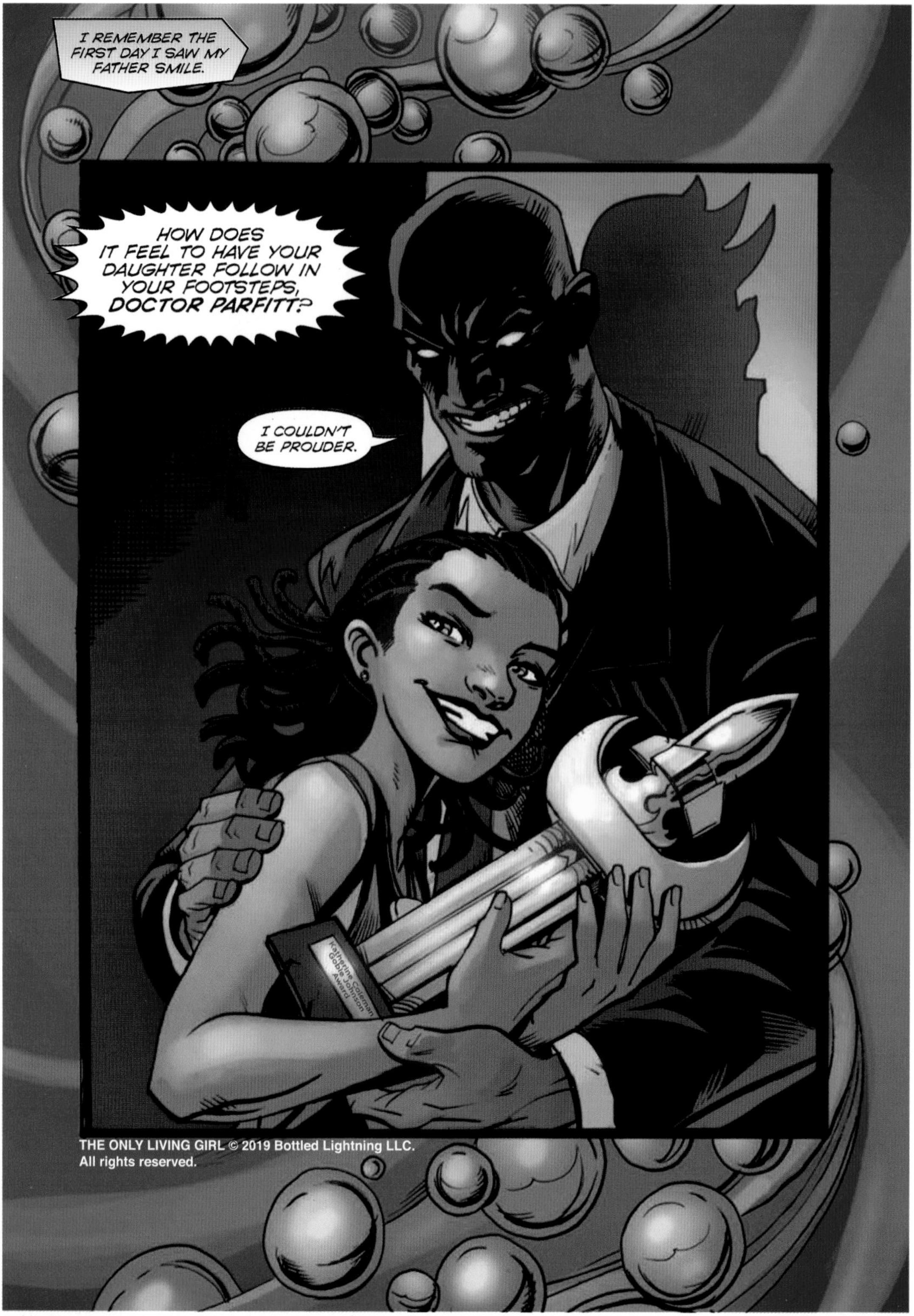

I REMEMBER THE FIRST DAY I SAW MY FATHER SMILE.
HOW DOES IT FEEL TO HAVE YOUR DAUGHTER FOLLOW IN YOUR FOOTSTEPS, DOCTOR PARFITT?
I COULDN'T BE PROUDER.
Katherine Coleman Goble Johnson Award

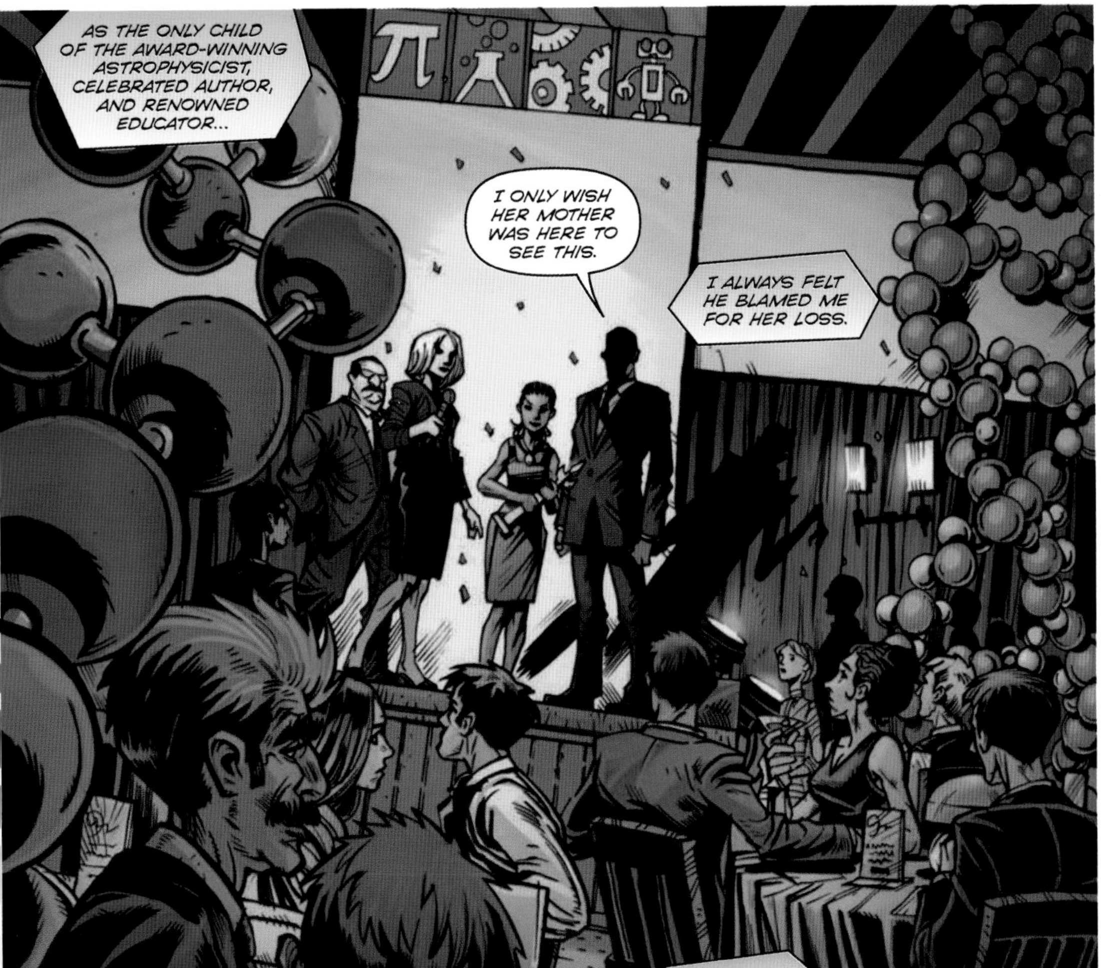
AS THE ONLY CHILD OF THE AWARD-WINNING ASTROPHYSICIST, CELEBRATED AUTHOR, AND RENOWNED EDUCATOR...
I ONLY WISH HER MOTHER WAS HERE TO SEE THIS.
I ALWAYS FELT HE BLAMED ME FOR HER LOSS.
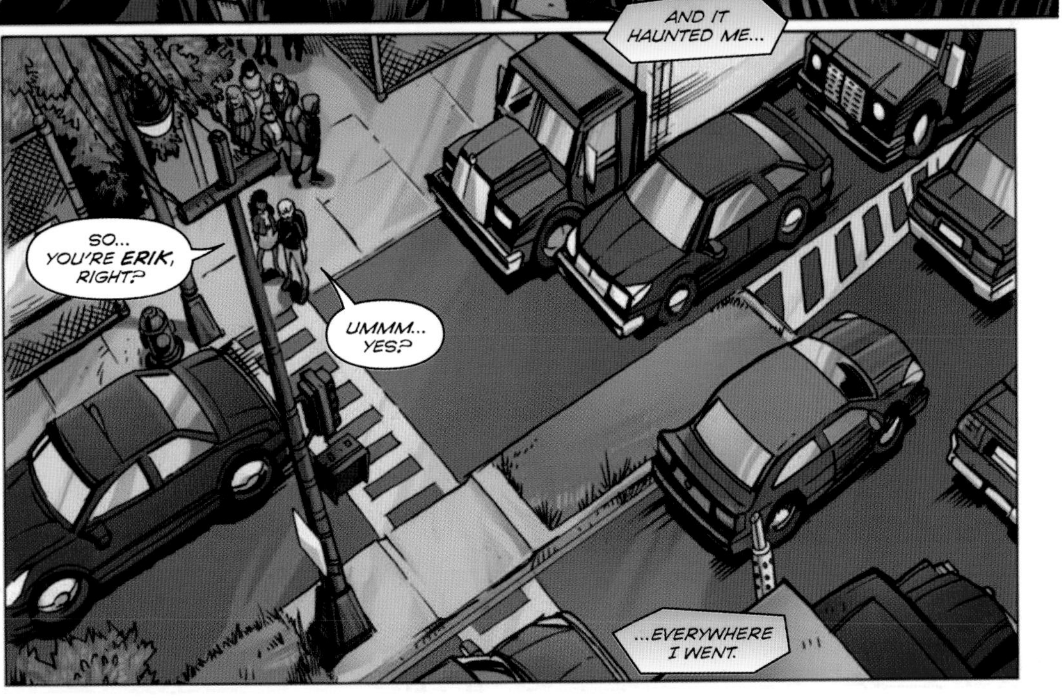
AND IT HAUNTED ME...
SO... YOU'RE ERIK, RIGHT?
UMMM... YES?
...EVERYWHERE I WENT.

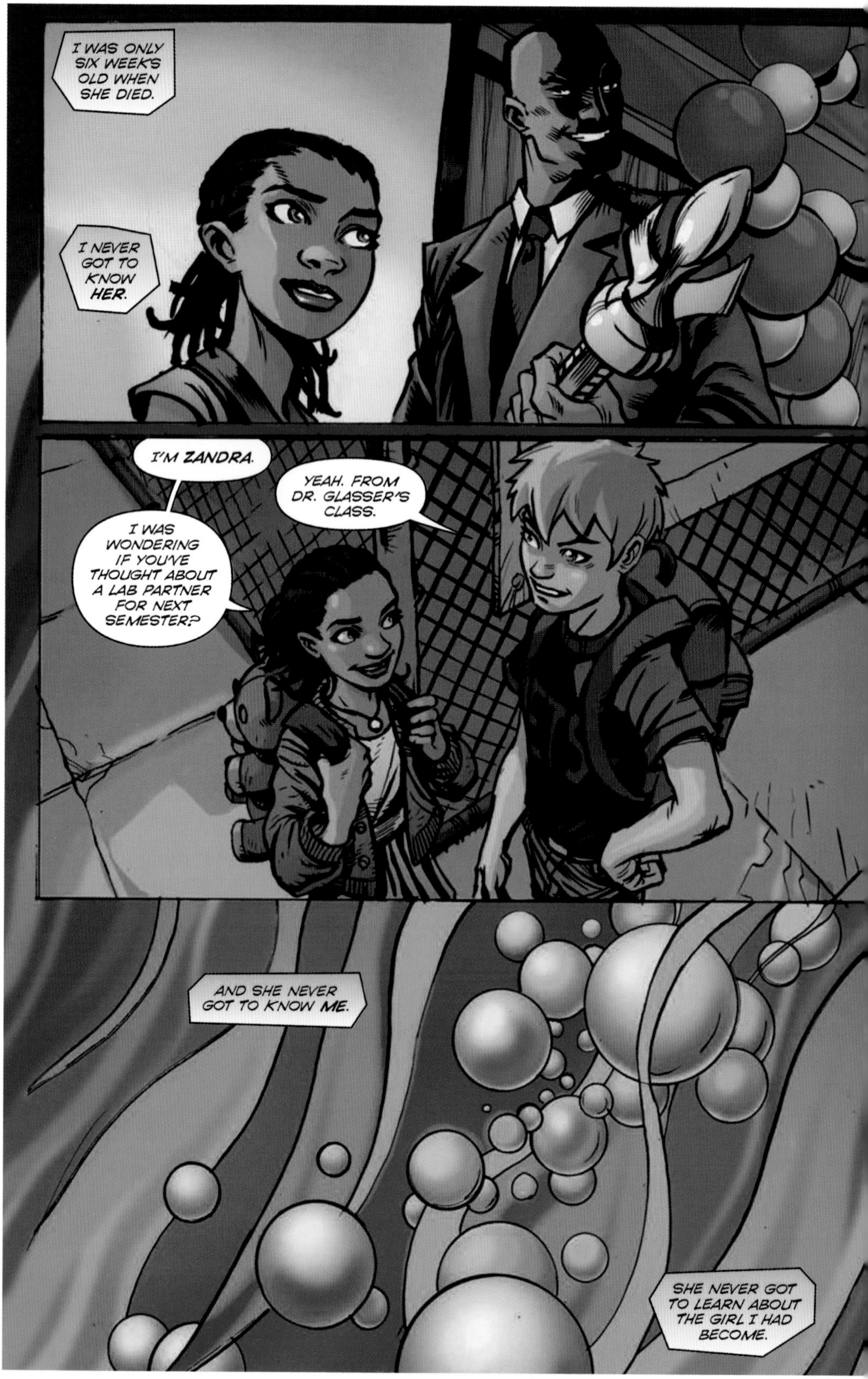

I WAS ONLY SIX WEEKS OLD WHEN SHE DIED.
I NEVER GOT TO KNOW HER.
I'M ZANDRA.
I WAS WONDERING IF YOU'VE THOUGHT ABOUT A LAB PARTNER FOR NEXT SEMESTER?
YEAH. FROM DR. GLASSER'S CLASS.
AND SHE NEVER GOT TO KNOW ME.
SHE NEVER GOT TO LEARN ABOUT THE GIRL I HAD BECOME.

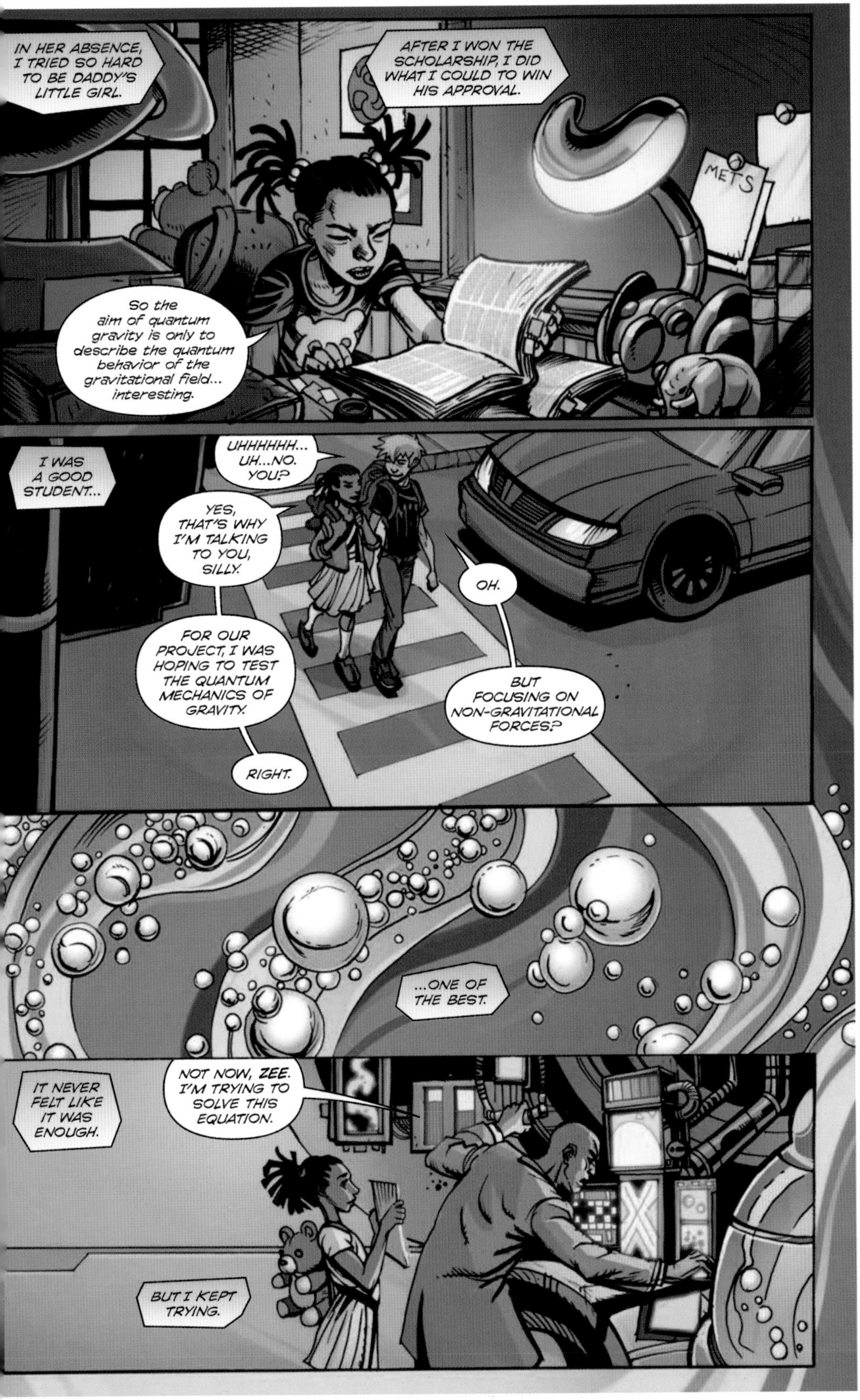
IN HER ABSENCE, I TRIED SO HARD TO BE DADDY'S LITTLE GIRL.
AFTER I WON THE SCHOLARSHIP, I DID WHAT I COULD TO WIN HIS APPROVAL.
METS
So the aim of quantum gravity is only to describe the quantum behavior of the gravitational field... interesting.
I WAS A GOOD STUDENT...
UHHHHHH... UH...NO. YOU?
YES, THAT'S WHY I'M TALKING TO YOU, SILLY.
OH.
FOR OUR PROJECT, I WAS HOPING TO TEST THE QUANTUM MECHANICS OF GRAVITY.
BUT FOCUSING ON NON-GRAVITATIONAL FORCES?
RIGHT.
...ONE OF THE BEST.
IT NEVER FELT LIKE IT WAS ENOUGH.
NOT NOW, ZEE. I'M TRYING TO SOLVE THIS EQUATION.
BUT I KEPT TRYING.

I LEARNED EVERYTHING I COULD FROM MY FATHER.

I KNOW QUITE A BIT ABOUT GRAVITY AND YOU SEEM TO KNOW A COUPLE OF THINGS ABOUT SCIENCE AND STUFF.

"MAKE EVERY DAY JEALOUS OF YESTERDAY" WAS HIS MOTTO.

ON THOSE BLEAK NIGHTS WHEN MY FATHER WOULD WORK LATE...

...I BROUGHT MY IDEAS TO LIFE.

MY ONLY LIMITS...

DONT WALK

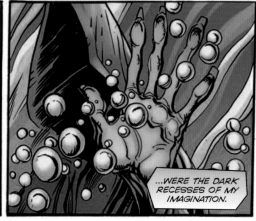

...WERE THE DARK RECESSES OF MY IMAGINATION.

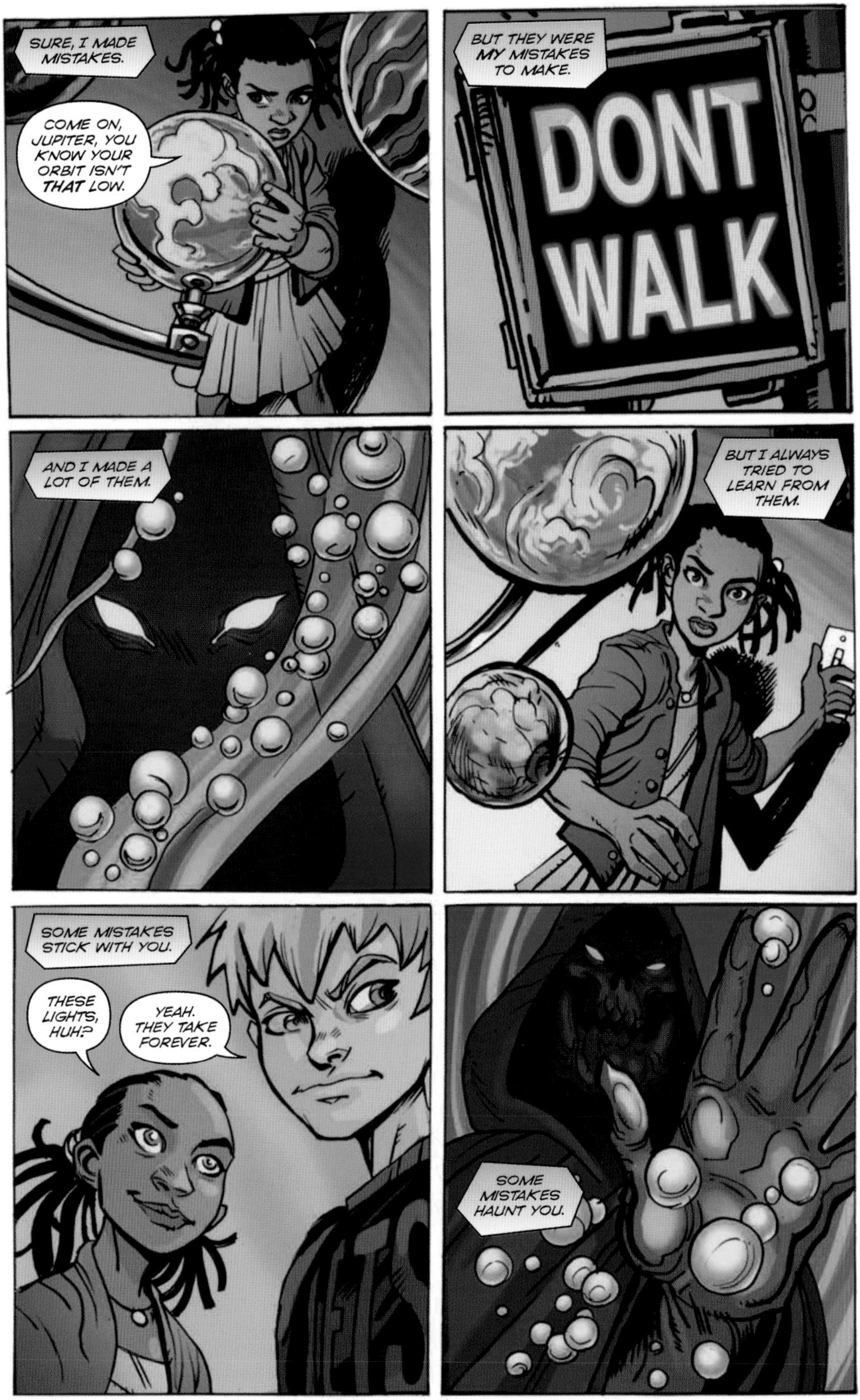
SURE, I MADE MISTAKES.
COME ON, JUPITER, YOU KNOW YOUR ORBIT ISN'T THAT LOW.
BUT THEY WERE MY MISTAKES TO MAKE.
DONT WALK
AND I MADE A LOT OF THEM.
BUT I ALWAYS TRIED TO LEARN FROM THEM.
SOME MISTAKES STICK WITH YOU.
THESE LIGHTS, HUH?
YEAH. THEY TAKE FOREVER.
SOME MISTAKES HAUNT YOU.

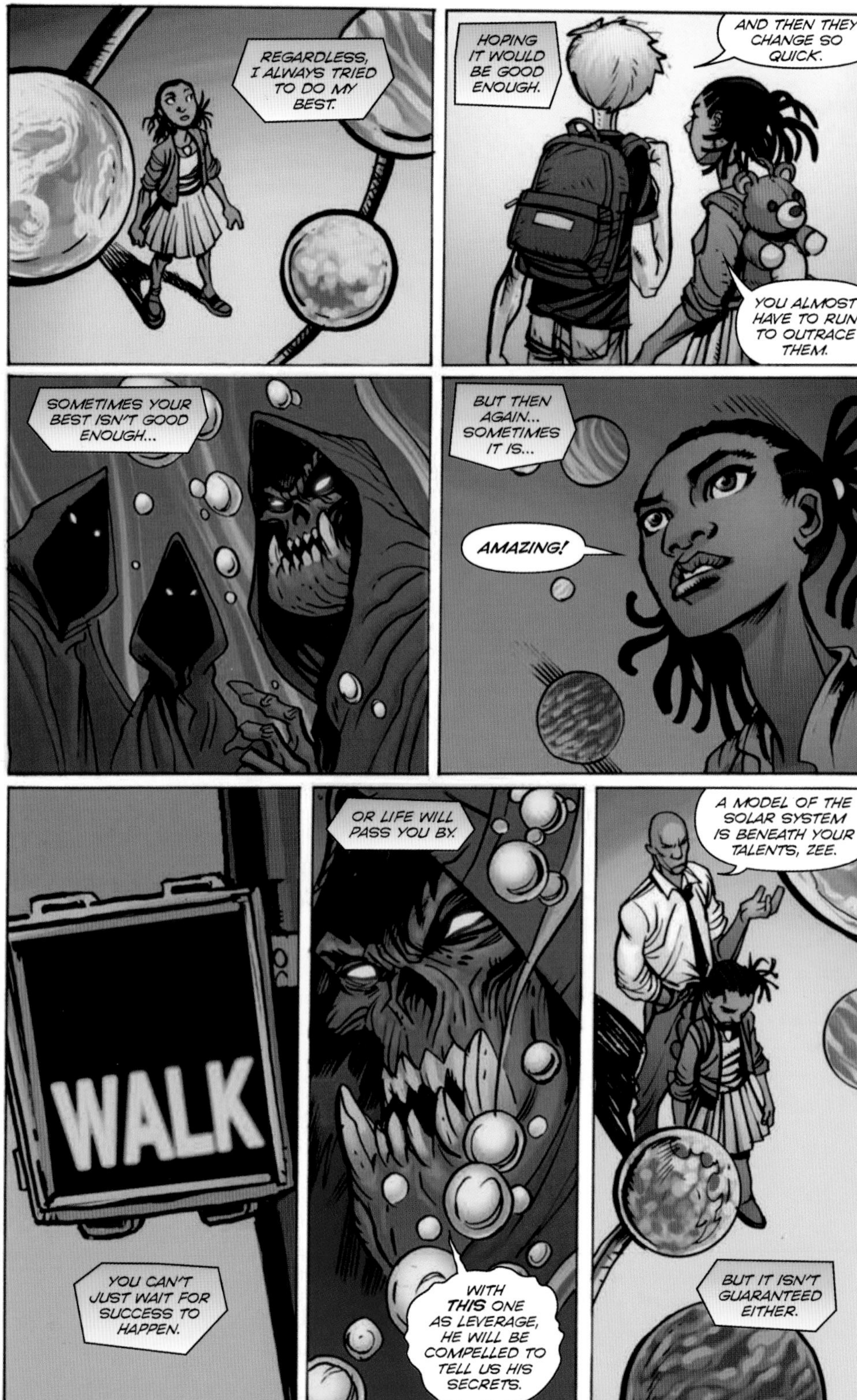
REGARDLESS, I ALWAYS TRIED TO DO MY BEST.
HOPING IT WOULD BE GOOD ENOUGH.
AND THEN THEY CHANGE SO QUICK.
YOU ALMOST HAVE TO RUN TO OUTRACE THEM.
SOMETIMES YOUR BEST ISN'T GOOD ENOUGH...
BUT THEN AGAIN... SOMETIMES IT IS...
AMAZING!
WALK
YOU CAN'T JUST WAIT FOR SUCCESS TO HAPPEN.
OR LIFE WILL PASS YOU BY.
WITH THIS ONE AS LEVERAGE, HE WILL BE COMPELLED TO TELL US HIS SECRETS.
A MODEL OF THE SOLAR SYSTEM IS BENEATH YOUR TALENTS, ZEE.
BUT IT ISN'T GUARANTEED EITHER.

Continued in THE ONLY LIVING GIRL #1, available now at booksellers and libraries.

Special Bonus Preview of
TRISH TRASH ROLLERGIRL OF MARS #1...

...here comes Betty Demonica...

...nice block by Deb O'Station...

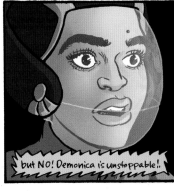

but NO! Demonica is unstoppable!

This is a historic moment, ladies and gentlemen!

In-credible! With five seconds to go...

WARNING

IMPEDIMENT DETECTED: FORE TO PORT

...did you see that block?
WAMI: DB is like the air—she passes thru
JIJI: grot that! she's DUST!
WAMI: haha

...Betty Demonica might just catch up with PDQ—again! If she laps her the third time...

EEP-EEP-EEP. Impediment detected.

Un-be-lieve-able! Betty Demonica, the league high-scorer, has just scored 19 points in one jam!

Alert. Clear impediment.

Her bout total is 76!

1.5 meters. Warning.

A more perfect bout could not be imagined...

.5 meters. Warning.

BAN

Crap.

GRIINDDDD

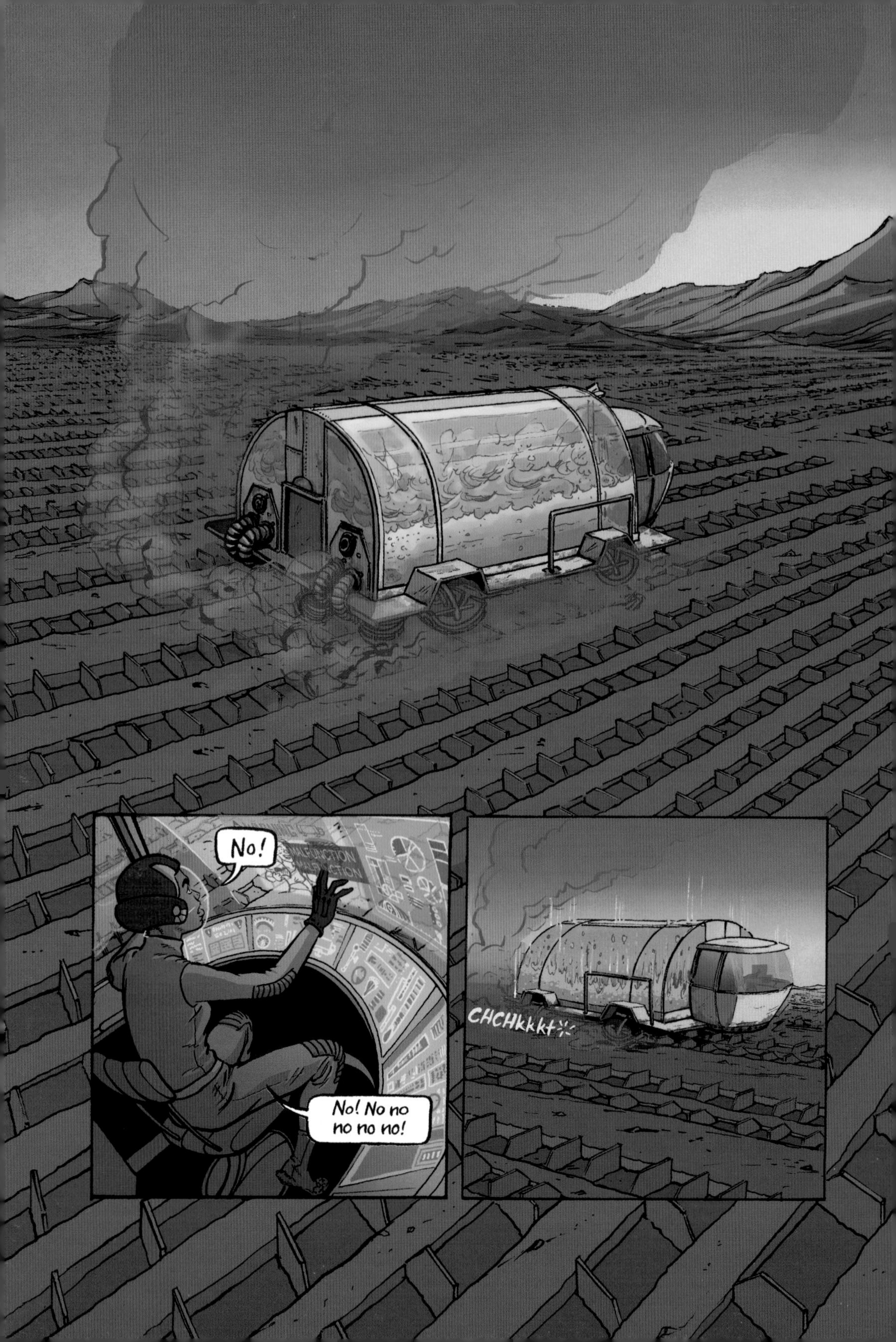
No!
MALFUNCTION
MALFUNCTION
No! No no no no no!
CHCHkkkt

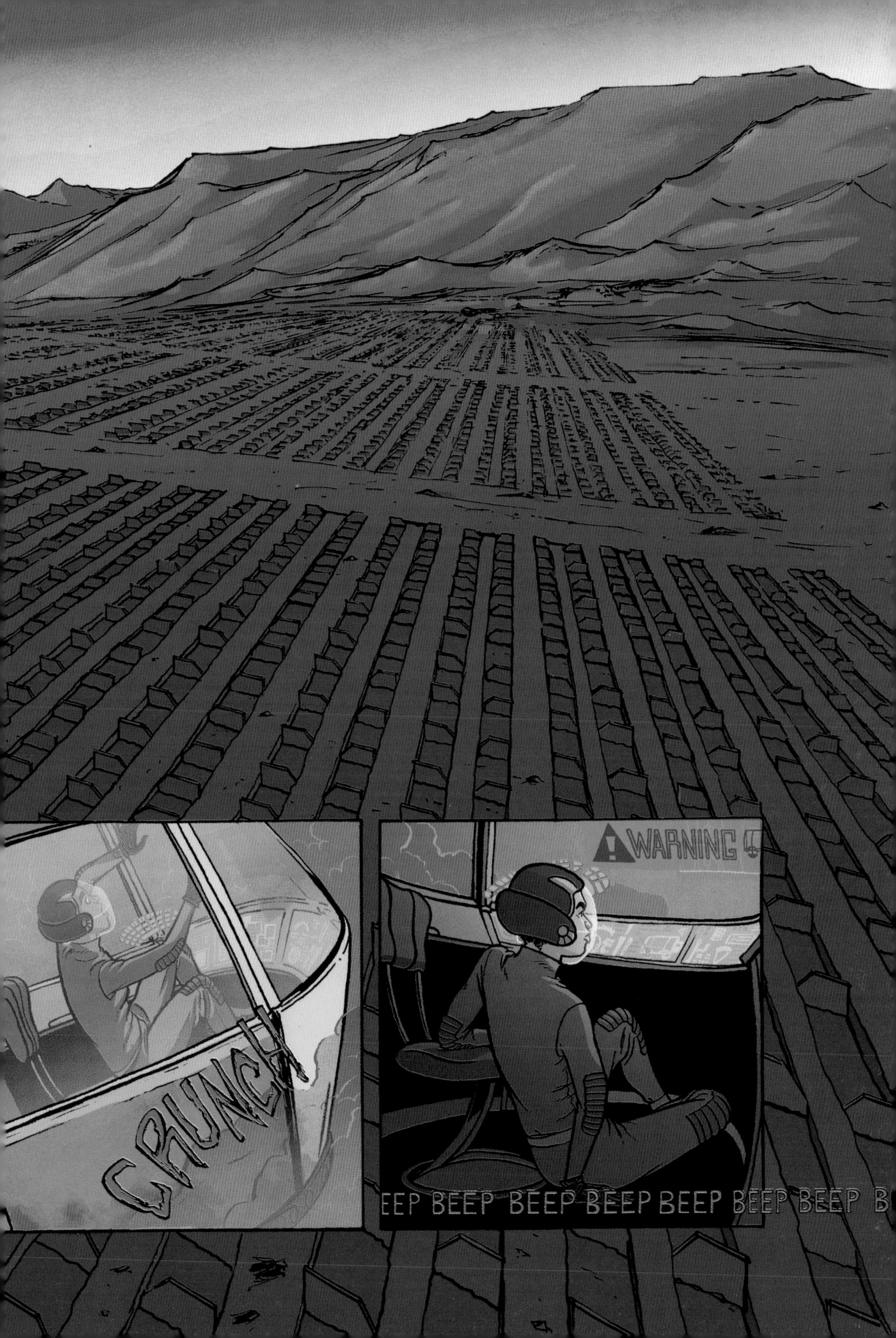
CRUNCH
WARNING
EEP BEEP BEEP BEEP BEEP BEEP BEEP

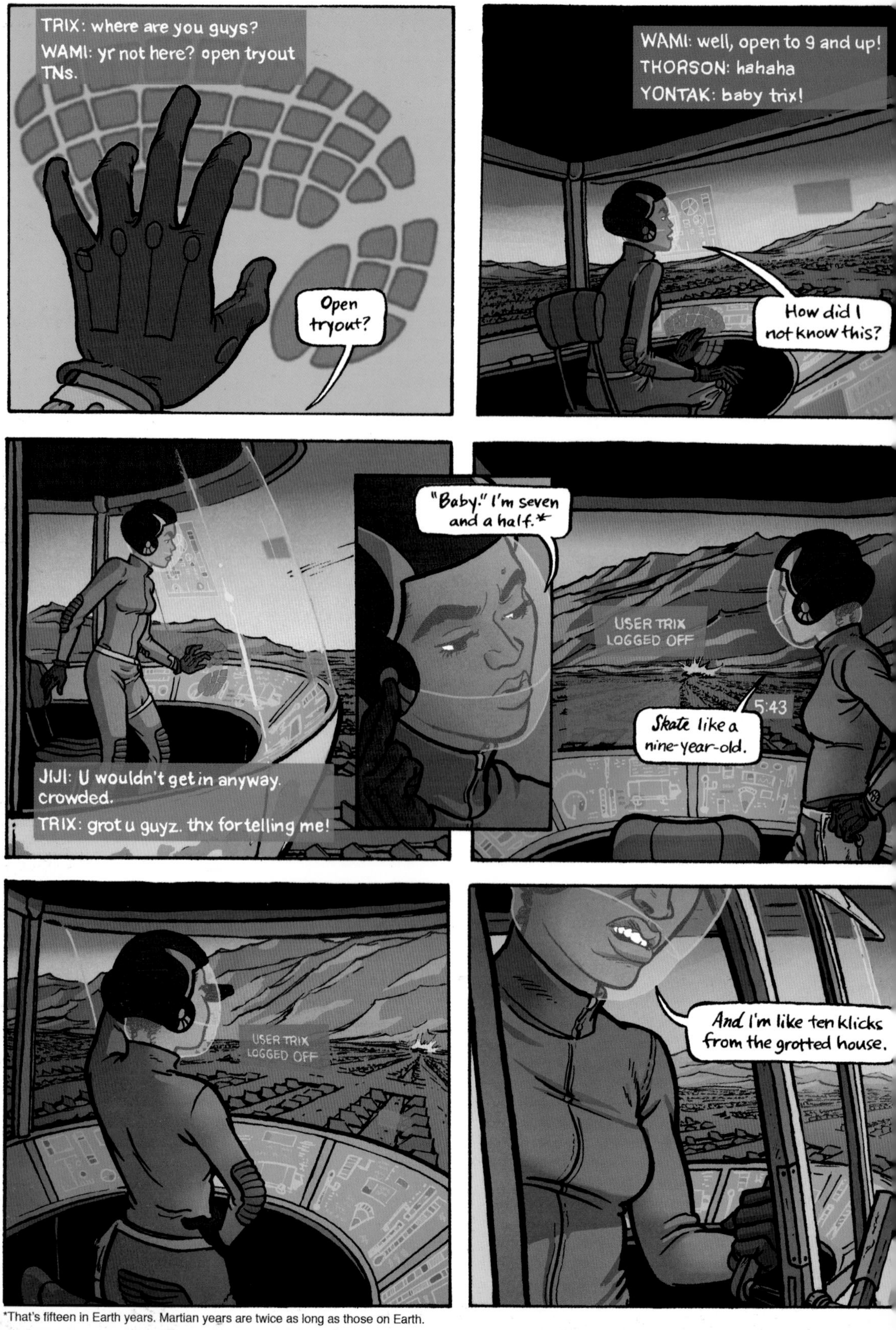
TRIX: where are you guys?
WAMI: yr not here? open tryout TNs.
Open tryout?
WAMI: well, open to 9 and up!
THORSON: hahaha
YONTAK: baby trix!
How did I not know this?
JIJI: U wouldn't get in anyway. crowded.
TRIX: grot u guyz. thx for telling me!
"Baby." I'm seven and a half.*
USER TRIX LOGGED OFF
5:43
Skate like a nine-year-old.
USER TRIX LOGGED OFF
And I'm like ten klicks from the grotted house.

*That's fifteen in Earth years. Martian years are twice as long as those on Earth.

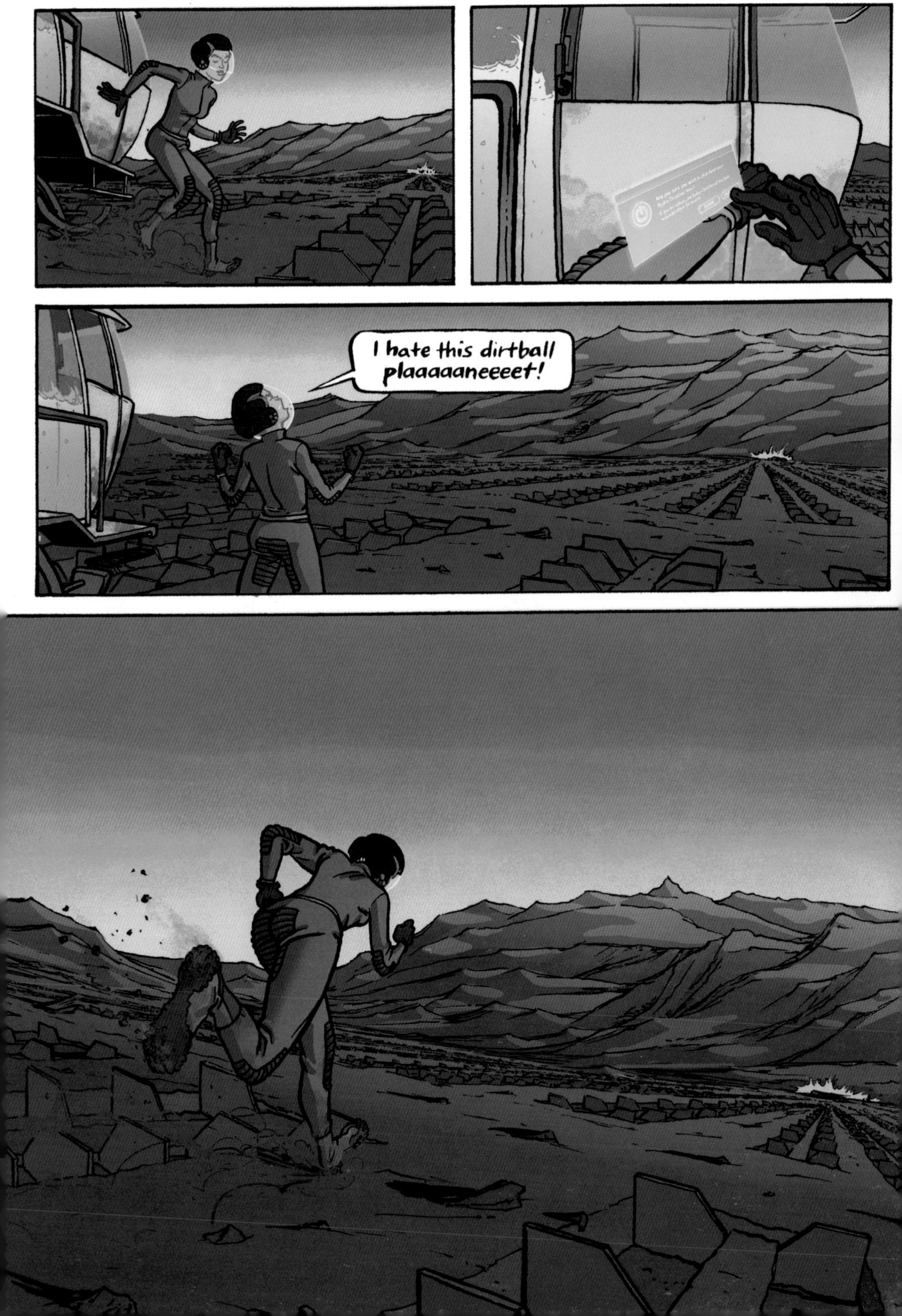
I hate this dirtball plaaaaaneeeet!

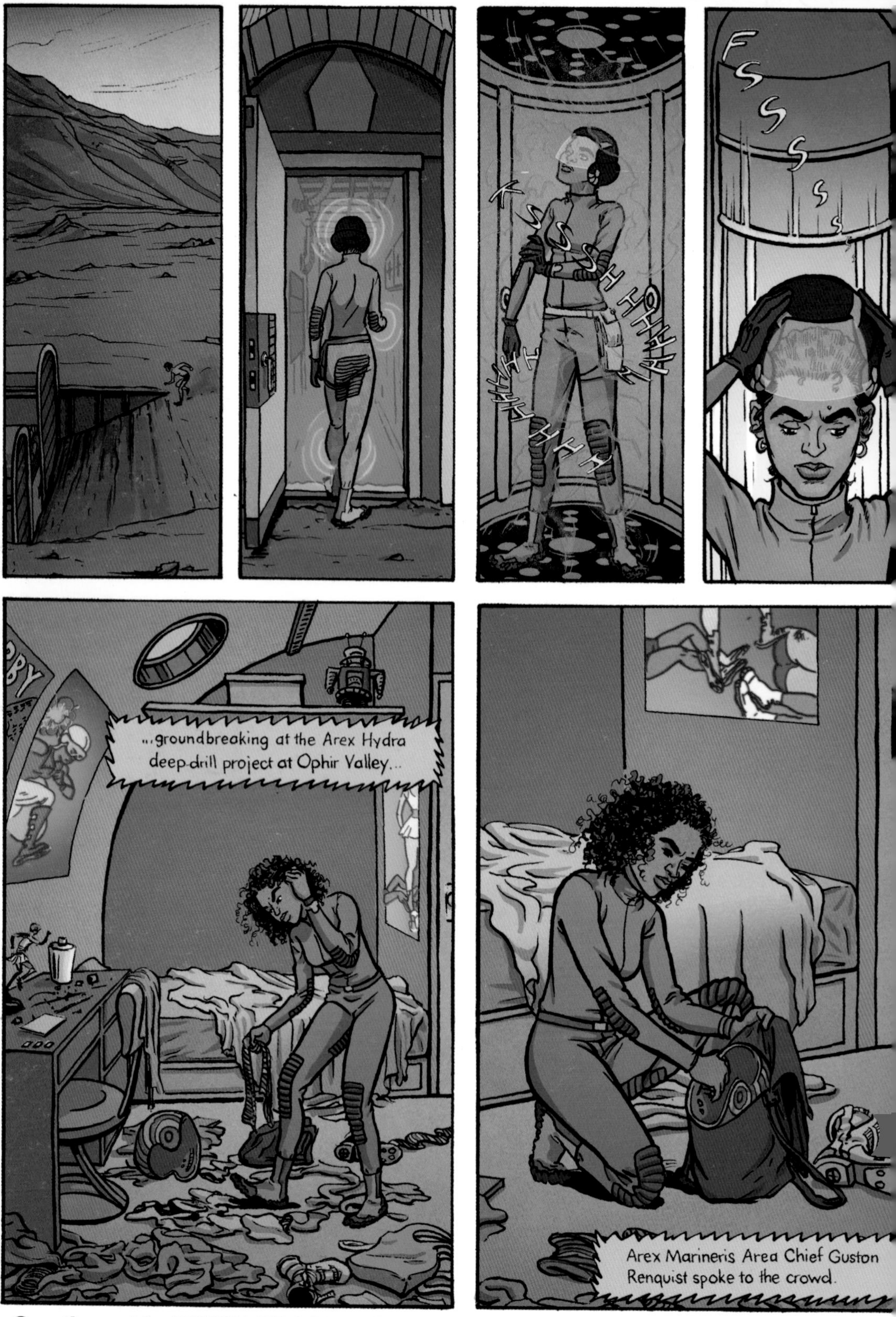
...groundbreaking at the Arex Hydra deep-drill project at Ophir Valley...
Arex Marineris Area Chief Guston Renquist spoke to the crowd.

Continued in TRISH TRASH ROLLERGIRL OF MARS #1 or TRISH TRASH THE COLLECTED EDITION, available now at booksellers and libraries.